LITTLE CULINARY TRIUMPHS

Pascale Pujol

LITTLE CULINARY TRIUMPHS

*Translated from the French
by Alison Anderson*

Europa
editions

Europa Editions
214 West 29th Street
New York, N.Y. 10001
www.europaeditions.com
info@europaeditions.com

Translated by Alison Anderson
Original title: *Petits plats de résistance*
Translation copyright © 2018 by Europa Editions

Library of Congress Cataloging in Publication Data is available
ISBN 978-1-60945-490-6

Pujol, Pascale
Little Culinary Triumphs

Book design by Emanuele Ragnisco
www.mekkanografici.com

Cover illustration by Mariachiara Di Giorgio

Prepress by Grafica Punto Print – Rome

Printed in Italy at Arti Grafiche La Moderna - Rome

FSC
www.fsc.org
MIX
Paper from
responsible sources
FSC® C131267

CONTENTS

LITTLE CULINARY TRIUMPHS

DOG FOOD

If Karine Becker had known better how to use the rhythm method, none of the following story would ever have happened. But she was on maternity leave, and due to budgetary restrictions, a temp was not hired. Sandrine Cordier, who had inherited the bulk of Karine's files, glanced grumpily over at the wall clock—an ugly digital model with red diodes on a black background which marked out the minutes backwards, like in a radio studio. 11:48: still an hour to go until lunch break, which lasted three-quarters of an hour. Then hang on until 5:40 P.M., the end of the day. Well, no, 5:25 actually, which was when the doors to the office closed and the crowd of pests receded until the next morning.

That was often the best moment of the day, when she saw Césaire heading toward the door the public used. He would post himself next to it, his hand on the electric controls, and activate the metal shutter that went slowly down over the glass door. A few last complainers were still dragging their feet in the hall; some of them lingered by the noticeboards or reached for leaflets. The most depraved slipped away to the restroom with a contrite little smile. But Césaire's booming voice hustled them all out—if he had to he'd flush them out by the sinks— "No dozing off! Let's move!" The metal shutter continued down its rail with the sound of a medieval instrument of torture—*greee, greee, greee*—and on a bad day Sandrine Cordier pictured it as a guillotine slipping down to tickle the neck of the last pests. *Shlap!* Struck off the list for all eternity.

Judging by the way the morning had started, that Tuesday might be one to file among the bad days, as it happened. But the worst was yet to come: now she had to deal with a few cases of newly registered applicants and transfers. To get herself going, Sandrine slipped her hand soundlessly in the top drawer of her desk to take out a cinnamon cookie. She'd brought the bag in the day before. Normally she would share them with her colleagues; she loved cooking and was good at it, and often brought in cakes or cookies after a weekend baking. But today she wasn't in the mood to share, given the pile of files that were waiting. She lingered a few more seconds before pressing the button that controlled the luminous signboard in the waiting room, then gave a little sigh: number 48 could proceed to office C.

She had skimmed through Antoine Lacuenta's file the day before, and it had left her with a headache. Thirty-five years old, a slew of diplomas and something of a chronic inability to adjust to the world of work. She'd reread his resume several times, and could not believe her eyes: he had a degree in history and geography, spoke fluent English, Spanish, and Italian—and even had a technical school certificate as a cook! This last qualification had piqued her interest, intrigued her. Then came a long-term nervous breakdown—that was less captivating. And he'd been a regular client of the public employment service for over five years, in half a dozen *départements*. Another stage winner for the Tour de France of the unemployed. He'd just landed in Paris and, worse luck, she'd gotten his file. All because Karine Becker would rather use natural contraceptive methods. But maybe it was just as well: she thought her colleague tended to be a bit soft with cases like this. Psychological approach, empathy, understanding . . . not Sandrine Cordier's thing. So she had decided she would make the most of this period to finalize a certain number of cases. Intimidation, threats, or, why not, an actual job (even if, judging by the client, such a possibility was by far the most fantastical): before long, Antoine Lacuenta would no longer be on welfare. Of course, she knew this was only a drop of water in a bottomless ocean, but the prospect of this little victory brought her a real anticipatory pleasure.

Truth be told, this was the thing she found most interesting about her profession—other than the fairly easygoing schedule, which left her some free time for indulging her passion for cooking. She had never found it all that interesting, helping good citizens to find a job, or a training course, or at least renewed confidence in their professional potential; she figured that only the weak and the parasites ended up in her office. The weak—those who had real difficulties integrating professionally, who'd suffered major mishaps in life—bored her stiff. The others, however, were much more interesting: good-for-nothings, shifty types, compulsive liars, a few cranks as well. It was not that she cared about the taxpayers' money or even the proper recording of public statistics on unemployment. But what she hated more than anything was for anyone to insult her intelligence or her intuition, which was particularly keen. Uncovering and getting the better of complicated strategies had initially been a delightful game that she excelled at, then it quickly became an addiction. She no longer saw the time go by when there was a chance to confound a guy who was working regularly under the table while claiming his benefits, or an executive rigging pseudo-professional interviews to get a few extra months of compensation. Long illnesses. Applicants who went in for one treatment after another: lungs in the spring, rheumatology in summer, digestion in the autumn. Freelance journalists were a real treat. Almost as delightful as the on-again, off-again theatre crowd! She'd been missing those down-at-heel actors since she left the office on the rue de Malte, but she'd learned to make do, with a certain pleasure, with the journalists, especially the freelance ones.

Just last month she'd nailed another one who thought he had the right to turn down a six-month contract at *La Revue du Cigare* under the pretext that for fifteen years he'd been a specialist on North-South relations for *Le Monde Diplomatique* and *Alternatives Économiques*. Yes, and so what? He'd bleated like a goat when she herself had arranged a meeting with the CEO of the venerable cigar publication to show him that she had unearthed the perfect candidate. *You'll see, he's an expert on Cuba*, she'd added disingenuously. *He'll cook you up a tasty little feature and it won't even cost you the airfare.* She was even beginning to have a bit of a reputation. When a newcomer in the waiting room was asked by his neighbor who his adviser was, and received the uncritical reply that it was Madame Cordier, the neighbor responded with a mute grimace which spoke volumes, before turning his head away—like at the beginning of the year at the lycée, when you'd ask about the math or philosophy teacher. Sandrine was, quite simply, formidable.

Her daughter Juliette, back in third grade, had asked her to explain what her job consisted of, for a class project. Standing in front of her awestruck, somewhat intimidated schoolmates, Juliette had declared that her mother was *a sort of sleuth, the secular arm of the government in the fight against rising unemployment.* Where had an eight-year-old kid come up with an expression like that? the teacher wondered, ill at ease. She'd had to console a little African boy whom Juliette had assured, her tone brooking no appeal, that *the only good unemployed person is the one who's been struck off the list.* Juliette's teacher hoped she'd never have to cross swords with parents like that.

Sometimes Sandrine was sorry she hadn't continued her studies at university, hadn't taken the bar exam or gone on to be a judge—she clearly had what it took. Or, at least, she could have gone for a master's, and after that she could have worked as a jurist, and maybe later as a private investigator. It would have been grander than this little job as a civil servant, which aroused her neighbors' skepticism when she told them what she did: adviser at the public employment service. What exactly was she advising? Moreover, law had not been her first choice. She would have preferred hotel school by far, but her parents wouldn't hear of it. Maybe because her grandmothers, both widowed in their thirties, had had to slave away at other people's stoves to raise their children. The Breton one as private chef for an upper-class family in Paimpol, and the one from Auvergne in an auberge in Rodez. Although they didn't know each other, the two women had dreamt of the civil service for their progeny, jobs that were modest but stable, obscure and respectable. The son of one had become an employee at the post office and the daughter of the other a teacher, and they in turn perpetuated the republican dream of social ascension by compelling Sandrine and her brother to take the competitive recruitment exams for a position in the administration. Oddly enough, the young woman's curious, impulsive, and mischievous disposition, along with a certain stubbornness, was a perfect fit for the austerity of the law, creating an unexpected but powerful alchemy. Since she couldn't work side-by-side with a great chef and then go on to open her own restaurant—her childhood dream—Sandrine gradually adapted to the subtleties of the codes and ruses of jurisprudence. But then at the end of her second year she fell in love with Guillaume; he'd charmed her with his bashed-up face and his six foot four—between boozy parties and rugby matches he was dragging his feet along a career path in social and economic administration. As a result, before she knew it she was married, with no more than a bachelor's degree in her pocket. Then, while her belly expanded, she dropped her studies and at the last minute took several administrative exams, before becoming a mother at the age of twenty-four. Her dream had been shelved but not altogether abandoned, for she put her considerable talent to use at home, even if she couldn't have her own little eatery.

* * *

The man who sat down across from her would have seemed totally harmless to any of her half-wit colleagues. And how wrong they would be! Sandrine Cordier knew from experience that he was anything but. First of all because, judging from his file, he was a Parasite, with a capital P. Then because he was far too good-looking to be honest. Dark, with trendy brooding looks, a three-day stubble and hair loose to his shoulders, slim, a slightly emaciated face dominated by huge dark doe eyes, and very red, moist lips. Not her type, though: she preferred sturdy blonds, men who took up space. She took a last bite from her cookie and tried to remember who the visitor reminded her of. A movie star? A TV anchor? One of those fashionable syrupy crooners? No, that wasn't it, he was simply the spitting image of . . . Jesus! The Jesus of the vintage catechism pictures she'd found not long ago when she was cleaning out her drawers. She had trusted in the natural regulation of the free market, where every offer has its demand, so she'd tried to sell those images during a neighborhood garage sale, along with other old things that had collected in the basement and in her wardrobes. Well, she hadn't really had much luck. She'd only managed to offload three of them to an old lady clinging to her Zimmer frame, who struggled to find her change purse at the bottom of her handbag. Later on, a gang of teenagers had fiddled with the remaining pictures, guffawing and nudging each other. After a few minutes one of them had asked her if she also had some pictures of the Virgin, but *wearing a string like that other dummy on the cross.* They ran off, screaming with laughter and slapping their palms together, little punks. As they moved off, one of them had turned around, and she thought she heard, *Hey, it's Aurélien's mom, how crazy is that!* One girl shot back, *I'm not surprised,* and their laughter grew even louder.

The straight nose, the gentle, sorrowful gaze, that fragile, almost feminine beauty . . . it was all there, but in the guise of a lingering adolescent: hoodie, jeans, worn-out Converses, canvas bag over his shoulder. She repressed a faint shiver and couldn't help but glance at his fine, white hands: phew, no obvious stigmata. As for his feet, his sneakers came up a little too high on his ankles for her to judge.

"Monsieur Lacuenta, you file has just been transferred to us. I'd like to go over the situation since you were last employed, which was the substitute position for a few months at the lycée Marie-de-la-Conception in Manosque, teaching history and geography. You see, I don't really understand why you left that position when you could have gone on working as a substitute. It was a perfect match for your skills, wasn't it?"

The man shot her a long, angry gaze, and he sighed, which Sandrine Cordier understood to mean that he found it difficult to speak of a trying episode. Another ultrasensitive guy, how annoying. Just wait, any minute he'd start up on those old schoolteacher blues.

"The pressure, you have no idea . . . you can't get kids to behave, they don't listen, they're not interested in anything, they have no respect for authority anymore."

No, of course not. As if you didn't have five months of vacation to recover, she thought, ready to say as much to his face.

In reality, above all Antoine Lacuenta found it hard to explain something that to him seemed obvious. But where everything else was concerned, he had no problem going over it in detail: he'd already had to do it many times, and he remained convinced he was in good faith.

"The school made absolutely no effort at all to convert to sustainable development. The heating was all electric, there were no local products at the cafeteria, and the principal had even installed the most anti-ecological device you can imagine: a coffee machine with capsules," he explained, with detachment, as if he were teaching a class at the blackboard. "No selective recycling, so as a result the waste wasn't put to good use. During civic education class I asked the pupils to sort the school's garbage cans and it caused a huge fuss, the parents even got involved. When I suggested at the faculty meeting that carpooling among the teachers should be made obligatory and that they should install dry toilets, everyone laughed in my face. They weren't even interested in the plans for a communal organic vegetable garden in an urban environment. And yet there were plenty of subsidies available. This failure to consider the problems of the planet and the urgency of finding solutions was quite simply intolerable. Teaching in such conditions was tantamount to condoning an irresponsible attitude, so by resigning I have made a statement whose impact is both educational and socially aware. Moreover, I've started a blog to explain why I acted as I did."

While staring at Lacuenta with a look that was both engrossed and severe, Sandrine Cordier lost the thread of the conversation. An organic vegetable garden in an urban setting . . . A rather nice idea, although she would not like to share her garden with just anyone. Her balcony ran the length of her apartment and was overrun with aromatic herbs, but it was hard to grow vegetables in such conditions. Dry toilets, on the other hand . . . What did that imply? She cautiously refrained from asking, for fear of being treated to a lecture on the subject, but her mind began to wander. Could it mean that instead of porcelain bowls, nesting reservoirs, and silent flush systems, the bathroom department at Leroy Merlin would suddenly be replaced by an entire aisle of giant plastic trays and bags of kitty litter? Vegetable, mineral, perfumed, family size, fifty liters minimum? Would kindergarten sandboxes be requisitioned and transformed into municipal *pissotières?* Having said that, if there were subsidies available, it was worth looking into. She noted the information in the *follow-up* box, cleared her throat, and sent him a polite but stern smile.

Antoine Lacuenta gave her a look that was both wretched and furious.

"You can see that I had no choice."

"Well, I cannot judge the heart of the matter," she said, going no further, for she was not sure she'd completely followed the thread of his explanation.

She turned a page in the file, read a few lines, frowned, then stared darkly at her visitor.

"Your militant ecological stance almost convinced me . . . But then, well, look, I read here that you didn't resign but that you were fired for hurting the school's cleaning woman. What's that all about? Maybe you suspected her of being a lackey for major investors? An agent infiltrated from Unilever who'd come to enlist your pimply teenagers? In my opinion, most of them already boycott a certain number of personal hygiene products, you know . . . "

"Didn't your grandmother teach you that all you need is a little bit of hot water, vinegar, and household soap to clean just about everything? She didn't? That's too bad," said Antoine Lacuenta, visibly annoyed.

Sandrine Cordier looked at his well-groomed hands and could not help but wonder whether he scrubbed his own toilet, dry or otherwise. He followed her gaze and hastily tucked his hands into his pockets.

"And yet it's simple," he continued, looking somewhat smug. "I explained this to her several times, but she went on using industrial products that are toxic both for her and for the environment. Not to mention the fact that they are very expensive and are often manufactured in countries that respect neither the moratorium on child labor nor even the right to strike.

All for the benefit of international companies, to enrich their financial investors. Of course I didn't attack her, I am nonviolent and she is practically my mother's age! I just asked her to hand me the window spray, and she was standing on a stool. I wanted to show her what the components were. And since she preferred to hang onto it rather than let go of it . . . she fell."

"Ouch. Her hip?"

"Among other things," he nodded, making a face.

Marta Pires spent several weeks in the hospital, wrapped in plaster from head to foot for multiple fractures, an enormous bandage on her skull. But the worst of it was that she nearly lost her right eye: in her fall, she landed on the ergonomic hollow handle of the squeegee, which then neatly slotted itself into her eye socket with a disgusting little suction noise: *shlup*. She'd been carried out on the ambulance stretcher with her work tool still planted in her eye and the window spray clasped in both hands like a big automatic pistol. She refused to let it go, and sprayed the paramedics more than once, straight in the eyes, with terrifying precision for such impaired vision and with twin fractures of the wrists. No doubt she believed she was aiming at Antoine Lacuenta, against whom she was chanting some sort of voodoo incantation in her Creole dialect from Cape Verde. At the hospital, given her refusal to cooperate, the emergency physician had to knock her out with a defibrillator in order to perform first aid.

"Actually, for all that you've been going on about local products and recycling . . . You do realize that the clothes you are wearing were surely not made in France, but by some malnourished children in Bangladesh?"

As she said it, an evil thought gladdened her: child labor was an abomination, of course, but sometimes, when she thought of certain adolescents . . . Those twins on the sixth floor who came tearing down the stairs, screaming whenever they could, at night, or at dawn on Sunday. Or Aurélien's friends: they were incapable of either a hello or a smile when they stomped grumpily through the living room on their way to sprawl in his room and shout and wail like lunatics. When they reemerged after a few hours, they again looked sullen and morose, and muttered a vague sort of goodbye, dragging their feet. If they found the front door it was by radar; they never looked up from behind their long, dubious bangs, and they left in their wake the sickly sweet effluvia of sleep and grime. Then there had been those kids at the garage sale: she pictured the little gang in the hell of a Chinese textile factory (toxic dyes, danger of mutilation and burns) or of an open-air quarry in Katanga (carcinogenic particles, landslides), and a faint smile crept onto her lips.

"On the contrary, my briefs were manufactured in France," replied Antoine Lacuenta, outrage in his voice.

Before Sandrine had time to realize what was happening, he had plunged his hand into his pants. He hunted around for a few seconds in front, then behind, before tugging out the stretch of cloth where the label was sewn. He stood up to show her, but with a placating little wave of the hand Sandrine asked him to sit back down. She really didn't need to see more. Given the size of the patch of cloth spilling out of his jeans, she got the unpleasant sensation that the rest of his underwear must be compressing him left, right, and center, or at least be very closely acquainted with the crack between his buttocks. A shudder went through her, and with a wriggle on her chair she checked that her own underwear was where it should be. Antoine Lacuenta sat back down without readjusting his clothes, the label still plain to see: either the damage was not as significant as she'd imagined, or he was used to such discomfort. Or maybe he enjoyed it? The man was definitely weird.

"Everything else—I wear only secondhand clothes," he continued, with a shrug. "Flea market, Salvation Army, discount stores, garage sales . . . There's plenty to choose from. And no need to go broke. Because in my situation . . . "

With his index finger he pointed first to his hoodie (Abercrombie), then his T-shirt (Diesel) and his jeans (Levis), enumerating the price he'd paid for each: 15, 10, and 25 euros. All three seemed to be in good condition, as far as she could tell, with just enough of a patina to look trendy. The computer that dozed perpetually in her brain suddenly woke up: to dress a teenager in those brands for such a sum would be a sign of real talent. Maybe this client wasn't as warped as he'd initially seemed, or maybe he was simply such a nutcase that he'd become interesting. In the end, her day was not totally wasted. You could even say that the week was starting to look positive. All morning she'd dealt with jobseekers of no interest, very drab in comparison to this Antoine Lacuenta. An accountancy director who'd just been fired for the fifth time, to start with, then a woman in her fifties who was hoping for a position as executive secretary after twenty-five years spent battery rearing her brats. The woman went away again sniffing into her handkerchief after Sandrine pointed out that her computer skills could not match even those of an average high school student.

"Do you have any good tips for buying Converses or Reeboks?" she asked, out of curiosity.

"Discount places, consignment stores, church fairs, I have loads of addresses all over the place. Even sample sales for the fashion press, if you're interested," he added, almost confidentially, leaning across the desk with a slight, sardonic smile.

She took no notice: Sandrine Cordier was incorruptible.

"Now it's clearer to me why, before Manosque, you worked at the treatment plant in Fougères-sur-Somme," she continued, a touch more professional, trying not to notice the label still sticking out of his jeans. "Recycling, sorting, sustainable development . . . You must have been in your element there, no?"

"Well, at least I felt like I was doing something useful, something that was in keeping with my values."

"What did you do there?"

"I worked in both collection and treatment. Dipping into every aspect of a trade is a very healthy principle. To start with, going around in the dump trucks with colleagues, picking up paper and newspapers on Tuesdays and glass on Fridays. Heavy stuff once a month. Alternately I did sorting at the site. You cannot imagine all the stuff that people throw out. Enough to furnish entire apartment buildings—toys, bicycles, appliances that are just missing a screw . . . "

"But you didn't want to stay? Because of the salary maybe, or the status? To end up a garbage collector when you have a degree in history and geography, that's not exactly upwardly mobile . . . "

"Oh, upwardly mobile! Typical petit bourgeois way of looking at things," sniffed Antoine Lacuenta with scorn. "I couldn't care less about status and I don't need much money to live on, especially as I do a lot of bartering. No, it was because of the trucks."

"Oh?"

"When I had my interview, the site director explained that before long the entire fleet of vehicles would be shifting to electric, or hybrid at the very least. The community of communes also communicated on the topic . . . We had a fascinating conversation about carbon footprints and renewable energy, and this convinced me to take the job. Six months later the fleet was still running on diesel and no one said a thing about electric or even hybrid vehicles. But I didn't give up: with some comrades from the union we got the word out, and I even tried get them to come out and march . . . "

"And you were let go after a little . . . accident? Another one?"

Sandrine Cordier looked up from the file and stared at him, frowning.

This guy really was a fraud.

Antoine Lacuenta shrugged and sighed. It was boring, going back over the past, a waste of time. But oh well, the little ferret would get her money's worth.

"After the elections, the president of the community of communes came to meet us at the end of one of our rounds. He insisted on climbing up on the dumpster to take a closer look at our working conditions, but above all he wanted a grandstand for making his speech. Like all politicians, he told us what he thought we wanted to hear. I asked him about clean-energy vehicles, and he avoided the question, I don't think he ever had any intention of talking with a garbageman, he was more the type who acts condescending around the proletariat. I got closer to ask him for an explanation, to remind him of what he'd pledged, but he obstinately refused to answer me and wouldn't even make eye contact. I made a gesture that was maybe a little sudden, he was startled, and he tripped on the running board . . . "

"Ouch. His ankle, I suppose?"

"Not only," sighed Antoine.

Philippe Petitjean had fallen headfirst into the giant dumpster just as one of the employees, at his request, had switched on the mechanism. The dumpster was full of household waste, which softened his fall, but he got his head stuck in a huge metal can which turned out to be a dog food container. The compactor continued its descent as the workers looked on, aghast. You have to realize, most of them had never seen an accident of this nature. Then the site director virtually flew across the five meters separating him from the truck, shouting and gesticulating as if he were performing a haka. He had scored with the security system, as if he were making a desperate try in rugby, for the beauty of the gesture, just as the ref was blowing the whistle. For a few fateful seconds Philippe Petitjean lay crosswise on his stomach, his arms trapped in a quicksand of refuse, his left leg beneath the enormous rollers while his right was making a sort of desperate, useless crawling movement in an effort to climb up the pile of garbage.

He'd roared like a boar, his cries muffled and distorted by the dog food can, but all he succeeded in doing was further stunning himself with his makeshift helmet. By the time they finally managed to get him out of there, his left leg was dangling at strange angles at both the knee and the ankle, sort of like a folding yardstick that's been badly . . . folded. The firefighters had to liberate him from the can in several stages, and initially they only opened the bottom so he could breathe. The rusty metal left him with a souvenir, a pretty little festoon all along his forehead, cheeks, and chin. One of his eyelids had nearly been sliced off and for the rest of his life it would droop lower than the other one, and this earned him thereafter the sympathetic and most appropriate nickname Fido. Since the incident his main political opponent had gotten into the habit of barking at him whenever they met. Petitjean was a good sport: in response he growled and bared his teeth.

Still, the town councilor's accident had not been without its usefulness, so to speak. On removing him from all the refuse, the firefighters had been dismayed and astonished to discover that the dumpster was filled with practically nothing but cans of pet food and extra-large, used, disposable diapers. The garbage round had been curtailed that day because of the councilor's visit, and the last call had been at a retirement home a mile or two from there. Now, other than five sorry, balding, little poodles, whose teeth were no longer in any condition to indulge in culinary fantasies, the establishment housed no four-legged friends. A health inspection control was ordered. Pet food, it turned out, had been the main ingredient of most of the meals for years: *pâté forestier*, meatballs in gravy, Shepherd's pie, *paupiettes*, spaghetti Bolognese, stuffed vegetables, ravioli, moussaka, chili con carne, goulash, and even *brandade*.

Moreover, most of the cans of pet food had expired at least eight years earlier, the date on which the Lithuanian manufacturer had gone out of business; at that point the retirement home had bought six tons of supplies for a song. It had all been stockpiled in a labyrinth of underground caves dug by the Germans during World War II, a gigantic rabbit warren underneath the garden at the retirement home that everyone had forgotten about. Among other things, the scandal had helped to shed light on the unusually high number of deaths from botulism at the institution, something that had hitherto been a complete mystery. Not a very nice story at all now, was it, particularly for a three-star retirement home accredited by the Social Security, with all the local upper-crust politicians serving on the board.

APPLE TURNOVER

"Psst, Guillaume!"

In spite of his considerable corpulence, the man speaking in a hushed voice managed to weave his way between the trolleys and piles of boxes cluttering the windowless little room, to reach Guillaume Cordier's desk. Cordier was struggling with an antediluvian computer that was reluctant to reboot. He looked up for a moment before dipping back behind his screen and the unsteady piles of cardboard folders stacked on either side of him.

"Hey, Marc, how's it going? I've got a bug here, sorry, I can't leave the keyboard, what with all these pathetic shortcuts."

"Yeah, sure, fine. Don't worry about the bug, the entire network is down. The IT people are overwhelmed with calls and I took the opportunity to get away, they'll think I've gone to help out somewhere."

"So I can leave the keyboard? Grrr, fucking stupid machine . . . Have you got time for a coffee? I have some left over from the marketing meeting this morning."

Two thermoses, some paper cups, and a basket of sorry-looking mini Danishes stood on a wheeled cart next to the desk. He poured two coffees and nudged one toward his visitor.

"Say, things are going well, by the looks of it. Usually the admins make off with everything at the end of a meeting. How are you getting on?"

"I'm getting on."

"I nearly forgot, you're in good hands at home, aren't you, you pig," chortled Marc, before swallowing his coffee in one go. "Yuck, your joe is lukewarm. Next time, call me when you get the thermoses so we can drink it when it's hot, okay? Already it's not the best in the world. Anyway, I came to see if you've got anything new?"

"Bah, not much, well, depends what you're looking for. Is it for you or for Isa? Maybe as a gift?"

"A gift, easier said than done; it's for my mother-in-law, we're having supper at her place tonight and it always softens her up a bit if I bring her one of those women's magazines, some fashion thing, maybe she won't make her usual remarks about how many glasses of wine I've had. Whatever you have will do, some cooking or knitting thing, that's fine, too."

"It's a bit slack at the moment, to be honest: I don't have the new monthlies yet, and almost no more weekly women's magazines. Let me just have a look."

Guillaume Cordier took a key ring from his pocket and unlocked the three heavy padlocks of a big metal locker behind his desk. It was a veritable safe, filled with newspapers and magazines carefully piled on the shelves or stored in hanging files. Labels on the edge of each shelf specified the categories: women's, news, leisure, etc. Guillaume rummaged delicately in the pile of women's magazines and took out the *Elle* from the previous week, along with *Psychologies Magazine* and *Gala*.

"This one is usually a hit, isn't it, full of celebrities and stuff like that?" asked Marc, pointing to *Gala*.

"It's ideal for your mother-in-law, it's what I'd take for mine."

In fact, his own mother-in-law, a retired teacher and die-hard militant feminist, had nothing but deep revulsion for women's and celebrity magazines; for her he reserved the more highbrow *Télérama*.

"One euro twenty," he said. "Otherwise, if you want something more intellectual, there's *Psychologies Magazine*. It's more expensive, two sixty, because of the little guidebook they give you. Hey, I just noticed the theme: 'Natural Medicine through the Rectum.' There must be an audience. I guarantee it's never been read, it's still in the shrink-wrap."

"If I take both, could you throw in the rugby paper for the same price?"

"I swear, you want to clean me out, Marc . . . Print media is really suffering already, or didn't you know? The price of paper keeps going up, competition with the Internet, crisis in advertising . . . That's not even half of it! Just because I'm not an official distributor doesn't mean I don't have my own little code of ethics, you know. Out of respect for my suppliers I can't set my prices too low."

"Yeah, really! You've got a margin of one hundred percent. And it's a good thing your little code of ethics *is* little, because if your suppliers found out, I think they'd really shove it up your rectum," added Marc with an obscene gesture that was not devoid of imagination. "And besides, I'm sure you've already read all the rugby news, no? You've recouped the cost once already, as it were?"

"Okay, then, since it's you," sighed Cordier. "Three euros eighty for all three."

Marc rummaged in his pocket and slid two two-euro coins across the desk, while Guillaume put the magazines into a big manila envelope. He pocketed the four euros and went back to fiddling on his keyboard.

"Hey, my change?"

"Sorry, no small stuff. Have a mini croissant instead?"

He held out a basket half full of pastries drooping on a smeared paper napkin. Up close they looked both dry and greasy. Some even looked like they must have been handled, or nibbled, then put back in such a way that any takers would notice only too late, once they'd already picked them up. A fat fly was dozing beneath a croissant and flew away with a buzz of annoyance when its improvised hammock was dismantled.

"Man, has the marketing budget gone down or what. Before, it was regal, but now . . . They entertain clients with this stuff? Are you sure these were fresh this morning?"

"If you don't want any, don't force yourself," said Guillaume, his eyes glued to the screen, as he began to reach for the basket. "I have takers who are ready to pay top price up in accounting and purchasing, you know."

The IT man was quicker: with one fat hand he grabbed a mini apple turnover, then changed his mind and pinched a soggy pain au chocolat as well. He swallowed both at once, before Guillaume had time to react.

"They're already practically inedible, I'm doing you a favor," he said with his mouth full, as he turned away with his manila envelope under his arm.

T-BONE STEAK

Marcel Lacarrière looked at the fruit of his loins with a heavy heart. Maybe it was always like this, after all, for "children with aging parents," as they used to say back in his day. He was already older than forty-five when he'd become a father, his genetic material was probably already deliquescent . . . The fact remained that thirty-two years later, he could not help but feel a twinge of bitterness at the thought that his only son had neither his mother's beauty (a magnificent Swedish model twenty years his junior, from whom he was long divorced), nor his business acumen, nor even a shred of intelligence. *Nada*. The fairies had not done their job properly, they'd gotten muddled after a rather boozy evening, or maybe those naughty girls had been bribed by the competition: the little boy had inherited both his father's considerably unprepossessing looks and his mommy's brains. A basically very banal mixture that Marcel Lacarrière had encountered all his life among any number of people he'd had to deal with. But it was hardly an asset for the future CEO and principal shareholder of a little press enterprise. Particularly in the middle of an economic crisis and the digital revolution.

This latest meeting with the management committee had just confirmed to him that he was not about to hand the reins of the group over to his sole descendant, at least not in his lifetime. As the notion of a legal retirement age had vanished, wasn't the number of necessary contribution trimesters constantly going up? Never mind—since he'd never get around to taking his bloody retirement! Lately he'd been brooding a lot, thinking that the odds of him kicking the bucket right after a board meeting or during some ordinary staff meeting, rather than lying next to his pool or in his bed, was increasing by the day. Something like thirty to one. He just hoped he wouldn't collapse in his private restroom next to his office with his pants around his ankles, he didn't want to be found in such a humiliating posture by one of his admins. He might be unattractive, but he was a great charmer: no way would the last woman to see him in his birthday suit find him about to surrender.

He gave a sigh as he glanced at the diagram the financial director had projected onto the white wall. For once, it wasn't littered with acronyms in English or stock exchange jargon, and the simplicity of the drawing spoke for itself. A geometrical work of art, a Mondrian in black and white: a perfect diagonal started from the upper left hand side and sliced gallantly down to the lower right, separating the sheet into two right-angled triangles. It was the sort of slope that would have delighted an amateur of cycling, a steep gradient in a straight line. Pure. Not an obstacle in sight. But dangerous, too. Moreover, it made not only the chairman but also the shareholder wince—as it happened, they were one and the same individual—for it represented the evolution of the company's financial results. And that diagonal line sliced through a horizontal one that figured right in the middle of the diagram, which signified as transparently as could be that the profits (once quite tidy, let it be noted in passing) had been transformed into losses, which would be very heavy in the short term.

At that intersection, the sudden shift toward the abyss represented the year in progress. Straightforward, right? Any slightly attentive primary school pupil could grasp this. But not his son, no, not the son of a Swedish model, a woman who with an inane laugh mixed up every pedal of every car he'd ever given her—and yet God knows he'd tried to keep it simple by sticking solely to automatics. No. Laurent Lacarrière had looked at the diagram, then at the financial director, with a stunned little air, before he turned to his father, one finger pointing at the white wall, and squeaked, *Dad, you see how it's going down?* Marcel had asked him time and time again not to refer to him like that in front of the employees or the suppliers. But whenever his son began to feel a little more anxious—and he must have realized that if there were losses he was going to have to do some hard work, and not just on the golf course—he got back into this habit, which in another context might have been perfectly touching. Around the table, the other members of the management committee felt a unanimous, furious urge to check their shoelaces, including the two women who were wearing high heels, and they all dove under the table as one man.

After the financial officer had finished his presentation, Marcel Lacarrière thanked him, along with the other executives who were present, and he adjourned the meeting. With a little nod he signaled to his son to follow him into his office. He also grabbed the arm of the deputy CEO, still not saying a word, indicating the same direction. What he had to say to them had to stay between them. He realized what a challenge it would be to have a discussion of this nature with Laurent, but he did not totally despair of teaching him a few tricks of the trade. *An old man's sentimental take on things; it'll be the death of me,* he thought. But he had only one son, after all, and not a great deal of choice.

He shot a look at Luc Bricard, the deputy CEO; as was often the case, Bricard had not yet said a thing, but was waiting for the right moment. He was Laurent Lacarrière's henchman and chaperone. Marcel had hired him five years earlier to keep close tabs on his son regarding every decision he might make, every appointment with a supplier, with a banker, every meeting with the trade union. He even asked him to keep an eye on his expense account, his neckties, and his amorous escapades—Laurent had always had multiple affairs, with little discernment, and he sometimes landed in embarrassing situations. Twice over Bricard had had to intervene to nip a nefarious affair in the bud; one had involved a series of naughty videos posted on YouTube. Laurent Lacarrière's bank account had the merit of causing women to overlook his charmless physique: a high forehead, already balding; a big, flat nose; deep-set eyes too close together. A premature paunch testified to his lack of exercise, rich diet, and extreme nonchalance—three vices to which Marcel had never succumbed. Laurent's height, the only shared legacy from both parents, did rescue his build somewhat, and there was about him the faint air of the degenerate aristocrat, all the same. In any case, the Lacarrière line would end with Laurent, as an untimely case of the mumps contracted in his late teens had deprived him of the ability to reproduce.

* * *

In spite of his official and semiofficial responsibilities, Luc Bricard managed to remain in the shadows. He was an intelligent man, consumed by ambition, but his modest origins—his mother, a nanny, had raised him on her own with a litter of seven or eight other children, and he had never known which ones were his real blood brothers and sisters—had left him servile and wary. But oddly enough, very loyal, as well. When he met old Lacarrière, he'd known right from the start that they wanted the same things. He had become the secret right-hand man, sufficiently calculating to remain satisfied with a position that many others would have found uncomfortable. Adviser to Laurent Lacarrière, that daddy's boy whose stupidity often attained abysses worthy of the Mariana Trench—in his case, it would be difficult to talk of summits—seemed to Luc one way like any other of reaching his goal of professional success, which could be summed up in three letters: CEO. So discreet he was almost shifty, and very efficient, he had made himself indispensable to the kid, and therefore to *Dad*.

Ever the crafty old devil, Marcel Lacarrière did however pay Bricard a bit less than he should have. Just enough to keep him under pressure, like a guard dog that is fed only in the morning so at night on an empty stomach it will be on the alert. Marcel made up for this with gifts, and because of his social origins, Bricard accepted them with admiration that was child-like, even though he was over forty-five: invitations to garden parties held by petty provincial nobles; admission to a Masonic lodge; unlimited access to the bar at the Lacarrières' private villa in Marrakesh, airfare included. But what was a must was the invitation to the grand barbecue the old man invariably hosted every year on his own birthday, at his hunting estate in Sologne: a little country feast, *simple as can be*, where the magnate himself, wrapped in a long apron, with a chef's toque on his head, stood turning the merguez sausages and T-bone steaks and seasoning the potato salad, then went on to serve his guests. There you would meet his family: three ex-wives with their current husbands and brood, and an entire string of nephews, nieces, and little cousins, all lured by the hypothetical inheritance; political allies who went way back; and personal bodyguards to whose rank Luc Bricard was proud to belong. Not really friends, opportunists of every stripe was more like it, with varying talents: the magnate carefully curated them all, while waiting for them to scratch his back.

The three men sat down in the chairman's office, a large, pleasant room with mahogany furniture.

"Right, I think the presentation was clear enough, we're headed straight for the wall, and at full speed," stated Marcel firmly. "Any concrete suggestions?"

"The sales team are doing everything they can, but the cost of advertising is still in a downward spiral," said Luc Bricard. "Same thing for distribution at newspaper stands. And every time I read an obituary in *Le Monde* or *Le Figaro,* I can be sure that we've just lost a subscriber. But we can blame the crisis: it's fairly obvious that things started getting worse since the launch of *Convictions* six months ago. We haven't stopped losing market share, while those bastards progress."

For three generations the Lacarrière group had been publishing *Le Libéral*, a little general newsweekly firmly situated on the right, whose readership was were over sixty. Its penetration in the affluent levels of the population between the ages of sixty and eighty-five—former executives, self-employed professionals, property owners, shareholders—was so successful that high-end retirement homes and manufacturers of hearing aids regularly rented the subscribers' mailing list to do their canvassing. For individuals over eight-five, who were far from marginal among their readers, it was funeral parlors, rather, who rented the mailing list. But all good pensions come to an end: senior citizens were no longer what they used to be. They got suntanned, went trekking, discovered cosmetic surgery and seemed to grow younger before your very eyes. They had learned to use a computer, then a smartphone, and now a tablet, and they'd gradually been abandoning traditional print media. Marcel was a living example: he often answered his emails on his iPad on a Sunday morning. In short, in the third millennium, readers wanted something new, but *Le Libéral* smacked of tradition, which was now slightly rancid.

Much smaller than mainstream news magazines like *L'Express* or *Le Nouvel Observateur, Le Libéral* had founded its editorial strategy on an unchanging triptych: economic liberalism; the art of the French way of life, provided one had a minimum of resources: fine wines, prizewinning restaurants, cruises, châteaux, and luxury hotels; and partisan, sarcastic political commentary—oh, those socialist Mitterrand years, what bliss! So much grist to the mill! All the staff writers still recalled them with a quaver in their voice, and several retired journalists had even offered free copy since Hollande was elected. At the back of the magazine a few pages were devoted to more frivolous concerns for Madame: a little fashion and beauty, some psychological advice, recipes, and decorating ideas.

To be honest, this new rival, *Convictions*, had not done much to update the formula, but it had made its stances and subjects more radical, in order to rake in a younger, more active readership. Its economic liberalism was even more liberal, so to speak. Its political attacks more virulent, flaunting all the while an opportunism which *Le Libéral* never allowed itself: under the cover of a "neither on the right nor the left" stance, sometimes they made eyes at the far right, sometimes it was the anarchists, or even the center, why not. Their travel features were more upscale and innovative; their fashion pages more glamorous and celebrity-focused. But where the new publication had scored a major hit, a veritable stroke of genius, was by replacing the psychologist—a bigwig in a white coat, retired from the faculty, looking drearily like someone's granddad—with a sexologist. Never mind that her qualifications were a bit murky, obtained at some unknown private institute in Belgium; this was largely occulted by her figure, like that of a reformed porn actress: an indecent breast size, fleshy lips, come-hither gaze, all reassuringly veiled by a pair of tortoiseshell glasses. Every week Annabelle Villemin-Dubreuil took two questions from readers, and already from the first issue her column had been a hit. But the editorial department of the magazine was caught up short by her success, when the pile of questions waiting to be answered began to grow exponentially. It made you wonder whether readers still had time to do anything besides confide in the press with their little plumbing problems!

Consequently, a special paid app had been created at the same time: *Intimate Convictions*, available for tablets. Under the cover of features on French heritage or pseudo-sociological surveys, the app also offered the addresses of partner-swapping guesthouses and luxury hotels in Europe that provided Swarovski handcuffs and Hermès switches to guests in search of refined frissons, at an exorbitant price. There were even comparison tests of sex toys and online shopping for naughty lingerie (from 59 to 250 euros per item, by the way, but well-made French or Italian lace never has been cheap). The stroke of genius in this particular case was not the choice of products, but the feature article that accompanied the photographs. The journalist in charge of the project had not hesitated to inter-view Monique Bonnier, emerita historian, professor at the Collège de France, and expert on costumes from the Middle Ages to the present day.

Convictions: Monique Bonnier, you have just published *Panties through the Centuries.* What, in your opinion, is behind a certain type of "sex-shop" fashion that is suddenly in all the stores?

Monique Bonnier: Contrary to what people might think, this is not the syndrome of a society where pornography has become the norm for sexuality and therefore, likewise, for its sartorial attributes, particularly where women's underwear is concerned. On the contrary, the return to crotchless panties, for example, reflects a desire for a certain traditionalism, a form of reassurance for contemporary women.

Convictions: What do you mean by "return"?

Monique Bonnier: In case you didn't know, until our great-grandmothers' generation, that is what our ancestors wore. Of course the style has changed; back then panties were big, loose things. Nowadays we have strings and tangas, rather, because we live in a society that favors austerity and the notion that less is more. But the choice to wear such an undergarment in 2013 is a way of reimmersing oneself into one's own family history and a respect for bygone generations. An attitude one typically finds during periods of crisis.

Convictions: Historically, how was this undergarment used? Has its use evolved?

Monique Bonnier: For centuries the practical aspect predominated. Women wore several layers of petticoats and long skirts which made access to the latrines rather complicated. This type of undergarment offered them greater freedom while ensuring satisfactory airflow and hygiene. Obviously this aspect of its use has become obsolete, principally because women dress differently: we no longer wear petticoats, but, more and more, jeans and leggings. It's the militant choice that prevails, now, rather than the functional one, even though the possibility for furtive coupling that a crotchless panty offers also has a certain advantage, as I'm sure you'll agree.

Oh la la! One can only take one's hat off to a publication that, to keep its readers informed, manipulates culture and impertinence with such brio. In short, a delicious perfume of bourgeois licentiousness emanated from *Convictions*, but all as if butter wouldn't melt in any journalist's mouth.

And the advertisers? They a-*dored* it. They couldn't get enough. So much so that the magazine was now selling its advertising space at auction. The links featured on the app, in particular, were breaking all records.

Dear Annabelle,
A few months ago Albert, my husband for over fifty years, put an end to our rolls in the hay because of his lumbago and

his hip replacement. What do you advise? You are our last hope . . . Madeleine.

Dear Madeleine,
Nothing is lost, on the contrary! A new life awaits (here, a link for a banking and insurance group). *Start by checking whether the thickness of your mattress is appropriate for Albert's back problems, and don't think twice about changing it if need be, along with the box springs* (link to an upscale mattress shop also selling ergonomic and medical beds). *After you've made the bed with some pretty percale or satin sheets* (links to two outrageously expensive Italian manufacturers of bed linen), *light a candle, or a diffuser with a few drops of essential oil* (pop-up for the leading European aromatherapy brand). *Slip on your most adorable negligee* (link to a designer specialized in outfitting biddies) *then ask your husband to lie down on his back in a comfortable position. You will then straddle him and, once you have his collaboration* (link to a famous brand of tablets for preventing erectile dysfunction) *undertake several series of contractions of the perineum while performing gentle movements with your hips. For enhanced muscular reinforcement, do not hesitate to contract your abdominal muscles at the same time. You can repeat the exercise as often as you and Albert desire, at your own pace. Best wishes, Annabelle.*

Not bad, is it? Annabelle Villemin-Dubreuil was preparing, moreover, to publish a collection of all her chronicles for the *Convictions Éditions* imprint: *Do Yourself Good in Order to . . . Do Yourself Good.* If the vivacious thirty-year-old is to be believed, all the minor complaints of advanced age can be repaired (or at least alleviated) by regular, tantrically inspired sexual activity. Does René cough at night? Nothing like the lotus position. Huguette has arthritis? Try the Thai wheelbarrow, very relaxing. Who could possibly want to contradict her? And even if they did, would those sexually disgruntled readers really go and complain to the Department of Competition, Consumer Rights, and Fraud Repression, or to the Social Security? What the hell, a little bit of daydreaming never hurt anyone.

Moreover, it could well be that the columnist for *Convictions* was on the right track: a polling organization had long been including questions about sexuality among senior citizens in an extensive monthly study, and recent findings were astonishing, to say the least. Ever cautious, the organization refrained momentarily from publishing their findings, but they were witnessing a weekly progression of:

a) the number of positions performed during intercourse (3.1 as opposed to 1.1 earlier; even octogenarians had gone beyond 2)

b) the monthly frequency of sexual relations (4 times as against 0.3)

c) the average duration of coitus (12 minutes compared to 4; in other words, roughly 4 minutes per position, so the director of studies mused, swearing she would try to shake her guy up a little that very evening)

d) sexual practices not approved by the Roman Catholic Church (a verbatim with a definite 1930s or '40s sound to its jargon accompanied some of the replies to the survey, particularly among the gentlemen; there was notably the question of "sitting on it and rotating", but not only that).

In short, while print journals were on the brink of ruin, *Convictions*'s gamble had paid off, thanks to a simple recipe: sex, buzz, sex, and more buzz. It was time to act.

Marcel Lacarrière gave a sigh and only began to speak again after a long silence.

"Right, the classical methods are not working. It's time to try something unconventional. To do things furtively. *Convictions* is well-established above all at the newspaper kiosks, so it's time for it to be a little harder to find. Stock shortages, unavailability . . . people forget quickly, it's only a very recent publication, without any real renown, it's just a passing trend. And besides, the shareholders cannot afford to suffer losses for too long, they've already gone through a huge chunk of their cash . . . So we will always represent a sure value, a mark people can trust," said Marcel emphatically. "We're the only magazine that people pass on in their wills, after all . . . "

Henri, Marcel's grandfather, had indeed invented the "emphyteutic subscription." Whoever took out such a subscription committed his or her direct descendants—or if there were none, privileged relations—to continue receiving the subscription at their expense without any possibility of retraction, for a period of ninety-nine years, tacitly renewable. With each death, the heir who took over the subscription was then known as the main subscriber, and the obligation then weighed on his own descendants or relations, *ad vitum aeternam*, so to speak. The little firm had always had crafty judicial and financial arrangements; the parties were bound by a contract drawn up according to the law of the Duchy of Luxembourg, eight pages in six-point type, written in 1923 by a somewhat underhand jurist. Among other improbable clauses, any notice of non-automatic-renewal had to be given three thousand five hundred days on the dot before the initial expiration of the ninety-nine years. Most subscribers got caught out because of leap years.

In reality, since its creation only a few thousand people had opted for this strange type of subscription, and the last major wave of new emphyteutic contracts dated back to over thirty years earlier. But in its heyday it had charmed a certain provincial bourgeoisie, who saw it as an enduring way to flaunt their opulence, like the noble families they were imitating. Moreover, this oddity of the French (and even global) press occasionally fueled some juicy lawsuit or titillating family quarrel, to the delight of all the media. Just last year the two heirs of a surgeon from Limoges had initially refused the entire legacy (2.6 million euros in real estate, treasury bills, and cash) because they did not manage to come to an agreement. The older heir had taken the younger one to court. Marcel Lacarrière, sensing a windfall, had offered a second subscription for the period of one year, long enough for the two brothers to come to terms about who would inherit the emphyteutic subscription. For several weeks the headlines of the *Libéral* had appeared on prime-time television, brandished by the two heirs' lawyers. In a period of housing crisis and recession, famines and wars in Africa, natural disasters in Asia and global warming, a good number of newsrooms had jumped on this amusing story, however trivial it might be, in order to entertain their readers and viewers. The attendant publicity had more than made up for the price of the subscription, thus giving *Le Libéral* a little renewed modernity and a new wave of subscribers. That crafty Marcel was still licking his chops. But unfortunately such an opportunity would not come around every day—or perhaps never again in his lifetime, as it happened.

"Make *Convictions* vanish from the newsstands . . . Clever . . . And were you thinking of anything in particular?" asked Luc Bricard, his tone indifferent.

"You have carte blanche, my little Luc," answered the old fox with a half smile. "Surprise me."

He got up and took a key from the pocket of his jacket hanging on the coatrack.

"Here, Laurent, I'm letting you have the Volvo station wagon, in case you need it."

"Your new XC90? Wow! Thanks, Dad!"

His son's face lit up with the smile of a poor man's son finding *two* oranges on Christmas morning. Laurent grabbed the key in passing as he might have caught the prize at a funfair, many years ago. *Not the brightest bulb in the box*, sighed Marcel, *but a good kid, all the same.*

CHICKEN WITH OLIVES

Mamoune! Do you think I should go into the history, about the Greek public debt and the crisis in Ireland? Maybe even go all the way back to the Treaty of Lisbon?" asked Juliette, slipping onto the sofa next to her grandmother.

"Later, sweetie, let me finish watching my soap. We'll have a look right after. Will you sit here with me for a while?"

Marité, known as Mamoune, put her arm around her granddaughter where she was sitting on the armrest, and swung her down onto her lap, kissing her on the neck with a little trumpeting sound. Juliette pulled away from her grandmother's embrace with a groan.

"No, Mamoune, stop, this is really important! It's about the austerity plan in Spain; the fiscal deficit won't go below three percent before 2016, the Spanish prime minister just announced the figures . . . All right, I'll start by listing the fiscal measures in detail, you know they're going to introduce special taxes, and after that I'll give a little rundown on the unemployment rate."

The girl wriggled out of her grandmother's arms and trotted off to her bedroom. Sandrine Cordier, who was preparing her succulent chicken with olives and cumin, peered around the door into the living room and gave her mother-in-law a suspicious look.

"What are you talking about now? Yet another one of those pathetic presentations? Public debt, housing crisis, pension reform, tax loopholes . . . isn't it a bit much? The other day it was tax exemption for working overtime, then the unemployment rate in the United States . . . I didn't even know these things were on the curriculum!"

"The curriculum has changed a lot since our days, you know . . . " said Mamoune, flipping the cap off a bottle of Corona with an indifferent air.

"Yes, well, maybe, we didn't exactly take our baccalaureate together, Mamoune, don't exaggerate."

"But you're right about the rest, Sandrine, these kids are swamped with work," continued Mamoune, ignoring Sandrine's remark. "At the same time, you know Juliette: when she's passionate about something she's a perfectionist, she likes things that are perfectly packaged, as Raymond would have said, may he rest in peace."

"Still, I'm going to look into this curriculum; as it happens I've got this jobseeker at the moment who has a teaching degree in history and geography. Then I'll make an appointment with Juliette's teacher; I'm convinced—and don't tell me otherwise—that he's gone off target. Yet another guy who wants to suck up to someone, I'm sure of it. I'll inform the principal, can't hurt."

"Don't be a fool, don't do that," said Mamoune, suddenly worried. "She'd be mortified if everyone found out about all the extra work she's putting in, and she's so brilliant, for sure the teacher wouldn't keep it quiet! Juliette's already top of her class, two years ahead of all the others, it would be enough to make her lose all her girlfriends, you know what girls are like at this age, real little bitches . . . No, I'll take care of it, don't you worry about it, you have enough on your plate with those good-for-nothing unemployed," she added in a syrupy tone. "I'm sure my little kitten will soon get over her obsession with the European economy. I'll have a word with her, I'll tell her she has to start going out and having fun, like other girls her age, do things with her friends, go to the movies, go for walks. You know she listens to me. Hey, why don't I take her shopping on Saturday afternoon?"

"Okay, thanks. I do have a fair number of cases at the moment, ever since my dear colleague got it in her head to get pregnant. But if the teacher goes on burdening them with his pathetic subjects, I'll go and see him."

"Oh, don't mention it, it's only normal, Sandrine. If I couldn't do at least that much, what good would I be, in the end . . . Just another useless mouth for you and Guillaume to feed . . . "

"If it were only just feeding . . . It's the drinking I'm worried about," grumbled Sandrine to herself.

"What did you say, dear? I don't hear very well anymore, you know," said her mother-in-law, pretending to sound indifferent, as she opened the fridge to reach for another Corona.

"No, nothing."

"It's hot, don't you think? It's so nice to drink something cold, after all."

Mamoune shot her daughter-in-law a winning smile and headed for Juliette's room. She closed the door soundlessly behind her and leaned against it before knocking back a lengthy swig of beer. Then she went into a fit of laughter, which she tried in vain to restrain, hiccupping for several minutes. Her granddaughter was giggling uncontrollably too, one hand over her mouth to keep from alerting her mother.

"Right, Juliet, we're going to have to be a bit more careful, your mother is beginning to wonder. She mustn't find out about our little secret, otherwise I think all hell will break loose where I'm concerned. I promised her I'd take you shopping on Saturday, we'll buy you those boots, how's that. Now let's get down to business: how far have you gotten?"

Juliette's grandmother leaned closer to the computer screen. She gave a quick look then used the mouse to scroll down the page, nodding her head with satisfaction.

"Well, hey, looks like you're doing really well here. Only ten more minutes. Are you okay, sweetie? Can you finish up or do you need me?"

"Yeah, it's okay, the audience keeps getting bigger. But the questions are so simple that I had to post some myself with fake usernames to raise the level . . . That way I was even able to get some stuff in there about the Treaty of Lisbon."

"Oh, good. You know who would have been really proud of you, sweetie?"

"Papoune-may-he-rest-in-peace?"

"Yes, treasure."

As she leaned down to kiss her adolescent granddaughter affectionately, Mamoune let out a little burp that had them both instantly in stitches.

"Mom says you drink too much, but I like it when you're like this, you know. And besides, everybody should have a grandmother like you. Emma's grandma stinks of old wardrobes and undigested medicine. She has hair on her chin, too; I won't let her near me."

"You're so sweet, my little dear . . . You know, Josy was never much to look at even when she was young, so I'm not surprised. Hey, you deserve a drop. Hang on."

Marité carefully tilted the neck of the bottle toward her index finger, then applied her finger just behind the girl's ears with a little wink.

"When we're all done with our project and it's a success, we'll get out the champagne, the way movie stars do, what do you say, honey?"

Juliette nodded, looking at her grandmother solemnly, before turning to immerse herself again in the computer screen: a blinking icon together with a little bleep had just informed her of an incoming message.

* * *

Marité Cordier had been living with her son and his family ever since she had been evicted, six months earlier, from the apartment on the rue du Poteau where she'd lived for over twenty years. Two years earlier the former owner, an insurance company, had sold the entire building, along with part of the city block, to a financial investor, who had set about getting rid of the tenants more or less legally, at the end of their leases or, most often, by means of some rather muscular negotiation. The aim was to renovate the property and put it back on the market to make an obscene profit. With a handful of neighbors—people like herself who'd lived in the quartier forever and would not have the means to move there nowadays— Marité had held out as long as possible while the building gradually emptied out. At the end, the final occupants had to climb over scaffolding to go in and out of the house. The sounds of sledgehammer and drill resonated relentlessly in the stairway; plaster dust had gradually invaded the space; and water cuts were more and more frequent and lengthy. At the end of a lawsuit, which received a great deal of coverage in the press, and mobilized aging hippies and old Montmartre residents who were completely on the same wavelength, the last hard-core stragglers had managed to win a small compensation to cover the cost of moving: thirty to forty thousand euros. A tidy little sum for most of them—modest retired people, former civil servants or craftsmen—but a laughable jackpot when it came to trying to find new housing in the quartier.

Marité had no retirement. And yet she had worked for more than thirty-five years, doing the books under the table for a major sex shop in Pigalle, the Pique-à-Boobs. But globalization had not spared small sex shops. When Maurice sold it, the new owner, a Chinese man, entrusted the books to a woman from Beijing who was formidably quick on the abacus. A tireless worker, in the evening she deployed her talents onstage in an entertaining number involving geisha balls.

Malicious gossips said that Marité hadn't done too badly from her years at the Pique-à-Boobs, but in fact she had always been a good girl, in spite of a figure that could easily have lured people through a heavy door on the Boulevard de Clichy or into a little striptease cabin. Tall, big-breasted, she had something of the singer Dalida about her—the same thick mane of hair and a slight squint in her eye, which the old magpies in the quartier suspected she cultivated deliberately—which she did.

Sometimes she was as dark-haired as a gypsy, sometimes as blonde as a Valkyrie, but she always had the same devilish air about her. In short, she was what they used to call a beautiful doll back in Raymond's day—may he rest in peace. By virtue of climbing up and down all the stairs in Montmartre on eight-centimeter heels, she'd acquired the gait of an African princess, and this had not changed as she aged. She did not go unnoticed when she went to pick Aurélien or Juliette up at day care or primary school. Even today, at the age of sixty-two, she still got wolf whistles in the street. She was a regular at the Négociants on the rue Lambert, the last real wine bar in the quartier, where every evening Rosa poured her a thimble of white wine. When she climbed down from her barstool to go home, there were men who sighed, a spark in their eyes and a stick of dynamite in their trousers.

She had been living alone for over ten years, and her eviction from the rue du Poteau posed a real problem: where was she going to live, now? Private rentals in the quartier were exorbitant, and even if she could qualify for public housing, it was all elsewhere, in the outskirts. And even then, who knew when she'd get a place, given the length of the waiting list. Her only income was Raymond's pension; he was a former railroad man who'd died of an aneurysmal rupture a few days after he'd hung up his cap, only fifty-six years old—may he rest in peace. But even with the little nest egg of thirty thousand euros she'd received, and her paltry savings, the prospect of being a homeowner was not something she could envisage, unless she were willing to go into exile and live in some dump in Seine-et-Marne or the Essonne.

But Marité didn't want to leave Paris, let alone Montmartre. She'd grown up there, gotten married there, worked and raised her son there. Even if the quartier no longer resembled the one she'd grown up in, when you still saw the greengrocers towing their handcarts. Even if the majority of hustlers and transsexuals she used to know back in the Pique-à-Boobs days were pathetic old scarecrows now, if they hadn't already kicked the bucket. The quartier's pulse went on beating inside her, every morning. *This is where I'll die*, she was in the habit of saying. *If one night I don't come home, just check around the stairways, I'll be bound to have missed a step on the rue du Mont-Cenis or the rue Lamarck.*

Her girlfriends had urged her to remarry an affluent widower (preferably), or to shack up with one (if all else failed), but Marité just laughed in their faces. A kept woman—no thank you; and yet, there would have been no lack of offers. The most eager was Roger, who used to sell paintings, and whom she'd known for forty-five years already, at least. He'd been courting her even before she got married; he'd buried two wives and had no children. He was the finest match in the quartier, in the over-seventy-five category. Mamoune was willing enough to be invited to lunch once a month at the Brasserie Wepler, but she spurned the aging beau's advances with a laugh, although she never stopped acting coquettish.

Contrary to all expectation, Sandrine had surprised everyone when she offered to take Mamoune in, at least until she found a more lasting solution. Not that they had room to spare in their seventy-three square meters at the top of the rue de Clignancourt—a long corridor, three narrow bedrooms, a living room full to overflowing, a kitchen where you could barely squeeze two stools, a lopsided bathroom, and a separate WC that was way too roomy in comparison. But a few months earlier they'd had the opportunity to put in a bid for a maid's room which was empty on the eighth floor of the building: perfect timing.

This real estate deal had kept Sandrine busy for months. She'd begun by harassing the tenant—a dark young man, dishwasher in a brasserie—to find out the terms of his lease, and she was not surprised to learn that they were purely verbal, and cash only. He got out of there in no time, afraid he'd be taken to court or have all sorts of bureaucratic hassles, the nature of which she had described to him in great detail—not the least of which was that she herself would make his life hell. For several weeks she had methodically removed all the notice of auction posters the notary in charge of the sale had put up. She'd confounded the property manager and the other co-owners in the building with questions about utility fees, percentages, and shares. Finally, she'd orchestrated a persistent rumor about a stench of urine and dead rat (supposedly stuck in the ceiling of the room).

The day before the notary had his planned open house for the room, she sequestered the neighbors' alley cat by feasting him on milk and kibble. Then at around midnight she placed him in a cat carrier and took him up to the eighth floor. There she managed to get him to piss on all the doors and doormats on the landing, which she had sprayed with bleach beforehand. Their mission was crowned with a certain success: potential buyers hurried through the room holding their noses; some even turned and left again the moment they arrived. It had been a hell of a job, but worth every moment: she was able to buy the twelve-square-meter room for a mere seventy thousand euros, transfer fees included.

Narrow, with a steep sloping roof, the room faced due west and had an incredible view on the Sacré-Coeur. It had two dormer windows, like doll's-house balconies, and a large built-in wardrobe. The oak floorboards, preserved for over sixty years by two layers of grotesque linoleum, had been restored. Guillaume repainted all the walls white. Marité moved in her bed, a dresser, a little desk, and a squat velvet armchair. She put the rest of her belongings in a storage depot—furniture, dishes, knickknacks, fashion magazines she'd collected for decades—and most of her wardrobe ended up at her son's place. She took the opportunity to donate the rest of Raymond's clothes to the Salvation Army—may he rest in peace.

She kept her most precious treasures close by, carefully wrapped and stored at the back of the wardrobe: a collection of watercolors, pencil or charcoal sketches, and little oil paintings by artists from Montmartre. She'd known a lot of them during her youth, when she used to pose in studios on the rue Hégésippe-Moreau or at the Cité Montmartre-aux-artistes. Moreover, she'd made some fairly sound acquisitions over the years, with Roger's help and thanks to her own good taste, which she'd nurtured over time. *You can sell it to buy me a padded mahogany coffin, with flowers and a plot in the cemetery,* she'd said, a bit tipsy, in front of Sandrine's parents at the most recent Christmas dinner, while brandishing a nude portrait signed Bernard Buffet. She was hardly recognizable on the painting, even though the foreground was taken up with an intimate part of her anatomy which none of the guests had ever seen.

* * *

Living under the same roof as her daughter-in-law—even if it was on a different floor—was no picnic. The only real compensation was the young woman's cooking, always delicious. As far as all the rest went—Sandrine stuck her nose in everything, bossed everyone around, and kept a tight hold on the purse strings. She thought that Marité, who no longer had to pay any rent, ought to be saving almost every centime of Raymond's retirement. But her capricious mother-in-law had her little secrets: white wine at Les Négociants, cigarillos, theater matinees, a few restaurants with girlfriends, Chanel No. 5, and the costume jewelry she dug up at the flea market and accumulated like a magpie. Above all, she loved to spoil her grandchildren, when she could, and without the parents knowing, which enhanced her pleasure: video games, books, trinkets, clothes—Juliette didn't care what she wore, and wasn't all that pretty, but Aurélien, very early on, had found himself a look that his grandmother delighted in and encouraged. To avoid having to explain anything to Sandrine, and also because it was a source of entertainment to her (and visibly, a means to keep young), Mamoune had found an additional source of income besides Raymond's little retirement—may he rest in peace.

Any other grandmother might have gone in for babysitting, ironing, or home knitting and crocheting. That was not Mamoune's style: the only knitting needle she'd ever held in her life was at the age of seventeen for a clandestine abortion, but at the last minute she'd decided against it, and she got her period again, miraculously, no doubt in part due to her extreme terror. No, there would be none of the typical granny stuff for Marité—volunteering at the parish, baking cakes for the school fair, or sorting clothes for the needy. Marité lived with the times, she worked in the digital economy, in the *cloud*. She'd started a bit by chance, answering an ad: a website for retired dog handlers was looking for an underpaid temp to supervise their forums a few hours a week. She'd had a great time there among the German Shepherds and their owners—as a rule they were former cops or gendarmes who posted hilarious videos of training sessions and swapped their best tricks. One thing leading to another, she'd found other little jobs on commercial websites or portals: community management, content moderation, viral marketing.

She worked mainly on weekends or at night, typing laudatory reviews by the kilometer for online shopping websites, or inserting tendentious commentaries on the forums of rival brands. One of her contacts put her in touch with an information site that was urgently seeking a replacement to moderate political and economic debates. She really got into it, and after four months had gone by she launched her own blog: economic policy as viewed by a blonde, crisiswhatcrisis.com, which earned itself a friendly little buzz. A way to combine work and retirement, Marité-style, and Guillaume and Sandrine knew nothing about it; she just quietly got on with it, up there in her little maid's room. And at her disposal she had the zealous assistance of the formidable Juliette, with her IQ of 172 and the talent of a hacker; her fresh twelve-year-old outlook on life was thrown in as a bonus.

SAUSSE, MEETBALLS, AND FRITES

Luc Bricard hadn't been back to the quartier where he'd spent his childhood and adolescence in years. The last time was when he'd helped his mother finish moving; she was going off to a little house near Lamballe she'd bought with her life's savings. *Lamballe, we'll have a ball, Lamballe, come one and all,* the siblings chanted sarcastically when summer vacation rolled around. The nanny dragged her brood there every summer by train, to a family holiday home, a sort of summer camp for low-income families where everyone shared kitchen and household chores in a spirit of good cheer. And it was there, in Plédéliac, to the southwest of Lamballe, that Bricard had spent his only seaside vacations until the age of seventeen. Although if you didn't have a car the ocean seemed a long way from that quiet little village. Around his classmates at the lycée he acted as if he'd been to Saint-Brieuc or Saint-Malo, embroidering on his scanty memories of excursions with his older brothers and sisters. But his mother remembered Plédéliac as one of her sole pleasures in a life of labor, and now she'd decided to spend her retirement there.

Oddly enough, it was first and foremost memories of Brittany that assailed Bricard as he was walking down the rue Custine, after parking in the only public lot in the place, on the corner of the rue Lécuyer. When he came to Château-Rouge he paused for a moment, stunned: the main intersection had been modernized, redrawn, with wider sidewalks, concrete traffic, islands, and bike paths. Access for pedestrians had been made safer with wide crossings, and Bricard had to restrain an urge to run straight across the street to the entrance of the métro, the way he used to as a kid. Looking distractedly down the rue Custine he noticed other changes, inroads made by the bourgeois bohemian lifestyle of the 18th arrondissement—even if the impact, for the time being, was not as noticeable as around Jules-Joffrin or Lamarck-Caulaincourt. Upscale bars with music and brightly-colored outdoor seating areas had replaced neighborhood bistros. Young designers' boutiques lived alongside Afro hairdressers and Turkish pizza and kebab shops. A number of traditional food suppliers had closed—at least two *charcutiers*, one cheese shop, a fishmonger's—often replaced by a trendy restaurant.

A wave of nostalgia came over him when he saw the crowd swarming toward the Dejean market: at least there nothing had changed. Like every time, Africa caught in his throat: the strong smell of fish, pigeons sitting tranquilly on huge baskets of exotic vegetables. Matrons wearing boubous clicked their tongues, don't try and argue, to put an end to the cosmetics vendors' sales patter, although they did go on examining the bottles and jars piled up on the makeshift cardboard display cases. Two kids zigzagged in and out, yelling, noses running, and bumped into him without an apology. Bricard missed the first one but managed to roundly cuff the second one: end of nostalgia session.

The deputy CEO of the Groupe Lacarrière was early for his appointment at the heart of La Goutte d'Or. He'd decided it would be better to park at a distance: his Audi with its leather seats would come across as a tad too middle-class for the neighborhood. Instead of a three-piece suit he'd put on his standard middle management uniform: wool trousers, somewhat worn, and a parka over a drab shirt, with no tie. For the occasion he'd taken on the identity of an entrepreneur from Dijon. Specializing in bottom-of-the-range by-products for

old-fashioned brands—calendars, key rings, magnets, pens—
he was on the lookout for a little warehouse somewhere in
Paris. He hung around for ten minutes or so, then went down
the rue des Poissonniers to La Goutte-d'Or, all the way to the
end.

The man was waiting for him, as agreed, on the corner of
the rue Tombouctou: early thirties, tight-fitting, cheap-looking
black suit, white shirt with a high collar, and pointed patent
leather shoes, the kind that Bricard thought of as *pimp's special.* His helmet tucked in the crook of his elbow, he was sitting
with his legs straddling his scooter, talking loudly on his cell
phone through a Bluetooth earbud, and smoking. He hadn't
noticed Bricard yet, who had cleverly posted himself on the
opposite sidewalk, pretending he was observing the tracks of
the Gare du Nord below him. The wind funneled down the
narrow corridor of the rue de Tombouctou, and Bricard raised
the collar of his parka, which sufficed to attract the attention
of the man on the other side.

"Hello! Samuel Benoliel, we were in touch via email," said
the young man by way of introduction, coming over with his
best commercial smile, hand extended.

"Yes, yes, of course, hello. Pleased to meet you."

"I've selected a few products that correspond to your
request—everything is just a few minutes' walk from here. If
it's not what you're looking for, we can stop by the agency to
talk things over in greater detail. Shall we go?"

Luc Bricard kept pace with the real estate agent, who was
taking long strides up the rue Stephenson, indicating a building a little further up. With the exception of the narrow door-
way that led to the residential floors, the ground floor façade
was covered along its entire length by a metal shutter, over ten
meters of shop window. Through the latticework a bare room
of roughly seventy square meters was visible. A little door gave
onto the narrow hallway of the building and it was through

there that the two men entered what had started out as a carpenter's workshop, then been converted many times over in the course of recent decades. The previous occupants must have been in the business of importing and exporting accessories, and a few old boxes with Chinese ideograms still lingered here and there. At the back, a little room a dozen or so square meters in size looked out through a narrow barred window onto a dark courtyard, or rather a light shaft which stank of a nauseating mixture of burnt fat and laundry. There was a cracked toilet bowl in one corner with, for company, an old three-legged chair leaning against a sink with a dripping faucet. All the walls were covered with obscene hyper-realistic graffiti, some of which looked as if they'd been made with excrement.

"The plumbing and electricity have been redone, and the rough side gives the place a certain charm, a very *street art* ambience that has loads of potential," the real estate whiz saw fit to point out.

Impassive, his client stood gazing at a very expressive *Sukk my dikk, bichch.* They sure like their double consonants, thought Bricard.

"The quartier keeps gaining in value, a lot of artists are moving in. Have you thought of buying instead of renting? It would be a good investment," he continued. "I might have some very interesting things to show you."

"I'll think about it, why not, but for the time being I'd rather rent."

The second property, on the rue Polonceau, was a veritable rat hole: access was through the two narrow courtyards of two connected buildings. The labyrinth took them past the concierge's loge and several dark little apartments as well as an acupuncturist's office. A stubborn smell of incense and greasy Asian cooking came from the open French doors of the office, which was concealed by a simple curtain of thick purple cotton. Samuel Benoliel pointed out that the acupuncturist lived there but was very discreet. *Yeah, sure, tell me another one*, thought Bricard to himself.

The space was a real eyesore, forty square meters stuck in the dead end formed by the third courtyard. The ceiling was low, seeping with moisture, feebly lit by a few glass tiles in the flat Fibrocement roof. The walls were irregular as they wound their way around the adjacent storerooms intended for garbage cans and bicycles. Old threadbare linoleum squeaked with filth underfoot. Curious, Bricard glanced at the description of the place: *Atypical space, no vis-à-vis. Numerous possibilities.* Oh, come on.

The third place was no better, a real jump from the frying pan into the fire. It was a former discount grocery store on the rue Doudeauville, at the foot of an insalubrious building that was being restored. The only advantage was the month-to-month lease, but the space was too large and too visible from the street.

Squatters had been living there recently, judging by the smell of feral animal that seized you by the throat the moment you went into the former store: excrement, urine, acrid residue of a fire where damp cardboard, tin cans, filthy fabric, plastic, and dope had been consumed. In one corner a ripped-open sleeping bag was bathing in a puddle of paint and turpentine. A bit further away a former refrigerated display case exhibited the remains of some rotten food: a can of ravioli, an open carton of milk, and decomposing fruit. Bananas? Pears? Going nearer, Bricard saw it was actually a rat, or some small animal. A sort of decadent Arcimboldo still life. *You want street art?* he grumbled to himself. Crushed beer cans were strewn across the floor and the pimp's special knocked over a half-full bottle of plonk: it shattered, splattering the real estate agent.

"Well, quite a place," Luc Bricard could not help but say, holding his nose.

Benoliel tried to contain the damage, rubbing his shoe and the bottom of his trousers with a dubious rag he found in a corner.

"It's in its original state, sure, but it's a proper basement duplex, with a loft potential to it that is in great demand. A good clean and you can move in, tremendous space to work with. Moreover, I've got two clients considering the place, for start-up offices and for a designer studio," he said, trying to direct his client toward the back of the room, where a little stairway led to the basement. "The cellar has all the amenities, good lighting and heating, tiles, a proper bathroom and toilet. The north wall, here, is built of stone, you just need to remove the roughcast," he added.

Adding action to words, he began scratching at the flaking coating with his ballpoint pen. The surface came away in strips, revealing a grayish mortar that was only distantly related to stone.

"You've got a good height there up to the ceiling, room to build a mezzanine, and it's a good price, what with the month-to-month lease."

"Right . . . Thank you very much but I think what you've shown me doesn't really correspond to what I'm looking for. Just get in touch if you think of anywhere else?"

Bricard deliberately left his sentence hanging. He knew these scum real estate agents only too well, and he was willing to bet five to one that the man would now pull a white rabbit out of his hat. Twice as expensive as the other places, but exactly what he was looking for. For a moment he stamped his feet out on the sidewalk, while he raised his head and considered which way to go, then he held out his hand to say goodbye. Samuel Benoliel shook it with a preoccupied air, frowning. He rummaged in his pocket and pulled out another key ring, and his expression turned conspiratorial.

"Now that I think of it, I might have another product, but

we haven't signed the mandate yet. Having said that, the owner has left me the keys, it's right nearby. Do you have a few more minutes?"

"Sure, let's go."

The two men went back down the rue Stephenson to the corner of the rue Myrha. Samuel Benoliel unlocked the automatic door of a medium-sized garage. There was a dip in the sidewalk along the entire width with room for a small van to enter. The place was empty, but clean and dry. Bricard was intrigued by its layout. The back gave onto a private courtyard covered by a sheet of PVC roof which protected it from any indiscreet gazes from above—even supposing someone might want to climb onto the toilet seat to try and look out the skylight rather than tranquilly having a dump. It was easy to get into with a vehicle, a discreet warehouse, hidden from view, with a private courtyard . . . No active businesses or offices nearby, just one restaurant next door that had been closed for ages . . . It was exactly what he was looking for.

As a precaution Bricard did peer through the window of the adjacent dive; a paper he initially thought was flypaper was stuck to the pane. In fact it was the greasy, splattered menu, which over time had become something of an anatomical chart for a natural history museum: fly shit, dead bees, spiderwebs. The prices were still in francs, and it was full of spelling mistakes: *sausse, meetballs, and frites.* Well, well, thought Bricard with a smile. An injunction from Paris City Hall, partly torn, was still posted on the door; it had surely been closed for sanitary reasons. The place was small, dark, and filthy, furnished with nasty plastic tables and chairs that didn't match. The open kitchen, just visible in the back, had not been brought up to code in over thirty years. In spite of the undeniable revival of the quartier, no trendy bar would be moving in here any time soon. And in six or eight months Bricard would be long gone.

"Well, I'm really interested in this place, it's a pity you don't have the mandate yet," he said enthusiastically.

While surveying the obvious advantages of the place with a knowing eye, he was careful not to abandon his role of the little provincial entrepreneur looking for an ordinary place to store things.

"Well, it's a bit complicated," said the agent, with a little wince of annoyance. "If you have time for a coffee I can explain it all to you?"

Aha, here we go, buddy, thought Bricard with an inward smile. He could have written the screenplay himself, how refreshing. He followed the young man into a bistro where they sat down off to one side, away from any prying ears. He listened to him serve up an epic tale of a widow, a family with joint ownership, children from a second marriage, a pending tax audit, an indiscreet notary, and even a little conflict with the local mayor, but that was about to be resolved—the works. Bricard punctuated his account with a chorus of Oh! Ah? No, really? and sympathetic frowns. Benoliel muddled up the entire story brilliantly, before reaching the climax: the owner—an elderly woman on her own, of great integrity, but who had been poorly advised and was out of her depth, was in desperate need of a serious, discreet tenant who would be willing to come to an amicable agreement. No lease, payment in cash. The price was good, but . . .

"A few extra euros would reassure her that the tenant is serious, as a sort of deposit. That is why we cannot offer this product to just anybody," said Samuel Benoliel, absolutely straight-faced.

Bricard felt like applauding but restrained himself. He just wondered who the desperate widow was: the guy's mother? Nah, that would be going too far. His mother-in-law? No, he wasn't wearing a wedding ring and he was still of an age to be messing around. Then maybe Auntie Benoliel? He'd find out someday, for the hell of it.

"A deposit?"

"Let's say, rather . . . an entry ticket, to seal the agreement. And just to set the record straight, we won't be making anything on this," he said, his hand on his heart. "We just like doing favors for good clients, that's all."

Bricard pulled a wad out of his pocket: two-hundred-euro bills that he'd taken the trouble to wrinkle slightly before coming. He counted out ten, carefully, looked thoughtful, then added three more, in a separate pile, smiling at Samuel Benoliel like some crafty peasant.

"Where I come from, we know how to appreciate a favor at its true worth."

The young man pocketed the bills and smiled in turn.

"You can move in as soon as you like, the last eight days of this month are on us. Would you like to stop by the agency tomorrow at opening time to pay the first month's rent and pick up the keys?"

"That won't be necessary: here are six months in advance. I'll come and see you again in the spring, if that suits your client. You have my contact information."

Another pile of two-hundred-euro bills appeared on the table as if by magic, much thicker than the previous one. Samuel Benoliel was still counting them when Bricard stood up to go, saying goodbye with a pat on the back. The rookie looked up from his Monopoly money a few seconds too late: the keys to the place and the client had vanished. *Shoot, I thought suckers like that existed only in films*, he thought to himself with delight. Not only had he rented out his aunt's place without going through the agency, but he had, on top of it, gotten six months' rent in advance, and made himself a handsome commission, in cash. Way to go, dude . . .

As for Luc Bricard, he was smiling with pleasure as he

walked back up the boulevard Barbès to the parking lot. He hadn't given his real name or his address, and the email he'd used was as bogus as the official company ID he'd had to provide. Same thing for the cell phone: a number that was impossible to trace thanks to a prepaid SIM card and an old Nokia he kept for private use. And he'd walked off with the three spec sheets he'd signed at the beginning of each visit. *Stupid asshole, grow up, you've got a few more things to learn*, he chuckled, almost audibly, as he rubbed his hands. For a start, he'd change the locks, that very evening: one of Marcel's amenable friends would do a first-rate job for him. Without batting an eyelid.

Cassoulet (the Castelnaudary Recipe)

uillaume Cordier moved his hand in the dark slowly toward Sandrine, who was curled up in the bed facing the other way. He stroked her back and felt her warm skin beneath the silky fabric of her nightgown. After all these years living together, his wife still had the same effect on him. She was a regular marmot and he loved waking her up just as she had dropped off, blowing gently in her neck and then pulling up her nightie. He would tickle her belly button, her smooth waist, her plump buttocks, lick the silky down on her slender thighs, turn her toward him, nibble her nipples, and then . . .

"Guillaume . . . " she murmured in her adorable sleepy little voice, slipping one expert hand into his shorts.

He didn't answer, let himself be overcome by the surge of desire. Her hand was soft and warm, and was moving with unbearable languor.

"Guillaume . . . "

"Mmmm . . . "

"You hear me?"

Her hand tightened its embrace and slowly increased its movement.

"Mmmm . . . yes . . . "

"You didn't give me your restaurant coupons this month, don't forget, tomorrow, right?"

Guillaume felt as if he'd been dipped without warning into an icy bath. But Sandrine had turned to face him and her other hand came in support, moving up his inner thigh to grasp him, gently but firmly, from underneath.

"Promise?"

"Well, I think I used most of them, honey," he whispered, as quietly as possible, while kissing her on the neck. "I only have what I need to finish the week."

Both hands came to an immediate halt: Sandrine was wide awake now. In the dark her cat eyes shone with a disturbing brilliance.

"Really? You used them all?"

"We'll talk about all that tomorrow morning, sweetheart," he said in an affectionate voice, reaching up to take his wife's breasts in his hands, seeking out her mouth for a voracious kiss.

Her breasts were both heavy and still amazingly high, as arrogant as a sixteen-year-old kid's. Nor had her two pregnancies changed her figure: on the contrary, it had blossomed with age—slender shoulders and waist, generous hips, flat belly, and these breasts, these breasts . . . A wave of love and desire overwhelmed him, which had the effect of hardening still further the part of his anatomy that Sandrine held in her hands. The back-and-forth motion had started up again very slowly, and this soft torture required all his attention.

"So, no more restaurant coupons for your favorite foodie?" she murmured, half-teasing, half-sulking, biting his earlobe.

Their embrace had relaxed, ever so slightly, and Guillaume now felt her nimble fingers tickling him like a butterfly's wings. At the beginning of their relationship, he used to explode in two minutes for less than that, and now he needed all his concentration.

"Next month, darling, promise," he managed to utter, between two gasps for breath amidst her caresses.

Dammit, if she didn't stop soon . . . Then suddenly the butterfly's wings vanished, as if by magic. Guillaume waited for a second with his eyes closed, his heart rate veering into the danger zone, then he groaned with disappointment and opened his eyes. In the beam of moonlight filtering through the shutters he saw Sandrine staring at him, lying on her side, her nightgown still pulled up—her adorable mons veneris covered in a dark down, there, so close, and the lace straps were so low on her shoulders that he could see the large areolas of her white breasts. He held out his hands but she was faster, tugging the duvet up to her neck with a rapid gesture, before she turned back onto her other side.

"Sweetie . . . " he whined, slipping one hand onto her hip. All he got for his pains was a sharp tap on his fingertips.

"Next month, Guillaume. Good night."

He tried a second approach and again felt a sharp little tap, more affirmative than the first one. He beat a retreat, buttoning up his shorts as he did so: you can never be too careful.

* * *

Sandrine had one great passion: food. Cakes, candies, but also Corsican or Italian charcuterie, Lebanese *mezze*, dim sum, sushi . . . Her eyes glowed with sensuous intoxication whenever she tasted a dish she liked or discovered a new one. She wandered up and down market aisles for hours, her nose on the alert like a wild truffle sow, ready to taste anything and everything they might offer her: old-fashioned vegetables with an earthy flavor, mountain charcuterie, matured cheese, crusts of bread. Early in the morning or at teatime, she could taste four or five olive oils by the spoonful—concentrating, her cat's eyes narrowed—before deciding which one to buy. To choose her pepper she would breathe it in, deeply, before delicately depositing a crushed grain on the tip of her tongue, like the finest of sweetmeats. It was enough for her to leaf through a cookbook to go into a trance—and there was no lack of them on her bookshelves.

She was also a peerless chef, with a delicate, creative touch; her dinners delighted friends and family. Moreover, she could apply great inventiveness to recycling leftovers, with infinite variations. Already as a teenager she used to spend her Wednesdays baking cakes, seeking inspiration in recipes that she adapted to her taste: honey instead of sugar; a pinch of spice; chestnut flour or cornstarch for lightness. But her parents had trotted out the same old thing all through her school years: they were a family of civil servants, that was all there was to it. They would not pay for anything else. Cook? Run a restaurant? When her grandmothers had nearly killed themselves, precisely so that the next generation could avoid such a calamity? What other nonsense did she have in mind! It was an exhausting profession, often precarious, with impossible schedules unsuited to family life: that was their constant refrain, and her mother reminded her that she had done her homework and eaten her meals all alone for many long years, while her mother was serving a refined dinner only a few miles away. And besides, they'd never have the means to get Sandrine started in a business. No arguments to the contrary had managed to dissuade them, and it was with a heavy heart that she had enrolled in the law faculty. If only she had known how to stand up to them. She could have worked to pay for her studies; but she hadn't dared try.

* * *

Her appetite, too, was a joy to behold. That was what Guillaume had found so charming about her the first time he'd invited her out to dinner—to see this slip of a girl wolfing down a cassoulet with such adorable gluttony. With hindsight he understood that his choice of venue, an auberge that specialized in food from the Southwest of France, might have been a catastrophe with any other female student. For sure another girl would have picked at or even refused such a tonic dish, with its white beans that made you fart and chunks of slow-cooked meat swimming in a rich sauce of fat and tomato—but Sandrine was over the moon. She licked her fingers without ever abandoning her regal air, and mopped her plate with thick chunks of rustic bread. That night they'd made love for the first time, in Guillaume's little studio, and Sandrine was as light and fresh as before the meal, and full of initiative. Guillaume on the other hand had been bitterly testing the unrivalled reputation of the white beans, and was obliged to make several nocturnal visits to the tiny bathroom for a jolly little improv trumpet concerto.

And what could you do—a girl who could eat cassoulet with that much pleasure, and not take to her heels after such a night of love: well, you were duty bound to marry her, naturally. Particularly when she had magnificent breasts, the body of a doll, and the most sensual mouth you'd ever seen. Moreover, he quickly realized that she made love the way she ate a meal: starter, main course, dessert, and sometimes even a cheese course. Her greedy curiosity brought little stars to her eyes; she loved tasting everything with her lips and her insatiable tongue, before dropping off, purring like a sated kitty.

Over the years she had gotten into the habit of taking a few restaurant coupons from Guillaume: how could he refuse her when she came and rubbed up against him, offering him her red lips as if they were cherries? She had started when she was pregnant with Aurélien, at the beginning of her maternity leave. She was feeling fit as a fiddle and during her long strolls around the Abbesses quartier she would buy mangoes and figs, Lebanese pastries or strange little Korean desserts that she nibbled at with green mint tea. None of which were generally recommended during pregnancy, but Sandrine had not put on much weight and her blood tests were perfectly normal, so why should she deprive herself of the little things she enjoyed?

When Aurélien was born, Guillaume's restaurant coupons, amid the familiar upheaval that accompanies the arrival of a first child, had served, evenings and weekends, to feed the parents, exhausted by their sleepless nights: sushi, pizza, ready meals from the deli. And then by the time Sandrine went back to work the habit had taken hold. Two coupons here for a big plate of cheese, three there for some pastries or a good meal out with one of her girlfriends. Over the years Guillaume had learned to make do with lighter lunches, fixing himself a sandwich at home, or even skipping the meal altogether. Until one day he realized he only had three coupons left to get through the rest of the month, and it was only the eighth.

But by then there was no going back. Restaurant coupons had become a way of life, or worse, an acquired, irreversible right, like a salt tax he paid, a conjugal racket from which he occasionally managed to salvage a few scraps, but scarcely more. To regain some wiggle room, he'd had to amputate his reading and smoking budget. The advantage—if there really had to be one—was that he'd learned to resort to his deepest hunting and gathering instinct to feed himself at midday. This was why he'd ended up loitering by night outside newspaper kiosks and newsagents' with a cutter in his hand to pilfer a few newspapers and magazines that he'd resell at a later date. Nothing spectacular in the beginning! He'd acted on instinct when he came upon a pile of the *L'Équipe* sports paper very early one morning when he was out for a jog, the day after the rugby championship final. He'd only taken one paper, for his own personal use. There'd been no plan just then, no premeditation, just the almost unconscious gesture of a man going past a pile of newspapers tossed outside a closed kiosk, who could not resist grabbing the one that was sticking out just that little bit, see, just there, with the ever so tempting headline about the victory of the Perpignan club.

The problem with little sins of pleasure that morality

condemns is the strong urge to reoffend when everything goes well a first time. Reading that issue of *L'Équipe* that Sunday proved to be particularly delightful. Like a schoolboy's petty theft, without consequence; perfectly modest forbidden fruit, after all; but for a man who was under the iron rule of a woman like Sandrine Cordier, it was already a significant, powerful act of emancipation. He reoffended the following week and also grabbed a copy of *Elle à table* for his nearest and dearest. Thus, one thing leading to another, he had become a modest but very active link in the media distribution chain in France, a little point of sale that did not figure on the Presstalis lists and was located in the basement of the headquarters of a manufacturer of orthopedic equipment in a northern suburb of Paris. Naturally the adjustment had been tricky: determining local demand, then non-local (spouses, families, certain acquaintances working in the same industrial zone), pinpointing stable suppliers while maintaining a wide diversity of supply, optimizing stock rotation, establishing a sound commercial policy: he'd had to learn it all from scratch.

He had quickly worked out what went on backstage in this world that was so new to him: the subtleties between the editorial policy of competing titles, the chestnuts that sold and the ones you had to avoid, the luridly appealing covers and the nefarious editorialists, the launches of new titles and new formulas. But also the likeable side aspects, such as the printers' and distributors' union, which several times a year would block the publication or distribution of a given title. He also took orders, now, thus reducing the risk he ran with oversupply, and consolidating customer loyalty. By chance, or coincidence, business at the two kiosks nearest to where he worked had fallen off so severely that they had no other choice than to close. In short, Guillaume Cordier was quite proud of what he considered to be his true professional success story, beneath the façade of being an assistant in the maintenance department of a medium-sized company—deep down, he considered it to be his primary career. In the space of a few years he had managed to generate the additional revenue of a thousand euros per month, with higher peaks during periods of enhanced news coverage: elections, royal weddings, Olympic Games, World Cups. And naturally this income was free of social and fiscal off-takes, but not of other charges, he affirmed: two or three times a week he drove all around Paris and the nearby outskirts, and fuel wasn't cheap. Not to mention the amortization of his vehicle and the hours of sleep he lost: all arguments he put forward when tactless clients tried to haggle with him.

But almost overnight finding publications had become tricky. Some sites were now guarded by night watchmen who had unfriendly pit bulls by their side: one morning, Guillaume found himself staring into the muzzle of a ferocious member of the species outside a Maison de la Presse in Levallois, one of his most important suppliers. He went away empty-handed, unable to go anywhere near a single pile of papers. Giving up this supply point represented a loss of income of two hundred euros a month, at least. He had noticed other security guards in Boulogne and in Neuilly, near the Relay store. Not to mention that the number of sales outlets seemed to be melting away: every day another Parisian kiosk vanished from the street.

He had adapted his rounds, concentrating on the north, south, and east, rather than the west, of the city, which prolonged his tours by several dozen kilometers. He then focused on little outlets inside Paris itself, locating isolated kiosks in fairly deserted quartiers, but the end result was still more or less the same. Either the newspapers were being checked by night watchmen, or they were put in a secure spot, or they were simply nowhere to be found. Sometimes the piles had been vandalized, torn open there on the sidewalk, scattered all the way to the gutter, and then the magazines could no longer be sold. There could no longer be any doubt: he had a competitor, and surely not an artist who worked as he did, delicately, with a cutter, opening the piles cleanly so he could just pull out a few copies. No, for sure this was a real saboteur, a gravedigger of the French print media—might as well call a spade a spade.

Over the last few weeks the seam had dried up like a barrel of water in deepest Sahara: Guillaume had even had to reimburse a few of his subscribers. To all of them he explained that the spread of the cataclysm was due to fantastical, mysterious reasons—gang warfare among distribution unions, factories blocked by Romanian strike picketers, a collective of bloggers basely attacking the good old print media, stocks pulped because of toxic smeared ink. He promised things would soon be back to normal and he dexterously rationed whatever meager booty he happened to find during his rounds. Unfortunately his offer was restricted above all to poor quality, low-end publications—specialized reviews that were of little interest to the general public: *RV Living, Mushrooms of Our Regions, Aluminum Lids, Blue Cheese of the Ariège Region*. To be sure, last week he had managed to offload *Firefighters of France* in the place of the leading gay magazine, but he wouldn't be able to get away with that kind of ruse for long. People would soon get weary, and he knew it only too well. A few more weeks like this and years of painstaking work would be wiped out. And as misery loves company, not only was Guillaume losing the business he had run so proudly for almost fifteen years, now here he was at one o'clock in the morning on his side of the bed with a hard-on like a donkey and Sandrine snoring next to him with a flyswatter in her hand.

THIÉBOUDIÈNE & BIRYANI

ntoine Lacuenta quickened his step on leaving the Simplon métro station: he was going to be late for the final. He strode up the boulevard Ornano and entered the labyrinth of little streets that led to the workers' hostel he'd moved into on arriving in Paris—well, now they were known as "social residences." They may be social, but don't expect the ladder, is what that bitch at Pôle Emploi would have quipped. She was a real pain in the butt, and clever on top of it: the worst kind. She wasn't ugly, either, with her lovely eyes and deep cleavage, even if she wasn't really his type. He'd always had a soft spot for tall blondes. In the end, by the time he got out of the interminable interview, she'd turned out to be less toxic than he'd feared.

Initially he thought he'd be struck off the list but, totally unexpectedly, she had upheld his rights. She then went on to suggest he take this eccentric, expensive training course in organic cooking. He'd opened his eyes wide when she'd made the proposal to him, but he actually rather liked it, when all was said and done. He wondered if she was trying to trip him up, he wouldn't put it past her, or was she simply seeking to fill up a course that was short on candidates? *Another string to your bow, one which fully respects your principles,* she'd said, with a sly little smile as he signed the agreement. She had waved a few pages in front of him, chattering endlessly, a veritable three-card monte that made his head spin. He was no fool, but she'd sprung it on him, so he felt obliged to give her a tip in exchange: there would be a big jumble sale at the Salvation Army the following weekend.

The four-month training course was held at a renowned institute where several prestigious chefs taught. His little group—fifteen or so unemployed participants of varying backgrounds—also had the opportunity to meet regional producers who had been promoting organic principles for a number of years. The course would give him a qualification, and paid a wage; participants were well-fed and had leftovers to share for supper; what more could he ask for? But tonight Antoine hadn't brought anything back to the Darcourt hostel: it was Saturday and he didn't work on Saturdays. He walked faster, since he knew they were waiting for him for the whistle. To be late would be a real gaffe, it would spoil the start of the celebration, and he would hear about it for a long time. There was no one outside the residence, a strategic spot for hanging around talking if ever there was one . . . Shit . . . Had it started already? He went through the door and into the hall, which was also empty. It was a concrete building, built fifty-odd years ago, with tall narrow windows. The façade, which didn't get much sun, had balconies here and there, according to no logic or obvious symmetry—as if once the work was done, because there was still some money left over, the architect had decided to tack on a bit of cheap fantasy. Antoine went in the direction of a distant hubbub, toward the cafeteria at the end of the corridor.

The final was played in the biggest room in the residence: a dreary space of sixty square meters that opened onto a courtyard that served as a terrace, with a view on a concrete wall. It was summarily furnished and had a few drink dispensers, a countertop, sink, storage cupboards, and a sluggish microwave oven, but no actual kitchen worthy of the name. Two sheets had been hung up like a theater curtain to hide that entire side of the room. The tables and chairs had been moved to the middle, along with a host of extra stools and folding chairs the residents had brought. Forty or so men were already waiting, sitting close together, and twenty more were standing in the corridor or the little courtyard. Others would replace them in the course of the evening, a never-ending flow of friends, acquaintances, cousins, and neighbors. Antoine's arrival was greeted with a murmur of satisfaction which spread rapidly through the crowd.

"Antoine, my friend! You almost gave me a heart attack, showing up late! Hurry and sit down, we're about to start!"

A huge, corpulent black man, wearing an impeccable tailor-made three-piece suit, came up to meet him. Toussaint N'Diaye was his name, and he grabbed Antoine with authority by the shoulders and deposited him like a parcel on a free chair at the central table. His neighbors, two young hatchet-faced Moroccans, wiry like long distance runners, squeezed over to make room for him. Antoine greeted them and looked all around him, responding with a wave or a word to other residents. Most of them had gotten changed after their day at work and had run a damp comb through their hair. Even though it was Saturday, a good number had switched to their second job—maintenance work, cleaning in high-rise buildings, construction sites without permits for private individuals. The tall black man clapped his hands and everyone fell silent. All gazes converged on the sheets hiding part of the room. A huge sign, roughly painted in clumsy letters with a spray can, announced the program. *Final: Senegal versus Tamil-land.*

* * *

There had been eight countries on the original scoreboard: Morocco, Algeria, Senegal, Mali, Portugal, Sri Lanka, Poland, and Turkey. For nearly two months, with one match a week on Saturday evenings, the participants in this singular competition

confronted one another through recipes, by preparing a traditional national dish. The simultaneous and/or consecutive tasting of the two meals went on until the middle of the night, and
the guests voted to choose the winner according to rules that
were as complex as they were obscure. The organization of the
tournament had been the subject of long debate among the
residents: should they risk a 100 percent African (Senegal-
Mali) or North African (Algeria-Morocco) evening right from
the start? Should the participants inform the others of the
menu ahead of time or keep it a surprise? Were they allowed
to reinterpret classical recipes in their own way—particularly
in the absence of certain ingredients that were hard to find
even in Barbès? Were there any forbidden ingredients? How
could they avoid the risk of allergies?

Initially, the management at the residence had been reti-
cent— "No collective meals allowed" was a rule cast in iron—
all the more so when the meal was a fiesta where the whole
neighborhood might come tramping through. The center was
not big, with forty or so rooms spread over six floors above a
ground floor with common rooms: a big hallway with letter
boxes and worn armchairs, a basic cafeteria, a laundry room,
and a computer room open six half-days a week. The residents
could check the Internet on ancient PCs donated by the Paris
City Hall; their near-obsolescence was a far better assurance
against theft than the ridiculous little padlock on the door. A
windowless cubbyhole hardly bigger than a closet served as an
office for the manager; and following recent cuts in the staff of
the association that ran the place he was now also in charge of
another residence in the 19th arrondissement.

After a first refusal he'd posted on the official noticeboard,
Antoine had agreed to come to the rescue. He'd arrived at the
Darcourt residence six months earlier, and stood out like a sore
thumb with his resume as long as his arm (although he'd never
mentioned it, information spread with the speed of lightning)

and his entertaining speeches about biodiversity, pesticides, and paper recycling. He'd shown up in the manager's office one morning without an appointment. A potent smell of stuffiness and rancid cabbage seemed to be encapsulated in the tiny room: one spark would have been enough to blow up the building. Hervé Schmutz, in his forties, had something of a Ukrainian shot-putter about him, slightly pudgy but still good-looking. Shaved head and sharp eye, he was sweating like a pig in a shirt that was stretched to bursting over his chest, biceps, and trapezius muscles, as he stared at a PC that was as dilapidated as the ones in the computer room.

"*Panem et circenses*, does that mean anything to you?" said Antoine, after a curt greeting.

"Monsieur Lacuenta, I have only a paltry degree in business administration, nothing as prestigious as your own CV. Incidentally, you will excuse me, but I did not download the Latin dictionary onto my smartphone because it's an old model and doesn't have a lot of memory. Having said that, I think I understand the gist of your irresistible witticism."

"So much the better. These guys work like dogs, for a pittance, and they're far away from their homes and their families. Most of the time they finish the evening in their tiny rooms in front of the television—when they've got the means to buy one."

"Kind of you to remind me. My luxurious working conditions had alienated me from that reality," said the manager, with a large circular wave of his arm that embraced seven square meters, a stained wall-to-wall carpet, a metal cupboard with no door, a neon overhead light, and a wobbly coatrack.

"They have come up with a joint project that is cultural and convivial: to introduce the cuisine of their home countries and share it with others. And you answer with health and safety regulations. Bullshit, in other words. The paternalist, castrating republic in all her splendor."

"Let's get one thing clear: do you intend to participate? Or merely act as a defender of worthy causes?"

"No, I have no personal interest in the matter, it's just a question of values and principles."

"Well, well, that's odd, I thought you were an advocate of shopping local. I must have got it wrong. Because the carbon footprint of authentic exotic cuisine is damn heavy. Plantains don't grow at the Dejean market, you know, nor do pimentos. Unless you intend to replace the rice with shell pasta and turmeric with beet juice?"

"But I know when to be flexible, and now I expect the same from you," insisted Antoine, beside himself. "Let them have their cooking contest; the initiative will strengthen group cohesion and improve the center's reputation—which isn't all that great, you know, it's hardly better than some flophouse in the banlieue. If you show you trust them, the residents will have more respect for the place. It's a win-win situation. Who knows, you might even get a bonus."

The manager burst out laughing and stood up from behind his desk, all two hundred and eighty-five pounds of him. For months he'd been struggling with financial problems. Because of the crisis, a handful of residents had fallen behind with their rent—but that was something he was used to, at a push. Above all, the owner of the building was preparing to renegotiate the lease on the basis of terms which, for the company managing the residence, would be crippling. The position of assistant manager had been axed already months before, and his own salary was rarely paid on time. The couple who did the house-keeping and reception part-time—he'd had to let them go, and he'd reduced the hours of the cleaning company that took care of the common areas. So, talk about a bonus . . . He stepped across to give Antoine, still standing there, a hearty pat on the back. He was at least six inches taller and a good hundred pounds heavier.

"You know what, Lacuenta, I like you. Where are you from, again?"

"You're saying *tu* to me now? Are you keeping a file on me for the prefecture?"

"Tsk, tsk . . . Don't go spoiling the beginning of a beautiful friendship."

"I'm a citizen of the world, if you can grasp that concept."

"Oh, oh! Spare me your global justice claptrap. Lacuenta, that's Spanish?"

"My paternal grandfather was from Valencia and my grandmother from Madrid. My mother's family is from Catalonia, and I grew up in the outskirts of Paris," recited Antoine in one breath, in a falsetto voice. "Will that do you, Schmutz? Or do I have to take my pants down to show you my foreskin?"

The manager closed his eyes and for a moment was lost in thought, joining his hands at the height of his face.

"Paella, *cocido madrileño*, and chorizo, right?" he continued. "Not bad, not bad, but not as good as a nice *choucroute* from Alsace, where I'm from, with all the trimmings, and cooked in champagne. Well, go ahead and have your contest. On one condition: you keep me a plate of each dish. But I warn you, from now on you're in charge of the project, so if there's the slightest hitch you'll get what's coming to you. Lights out at two A.M. Go easy on the booze. Cafeteria spotless afterwards. No scenes with the neighbors, we already have enough problems as it is. Deal?"

"Deal."

Antoine Lacuenta held his hand out to Hervé Schmutz, something he'd avoided doing on his way in, out of caution. Now Schmutz crushed his knuckles with a good-natured smile. Not such a bad guy, Antoine concluded, suppressing a wince of pain.

"Your sissy little cold cuts, those little bits of *pata negra* that melt in your mouth, they're not bad with the aperitif," conceded the manager with a final nod. "But a good, greasy Montbéliard sausage and a chunk of smoked lard over a pound of sauerkraut—and don't forget half a dozen frankfurters—now there's a meal for a real man. I'll have to invite you over, you look like you need fattening up."

Antoine hurried out before Schmutz had a chance to give him another rather too virile show of affection. A few days later, Schmutz pulled some institutional crockery and two professional gas hotplates out of his hat, on loan for the duration of the contest. And Antoine became the resident mascot and official patron of the competition.

* * *

Before collapsing on a folding chair that sagged beneath his weight, Toussaint introduced the candidates in his stentorian voice, rolling his "r"s luxuriously like a fairground magician.

"To my rrright, for Senegal, my brother Saturnin Doucourrré with his fantastic *thiéboudiène*, here to serve you. A true delight for those who know it, and a surprise for everyone else!"

Saturnin Doucouré was a tall, thin man in his sixties, with very dark, pockmarked skin. A scar ran along his left cheek from the edge of his lips to the top of his cheekbone. Whenever he tried to smile his expression froze in a disturbing grimace. He was a security guard at a shopping center in the outskirts of Paris. Half the evil gossips said that he'd found his recipe while leafing through the cooking magazines at the supermarket, and not in the family pot, as he'd claimed from the start. The other half swore that this was impossible because Doucouré couldn't read. He greeted the company with a few dance steps, which contrasted with his forbidding air. A salvo of shouts and whistles came from the audience, which had grown even larger; hands and feet tapped on makeshift percussion—metal bowls, spoons, table legs and surfaces, backs of chairs. An African man conjured an enormous boombox as if by magic, playing a nasal hit by Youssou N'Dour. Doucouré enjoyed the unconditional support of all the Africans in the residence, even the North Africans, as well as that of the small West Indian community. As he'd been living at the Darcourt residence for over three years, he was, so to speak, playing to a home crowd.

"On my left, from his far away, mysterious Tamil-land, here is Vairam Navaratnarajah and his biryani! He has promised to take our tastebuds on an exotic journey, so hang on!"

Although they were not as numerous, the Tamil's supporters heartily made their presence known, letting out a long, hoarse, ever-louder cry that ended up like the howling of a wolf, before chanting *Vai-ram! Vai-ram!* to drown out the Senegalese music. He was a real outsider: not only did no one know exactly where his country was located, but he'd been living at the center for barely two months, and had hardly gotten to know anyone. A handful of Pakistanis and Sri Lankans made up most of his fan club. But ever since the semifinal, where he'd wiped out Morocco, which had beaten Portugal in the previous round, he also had the staunch support of the little Portuguese community. Without realizing it, they had reconnected with what had been, for the era, a very fruitful alliance where international gastronomy was concerned. He was a short, round man, much younger than his opponent, reserved, with a darting and very clever gaze that lit up his appealing face. He had a short, bushy mustache and his skin was a bluish brown.

"My friends, may the best man win!"

The master of ceremonies tore down the sheets: two enormous recipients had pride of place on a solid table. Piles of Arcopal plates had been set on the countertop, next to two huge containers, one filled with cutlery and the other with cafeteria glasses. Saturnin Doucouré lifted the lid off his pot with a little war whoop and waved a ladle as if it were a machete. A familiar odor wafted into the room and the Africans rushed up to be served generous portions of rice, sauce, and fish. Everyone was familiar with Doucouré's *thiéboudiène*, because he'd already cooked it for the quarter- and semifinal. This time—hoping to make *the* significant difference, and to the delight of the Senegalese diners—he had added some *guedjef* and *yete*, traditional dried fish and shellfish.

While dishing out the meal and passing the plates from hand to hand as soon as they were filled, he glanced over at the strange little man next to him. Vairam had not yet served a single spoon, and was taking his time without the slightest concern for what was happening around him. Doucouré moved over slightly to peek into his opponent's pot. Oh dear, the rice looked all dry, he must have screwed up the recipe, poor guy probably wasn't used to this. His making it to the final was simply beginner's luck, but that was about to come to an end. He almost felt sorry for him and was thinking of handing him a plate of *thiéboudiène* to seal his his own victory, but just then Vairam, with a precise gesture of his big serving spoon, broke the crust of rice on the biryani. Unfamiliar aromas, as delicate as they were potent, drifted into the room like a genie from his lantern. Every delicate wave banished the previous one, with each successive, deeper dip of the spoon into the biryani revealing the subtle construction of the dish in successive layers: green vegetables, rice, potatoes, and various meats. There was a sudden, pervasive silence, and before anyone had even tasted the biryani, Doucouré knew he had lost the final.

Caviar, Lobster, and *Macarons*

uc Bricard listened distractedly as Laurent Lacarrière related his jaunt to Deauville the previous month in the company of two models. Two professionals, I swear! Bricard had seen the receipts, as usual: the royal suite, twelve magnums of champagne, caviar and lobster, all room service over an entire weekend. One of the damsels had expressed an urge for some black currant-rhubarb *macarons* from one of those stars of Parisian patisserie: its name hardly mattered. Laurent had asked the manager of the hotel to send an employee to Paris at once to pick up a box. One advantage of luxury hotels, among other things, is that nothing is ever impossible. The manager did not even raise an eyebrow; every day he was confronted with demands that were far trickier and more eccentric, and the hotel had merely added one thousand euros to the bill (in addition to the price of the box of *macarons*) for the little favor that took half a day. Almost twice as expensive as the daily rate of those strategy consultants who came sniffing around the old man every month to offer their services! Those models had scented a sucker and they wouldn't stop there. Luc Bricard conducted a quick little investigation into the pretty young things: demimondaines haunted by a few scandals. Then he'd appointed an intermediary (a former boxer, as sinister-looking as they come) to refresh the ladies' memories regarding a few unfortunate incidents, and that had convinced them to leave at once for the Riviera. Ever Mr. Nice Guy, Bricard had even paid for their plane tickets.

The details of Laurent's hotel suite romps annoyed him on several counts. The boss's son's shenanigans with two adventurous little bitches reminded him of how deadly dreary his own sex life was at the moment. So it goes. But above all, there were bigger fish to fry: business was not going well. Ever since that private conversation in Marcel's office, things had gone from bad to worse. The cost of postage for print matter was set to go up again this year, crippling media companies even further. The most recent renegotiation of printing rates had yielded poor results, and the cost of paper had soared yet again. The competition was hurting too, of course, but *Convictions* was still maneuvering more successfully than everyone else: the novelty effect had not yet worn off. Annabelle Villemin-Dubreuil's column was a huge hit. Once the initial excitement was over, their plan to spirit the magazine away from the kiosks was proving more difficult to implement than they'd projected. For several weeks Bricard had displayed incredible ingenuity, coming up with the most extravagant plots to get his hands on a considerable supply. The best method would be to be nip distribution in the bud, at the printer's: bomb scares, fire-setting, flood, nighttime breaking and entering . . . He'd envisioned them all. The hardest thing had been to dissuade Laurent from trying to get himself hired at the printer's: he wanted to sabotage the rotary presses himself, which he would have managed to do very easily since he was so incredibly clumsy.

In the end, they managed a raid at the printer's one Wednesday evening at dusk, just as the rotary presses were going full steam. They had secured the complicity of a former worker through a series of discrete intermediaries, which made it practically impossible to identify them. The two men had lain in ambush in a field of beets just next to the warehouse, their car covered with a military camouflage net. A huge panel had been neatly cut in the fence before they arrived: all they had to do was move it then put it back. The former worker had been well paid to take care of it. Two towering pallets of magazines were waiting for them just beyond the fence. The risk was reasonable: it would take only a few minutes to shift them to the car. They filled the Volvo to bursting, and at the very end they covered the magazines with the camouflage net. Bricard resolved to rent a little commercial vehicle the next time round.

This first booty was encouraging: several thousand copies spirited away. It would be hard to find *Convictions* on the newsstand the next morning. But when they got to Barbès, the two apprentice thieves had a rude awakening: at least a good third of the stacks their accomplice had prepared for them consisted of other magazines. Bricard, who felt as swindled as if a dealer had sold him coke mixed with powdered sugar, ranted all evening long. All that for this! Besides, he knew it would be impossible to perform the same exploit every week. So then he turned to the big depots in the suburbs where the magazines were stored before they were shipped to the kiosks. Once again he resorted to the services of an accomplice on the inside (Marcel's network was inexhaustible) who unlocked an emergency exit and prepared freshly packaged stacks. The operation went smoothly, and they repeated it several times over. But the bounty was limited, and here too it had been trafficked: sometimes it was women's magazines they picked up, or home décor glossies, or crossword books. Bricard had stored everything at the place in La Goutte d'Or, until a better solution came to him. Should he throw them out, or burn them? The prospect of having to move everything to a dump in the outskirts wasn't exactly thrilling. Unless he just abandoned them there, since neither the owner nor the real estate agent would be able to trace him?

They were getting ready to drop off the previous night's plunder at the garage; this would surely be the last time. They avoided coming at night and preferred to stop off when the neighborhood was teeming with activity. The traffic was heavy. Road work on the tram along the boulevard des Maréchaux was backing the cars up as far as Barbès. Laurent, at the wheel, was sharing some juicy details about his weekend in Normandy, while eyeing all the young women they drove past. At last they reached the rue Myrha, and Bricard pressed the remote that opened the garage door. It took only a few minutes to empty the station wagon, with the engine idling, and back out of the garage. A pretty little brunette was walking along the sidewalk toward them with a smartphone in her hand. She had a curvy hourglass figure, and her gait was light and sensual. Laurent flashed her one of his charmer's smiles, along with a wink. The young woman stared back at him and her eyes grew as round as saucers.

"See that, Luc, they cannot resist me, not a one. Even in Barbès . . . "

S andrine locked her bike to the nearest pole and walked up the sidewalk a dozen yards or so to the glass door. Her heart was pounding, and she had trouble finding the keys in her pocket, then choosing the right one: a simple flat key that initially turned without catching. She pushed open the filthy, creaking door and entered a stuffy, sour-smelling place. It was already familiar enough to her, but this was the first time she'd come on her own. A month from now, at the most, and everything would be finalized. But she didn't really feel at home yet: to get the keys she'd had to act her most persuasive self with the little jerk from the real estate agency, in his ridiculous pointed shoes—well, anyway, they all looked alike in those agencies, with their cheap black suits, their white shirts open at the neck, and the latest model smartphone stuck to their ears.

This one was rather beefy, bursting out of his too-tight trousers that came straight from the Sentier garment district. He talked about *products*, and *good dope*, and *what a high*, so much so that the first time, Sandrine wondered whether he didn't have a parallel career as a dealer which had caused him to adopt a sort of universal language around his clients that made life easier. Given his gloomy, unmotivated look this morning she supposed he'd already gotten his commission and that it wasn't very hefty, whence his reluctance to help her out. When she'd assured him that she could manage very well without him and would get the keys back to him by noon, he suddenly became more conciliatory. But she basically understood that he really didn't give a damn if she lost the keys or even moved some squatters into the place.

She checked the main switch on the board by the entrance to the kitchen: still no electricity, she'd have to call the electricity company. No trouble with the water, however: she could hear a faucet dripping in the kitchen. She'd have to see to that with the plumber. She took a little notebook out of her bag and started jotting down the jobs to be done. The most important things had already been noted in detail but she felt a constant urge to improve her list, which to her represented the promise of a new life, full of possibility, far removed from her job at Pôle Emploi. The kitchen was top priority. She'd have to get rid of all the old equipment and remove the tiles, scrub everything thoroughly, bring the electricity and gas up to standard, repaint, have new tiles laid, and finally install a stainless countertop and brand-new equipment: range with several burners, cold rooms, ovens and a slow-combustion stove, ventilation, deep-fat fryer. The room was fairly big, with a window, and a door leading out onto a little inner courtyard that also connected to the hall in the building. The restrooms would also be destroyed and rebuilt, immaculate, with pretty mosaic tiles and a soft light—but not too dim, either. She knew the filthy habit most men had of marking their territory wherever they went, like cats, leaving concentrated drops of urine with a potent smell. She hoped that her future clientele would know how to behave and that adequate lighting (as well as amusing toilet bowls that would reveal a decorative target when the lid was lifted) would encourage the clumsier fellows among them to aim at the right spot. With perverts, it was another story.

The main room, too, would have a new appearance, a radical change. The old bar counter from the seventies would disappear, freeing up the space for a long dinner table. Under the fake ceiling, where one tile had already fallen down, to her great delight Sandrine had discovered a crimson and gold rococo décor, in perfect condition, that must date back to the construction of the building: enhanced by some modern lighting it would give the place terrific character. She hadn't chosen the flooring yet, hesitating between colored concrete and a dark parquet floor with wide boards, with a preference for the concrete, which would be cheaper and easier to maintain. The storefront would also be completely renovated with wider windows and a dark sign. Inside, antique and flea market furnishings and dishware would mingle Scandinavian influence with the spirit of a New York loft, with a hint, just a hint, of the boudoir. A dark velvet curtain behind the front door and one or two squat reupholstered armchairs around a coffee table would do the trick.

With her pencil in hand and her nose in the air, still standing in the middle of the grimy kitchen, Sandrine allowed herself to be borne along on her sweet dream, now taking shape. *Her* restaurant, after so many years of thinking and hesitating. At the age of nearly forty she had at last decided to fulfill her dearest wish and to break away from the path her parents had set her on: university, administrative entrance exams, church wedding, children. To be sure, she'd done remarkably well with all of that, and she still loved Guillaume and enjoyed their life together, but she wanted more. Or rather, she wanted something that would be hers, and only hers, and where she would not be beholden to anyone. She'd spent years examining the problem from every angle without finding a solution, and then suddenly, in the space of a few months, all the pieces of the puzzle began to fit together, one by one, with disconcerting ease. Her meeting with Antoine Lacuenta and his diatribe about organic produce and recycling had struck home— why deny it? He claimed that another social model was possible, based on negative growth, and a new attitude toward work and consumption. Okay, why not. For her, too, another model was taking shape, but on a more modest level: to open her own restaurant and make her delicious cooking available to everyone.

When by chance, leafing through brochures at the office, she had seen that the Paris City Hall was launching a program to purchase premises and commercial leases in quartiers undergoing rehabilitation, her antennae had vibrated. A similar operation had been under way for a number of years already with independent bookstores, to help with the reimplantation of this economically fragile sector. But now all sorts of activities were concerned, provided they were located in the targeted quartiers—and the 18th arrondissement had been singled out, from La Goutte d'Or all the way to the Porte de Clignancourt—and that a sustainable approach would be adopted. Thrilled to her fingertips, Sandrine went through the application process she had downloaded from the website.

The program was the fruit of lengthy negotiations between the socialist deputies and the Green Party, and it offered generous subsidies, but it had not received a great deal of publicity: in Sandrine's opinion, this meant it was too good a plan not to fall prey to some scheming and personal connections. To have one's project chosen would require, therefore, cleverness and strength of conviction in equal measure—two qualities she possessed in abundance. Under cover of her position at Pôle Emploi, she met with an economic development adviser at the town hall of the 18th arrondissement whom she had encountered at job forums from time to time; she hoped he would give her a few leads. With his eyes riveted on her bountiful décolleté, Christophe Lebret had been forthcoming beyond all expectation. He filled her in on the type of project they hoped to fund. For a start, any business with a social nature, like child-care centers run by the parents, or day nursery associations, but also more "classic" businesses: groceries that were organic or specialized in free trade, restaurants, designer boutiques. Cooperative and participatory associations were much sought-after, as were projects that enabled people in difficulty or the long-term unemployed to reenter the job market. Considerable amounts of additional aid, moreover, had been earmarked for precisely these activities.

According to Christophe Lebret, the applications they had received thus far had been fairly poorly presented and disappointing. But he also hinted that the Green Party members were getting impatient, things were moving too slowly, and the next meeting of the commission was scheduled in eight weeks' time, when they would decide on at least two projects, even if they were mediocre. The program brought together several head offices with rival interests at stake (real estate, economic development, employment, environment), which hampered its smooth operation, given the squabbles hatched between clans in the plush corridors of the town hall. Six months after launching the program, those in charge of the real estate sector had found no more than a dozen buildings to buy, and a similar number of commercial leases to preempt, in the four arrondissements concerned. Over dessert, Sandrine learned that there were three locations in the 18th arrondissement. After coffee, she made appointments to visit them. The third one, right in La Goutte d'Or, was exactly what she had been hoping to find. A site closer to Jules-Joffrin would have been even better, but the place met the criteria she'd set herself all the same.

After careful consideration, she concluded that the ideal project had to meet four conditions, in order to satisfy each of the sectors involved: rehabilitation of the urban environment in a disadvantaged quartier; reimplantation of a neighborhood store with a solid business plan; employment of needy individuals; and a realistic, sustainable approach that was also innovative. She'd put her application together shrewdly, and she'd hit the jackpot, though not without a leg up from Christophe Lebret, who'd managed to put her file on top of the right pile.

Sandrine's project for an organic restaurant had been awarded an investment grant of forty thousand euros.

The additional stroke of luck was that the premises were among those the town hall had purchased through an ad hoc semipublic company. As it was located in a quartier classified as a top priority zone, it came completely rent-free for twenty-four months, then after that, they would ask the going market rate. A regional subsidy for a company start-up as well as an interest-free government loan rounded out the financial setup. But it was not all settled, far from it. The sixty thousand euros she now had would cover only part of her needs, and she'd have to dig into her own savings as well as take out a bank loan. She was also getting ready to apply for unpaid leave from her job in order to start up her business. But thus far her plan to change her career was coming along nicely.

* * *

Sandrine emerged from her daydreaming with a smile on her lips. She still had a few measurements to take and she went on poking around. An old refrigerator took up the space at the back of the kitchen and she shoved it aside a few inches to see what sort of condition the wall was in: on the ceiling there were old marks from water damage, and she was afraid some of the walls might have been affected. She'd have to take that into account in her estimates with the painters, and keep a close eye on the work. She managed to push the fridge out of the way and discovered rings left by a damp spot on the dirty paint job. She scratched the surface with a screwdriver she'd found the other day under the bar, in an enormous ashtray, in the middle of a jumble of metal objects: rusty keys, promotional key rings, paper clips, small change in the old currency.

The plaster came off in huge chunks, laying bare a plywood wall. That was odd. She banged her screwdriver on the plywood and got a hollow little sound: the wood panel seemed very thin, as if it were placed against a harder surface. Sandrine stepped back for a better look, not easy given the lack of light, but eventually she could make out the shadow of a rectangle roughly two meters thirty high by one meter wide. With the screwdriver she found the joint on the right-hand side and dug a deep groove from the ground to a height of about one meter eighty. She scraped and dug until the plaster gave way all along the length of the groove, then using the screwdriver as a lever she probed between the plywood and the wall, then did the same thing on the left-hand side. With a sharp crack and a hail of plaster the plywood sheet eventually gave way, unveiling the metal cellar-type door which it had been fastened to. There was no door handle, and the keyhole, fairly basic by the looks of it, seemed to be locked.

Initially Sandrine thought it must be a wine cellar; but then why had the former owner walled it up? The blueprint of the premises, which she had studied meticulously, corresponded in every detail with the layout she herself had mapped, and did not indicate anything at this spot. So the space behind must be very small—a storage space, a broom closet? Or maybe some old-fashioned Turkish toilets, like the ones you still found in numerous cafés in Paris? A slight draft made the theory of a closet or even toilets unlikely. She tried, to no avail, to look through the keyhole. Then she remembered the jumble of things under the bar and went to fetch the heavy ashtray full of metal objects. She eliminated the bigger keys and identified a dozen that might actually work. None of them fit the bolt. She took the key to the front door, which she had in her pocket, and it went soundlessly into the lock and turned twice. Given that there was no door handle, Sandrine used the key as a lever and tugged the door toward her; it was fairly heavy. She could always say it was unlocked if she suddenly found herself face-to-face with someone. Holding her breath, she stepped into what seemed to be a medium-sized warehouse or garage. The adjacent premises.

"Hello, excuse me, is anyone there?"

Her voice echoed but no one answered. The place was empty, there were no cars or tools or any sort of equipment. Well, not quite, she noticed, as her eyes gradually adjusted to the gloom. Tall bales of paper were stacked against the walls, sometimes several rows deep, most of them still tightly bound, as if they had just left the printer's. Magazines. That's odd, I didn't see any newsstands anywhere in the street, she thought, surprised. She went closer: there was one title that came up again and again, *Convictions*, a magazine that had launched a few months earlier, some sort of right-wing rag according to Guillaume, but which was selling rather well. At a rough guess there were hundreds, even thousands of copies.

She glanced into one or two open boxes and found they too were filled with newspapers and magazines, *Convictions* yet again, but also all sorts of publications that seemed to have been selected at random. Some were spoiled, others were in perfect condition. Issues that hadn't sold, in all likelihood? If Guillaume got a look at this . . . He'd been having so much trouble getting supplies lately . . . Maybe she could bring him here from time to time. She was lost in thought when a car braked and stopped outside the building. She jumped when she heard the electric garage door grind into action. She beat a hasty retreat, locked the door behind her, and stood there listening, her heart pounding: not a sound filtered through from the garage next door. Her curiosity got the better of her: she took her notebook and her bag that she'd left behind the bar, and left the restaurant, double-locking the front door. A huge spanking new black station wagon was just pulling into the garage, too quickly for her to take note of the license number, other than the *département*: 92. Probably some merchant from Barbès who was rolling in it. But then why would they have all those stacks of magazines? Well, in any case she intended to invite all the neighbors to a party for the grand opening, that would be the opportunity to dig a bit deeper.

With her sunglasses on her nose, she strode down the sidewalk pretending to be on the phone, listening out for any noise from the garage. She went up the street to the corner, then when she heard the car engine and the mechanism of the garage door she turned around and came back down. The station wagon was on its way back out; it had stayed only a few minutes. Two men sat inside and she gave them a surreptitious glance when the car came to the stop sign at the corner of the street. They hardly looked like local tradesmen, more like well-to-do management types. Her gaze lingered on the passenger first, an ordinary fortysomething man, grumpy-looking. The guy at the wheel was taller and younger, wearing peccary-skin driving gloves. He turned to look at her and gave her an intent smile and a little wink. She shuddered when their eyes met, and held her smartphone over her mouth to stifle a cry.

Bouillon, *Choucroute*, and Vindaloo

Not for one moment did Vairam Navaratnarajah doubt he would win. He came from a long line of chefs whose roots went back to the eminent servants of the Mogul emperors. According to family legend, one of his ancestors had married the daughter of a king who wanted to bring him into his house—she wasn't the loveliest of the six princesses, to be sure, but she was of royal blood all the same, and came with a rich dowry. At the height of his glory this ancestor was in command of a brigade of over thirty qualified chefs who had come from the four corners of the Indian subcontinent, and double that number of kitchen boys and other helpers, up at three o'clock in the morning on banquet days. He had at his disposal a walled-in kitchen garden, where there grew herbs and spices and rare vegetables he kept jealous watch over. Several times a year he was visited by voyagers from afar—monks or explorers from Portugal, Spain, or France—who came to offer him seeds, tubers, or fruit from Europe and the New World, and whom he thanked with a memorable feast.

For grand occasions he prepared menus of several dozen dishes, which high-ranking guests enjoyed night and day without interruption. Some feasts, moreover, had been recorded in the virtually hagiographic memoirs of the master of the house. Even the royal family's everyday fare rarely consisted of fewer than twelve dishes of the highest refinement, not to mention the desserts. The chef himself however ate like a bird, surviving above all on clear broth, and roots and herbs, which might explain his exceptional longevity and abundant progeny, whom he initiated into his art. For years his main rival tried to uncover his recipe for vegetable consommé with spices, handed down to posterity with the poetic although slightly excessive name of the "bouillon of a thousand bouquets." Its subtle flavors bordered on perfection, without the slightest ingredient being revealed by the filtered liquid, which was pure and amber. After a final failed attempt (which he thought, however, would be the right one), the rival chef committed suicide, which consecrated the ancestor's reputation for good, and ensured he would become a legend.

Vairam did not really *learn* to cook: in his veins there flowed three and a half centuries of grandiose know-how and the fascinating history of Indian gastronomy. Three and a half centuries of culinary blending from the north to the south of the subcontinent. In 1980, when civil war broke out, his paternal grandparents left Colombo with their seven children to settle in Madras with a distant relative. In a soft pouch that did not leave his side during the entire journey, the grandfather, chef at one of the best restaurants in Colombo, carried seeds and spices. In Madras (not yet known as Chennai in those days), Vairam's father married Namita, who was from a family where for generations the women had been the guardians of a renowned Ayurvedic tradition. The two families had contracted the alliance in full knowledge of the facts. For both families cooking was not simply a matter of human survival, but belonged to a truly spiritual realm, a sort of magic, a powerful alchemy that must not be taken lightly. Vairam was born with this heavy responsibility already on his shoulders, eighteen months after his parents' wedding. It was in the late 1980s, in the kitchen of his paternal grandfather's restaurant, already much lauded, that he learned to walk.

At the age of ten he was already meeting with suppliers with his grandfather, and he did not hesitate to send something back straightaway, with a simple nod of his head. By the age of thirteen he had picked up the old man's knack at almost everything, and under his maternal grandmother's firm rule he had begun the long initiation into Ayurvedic philosophy. When he was nineteen the family sent him on a tour of the country to discover other regional cuisines. He traveled for almost two years from restaurant to inn, enriching his experience, already impressive for his age. Some of his best recipes came from the grand restaurants where he had perfected his training. Others he found in poorer quarters, in tiny holes-in-the wall where a single steaming pot kept everyone fed, all day long—craftsmen, workers, and penniless students.

This long apprenticeship left him with a love of travel, and when he got back to Chennai he felt confined. One year later he left to join a cousin in London, then followed another one to Paris, where he now lived. For a long time he had dreamt of working for an award-winning chef, in order to wed French gastronomy with his own know-how, and reinvent haute cuisine. He certainly had the ability, but his dark skin was an insurmountable handicap when it came time to knock at the service door of this or that grand establishment. For many of them he was just another one of those *commis* from the Indian subcontinent who had invaded the capital over the last few years. One day a second-in-command had asked him if he knew how to cook curry. Vairam had tried to point out the subtleties of his national cuisine, explaining in his peculiar French (one branch of his mother's family was from Pondicherry, but his accent was still very strong) that the notion of curry was above all a Western construct. The man had snickered, not even bothering to see him out, and moving on to the next candidate. Although he was the custodian of an art he had never stopped perfecting, in homage to those ancestors whose benevolent ghosts haunted every kitchen where he had ever worked, Vairam still had to make do with dishwashing or potato-peeling in brasseries on the *grands boulevards*. But he was determined to succeed.

Neither Toussaint N'Diaye nor Antoine Lacuenta nor even Hervé Schmutz knew of the great tradition of Mogul chefs. But all three were communing in silence over a vindaloo. Standing back, Vairam observed them with a smile of satisfaction. Like his ancestor—even if his round little build suggested quite the contrary—he did not need much to satisfy his appetite, and he'd finished eating long before the others.

"*Gghro* . . . shit," said Schmutz.

A long sonorous fart resounded: flatulence, for Schmutz, was a natural expression of satisfaction or pleasure. Obviously, it was not always a good thing, particularly if he was with a lady friend.

"He's like José Bové in velvet trousers, don't you think, Antoine?"

"That's it for your *choucroute*, old man. No offense to your wife, mind," said Antoine, his tone contemplative. "Citizen of the world, as I said, that's the only way to go."

"Ooh la la, brother," sighed Toussaint N'Diaye, getting to his feet to go and hug Vairam with his arms that were as thick as tree trunks.

In the middle of the meal, belying his reputation, Toussaint had removed his jacket and unbuttoned the vest stretched tight over his big stomach. Because his image of impeccable dandy, Savile Row variety, meant a lot to him. No one in the hostel had ever seen him in jeans or a tracksuit; when he walked around the place in the evening or at night, he only ever wore a velvet dressing gown that closed with a smart tasseled sash, over a pair of freshly ironed satin pajamas.

"If you were a girl I'd marry you right now, on the spot. Don't you have a sister? A cousin?"

Vairam extricated himself with a laugh. It wasn't his style to go in for false modesty; he'd known for years the effect his cooking could have on people. And besides, he'd whipped this one up in a hurry, on the electric hot plate in his room, and he hadn't even found all the ingredients he needed. Ever since he had won the cooking competition, hands down, the other residents greeted him with respect and curiosity, peering into his room the moment he began to cook, ever on the lookout for an invitation to have a taste. Saturnin Doucouré alone sulked, annoyed that he had lost to a kid no older than his youngest son, and who came, moreover, from a dubious country (the man from Senegal had searched everywhere for information about Tamil-land, to no avail, and would tell anyone prepared to listen that he was going to appeal the results of the contest, on the grounds of fraud). Initially he'd refused to taste the biryani, claiming he'd lost his appetite and had acid indigestion. But at the end of the festivities, as soon as Vairam had his back turned, Saturnin had rushed over to scrape the bottom of the bowl. He'd come up with a skimpy spoonful of rice; every grain, perfumed and toasted, melted in his mouth. He'd licked bare the last mutton bone he'd found at the bottom of the pot, sucking out the marrow, savoring every drop of juice, trying in vain, like back in the days of the ancestor's unlucky rival, to unveil the recipe's multiple ingredients and spices.

* * *

The men sitting in the cafeteria made a strange quartet. One elegant, black-skinned giant, as comfortable as a lord in the plushest private club in London. Another giant, blond and pink as a piglet, cramped in cheap clothes that were always too tight and smelled of cabbage, regardless of the day's menu (it was the fault of the laundry, he asserted). Both of them had close-cut hair and rivaled one another where their paunch was concerned. Next to them the handsome man in his thirties, with brown curls and a dark gaze, dressed like a belated adolescent, appeared downright skinny. And finally the man who had brought them all together that day: a round little fellow whose skin was almost black, cinched in a kitchen apron that came down to his ankles, as solemn as a pope with his serving spoon in his hand. The likelihood of these four men meeting and becoming friends was virtually zero. And yet they had. Could workers' hostels be a sort of social laboratory, a melting pot for secular, republican integration? They weren't, however, cloud-cuckoo-land. The dark clouds that had been gathering over the Darcourt hostel for several months had not dissipated and were threatening to bring a major downpour.

"Okay, I don't want to spoil our picnic, but . . . "

Three pairs of eyes turned in unison to look at Hervé Schmutz, who had just lit a cigarette and was greedily inhaling his first puff. Smoking was not allowed in the common areas and everyone knew he hated tobacco.

"In three months' time at the most we're closing up shop. The rent is no longer affordable and the pile of outstanding payments keeps growing. The owner wants to renovate the building and transform it into I-don't-know-what, and the association doesn't give a damn. It's curtains for the Darcourt hostel," he sighed.

The building housing the hostel belonged to a major player in the sector, the Francilienne Sociale, which since the 1950s had been working the seam of temporary housing in Île-de-France and Normandy: accommodation for young or casual workers, migrants, and foreigners. Before it was turned into a workers' hostel the Darcourt residence had been a dingy little hotel, then a student residence that was hardly any better, but none of the projects for the place had lasted very long. Several associations had stepped in one after the other, the latest one having also been in charge of hostels

104 · PASCALE PUJOL

in the 19th arrondissement and in the south of France. But none of them had managed to sustain the activity satisfactorily. At fault were the center's limited size, its lack of amenities, its dilapidation, and the layout that meant it could only house single men. A certain amount of renovation and upgrading to meet the norms in vigor had become indispensable, but the Francilienne Sociale didn't seem in any hurry to get the work done. In spite of its shoddy state of repair, the value of the property had increased tenfold, and the company was thinking, rather, of selling the place for a hefty profit. To make things worse, the current property management were going through a major restructuration, and they'd handed the reins over to Schmutz long ago, leaving him to deal with all the problems on his own.

"You must be joking," said Antoine, alarmed. "But what will become of the residents?"

"For months I've been looking for housing in other centers in Paris and the banlieue, and I've also got a few requests pending with the low-income housing bureau in inner Paris which should go through. If all goes well, everyone will have a roof over his head by the first of the year. But as far as the cooking contests are concerned, I can't guarantee a thing, guys."

"Are you telling us we're going to be spread out all over the place?"

"Shit, Antoine, are you thick or what? I'm telling you that I have been bending over backwards for six months or more to find everyone a place to sleep by the time I have to hand over the keys here. And I'm really proud of the fact that I've managed. Thirty-five single guys, mostly immigrants, when there are waiting lists as long as Toussaint's arm here, do you really think that's something you can pull off with your eyes closed? And in principle all three of you will be at the same place, I'm just waiting for confirmation."

Antoine Lacuenta frowned before returning to the attack. The other two followed the conversation attentively, not saying a word.

"And what about you? Are you going to go on with your boring little job in another hostel? Maybe moving to the 19th, with scenic view over the Buttes Chaumont? Will you come see us out in the banlieue, or does it stink too much for you?"

"Nah. Not even close."

"Aha! Rats deserting the sinking ship, you're done with social work, is that it? You're gonna find a cushy little civil servant's job? Going back to sauerkraut-land? Hate to inform you, you're too old to take the entrance exam to become a cop."

"Asshole! And you're nowhere near."

"No way . . . you found an even cushier gig than civil servant?"

"Ah, getting warmer. Yes, very cushy. I'll have all the time in the world to work on my resume, as it happens. Because this job is going to be axed, and the only placement those swindlers offered me is in Provence, in Brignoles. And you may laugh, but I wasn't too hot on Brignoles."

"The climate, maybe? You afraid of getting sunburnt?" said Toussaint, giving Schmutz's nearly shaven head an affectionate little pat—the sort of pat that would knock a donkey to the ground.

"Yeeeah, that's it. I don't like olive oil, either."

Hervé Schmutz collapsed into a fit of noisy, uncontrollable laughter (as always accompanied by his charming little farts), and the other three quickly joined in. Even Vairam, who was fairly reserved by nature, was hiccupping fit to choke, his face buried in his apron to hide his tears of laughter.

"Okay, are we having fun yet, guys? Are you pleased to hear I'll be joining the ranks of the welfare scroungers? But I've got a plan B for the center. You want to hear?"

SEAFOOD PLATTER

S andrine Cordier glanced one last time in her compact mirror, pinched her lips to spread the transparent lip gloss, and tidied a lock of hair. She could hear the click of high heels approaching.

"Madame Cordier, if you will come with me . . . "

Sandrine followed close behind a superannuated Barbie doll wearing a skirt that was both too tight and too short. She could not help but think of Marité: although she was several years older, her mother-in-law had an altogether different style. The Barbie doll knocked on a door, opened it without waiting for a reply, and stepped aside to let the visitor go in, before closing it soundlessly. The room was imposing, with tall bookshelves and thick carpets, but it would take more than that to intimidate the likes of Sandrine Cordier. Behind a wide mahogany desk an ageing beau was struggling with a computer mouse. He was dangling it in front of the screen and shaking it like a maraca. Parkinson's and Alzheimer's combined, this should be interesting, thought Sandrine.

"Madame Cordier, please, have a seat," he said, pointing to a round table with his free hand. "I'll just send this email and I'll be right with you."

Sandrine sat down and took a cardboard file folder from her bag. Behind the desk the man was still muttering to himself, while the computer refused to respond. Finally he put the mouse down next to the keyboard and tried a few seconds more, shaking his head, until finally the computer gave in with a little beep.

"Forgive me, I'm not very good with these machines," he sighed, sitting opposite her. "Anyway, I had a look at your email," he added, waving a sheet of paper he scanned quickly. "A program run by Pôle Emploi to support struggling sectors . . . two years' relief from social contributions for the hiring and training of the long-term unemployed . . . creation of positions in the field of new technologies . . . Very interesting, I have to confess I'm enthralled," he said, ending with his most gallant smile, calculating on the effect of the double meaning of his words, for his visitor was rather to his taste. "We would like to be part of the pilot phase. Tell me more."

Opening her file, Sandrine came out with her most persuasive smile, too.

"You'll see, it's very simple."

She slid a photograph across the table.

"Yes?" He looked up, surprised. "That's my son. Do you know him?"

A second photograph appeared.

"And this is my husband, Guillaume," she said.

"Forgive me, I don't understand, what does all this have to do with Pôle Emploi?" He frowned as he looked at the young woman, who really did suit his taste. "Is your husband looking for work? Have him send us his resume. I have no time to waste on these little schemes. Please get to the point."

"Indeed, I will grant you that none of this has much to do with Pôle Emploi, even though I do work there. But please do take a closer look at these two photographs."

He gave Sandrine a harsh look and put on his reading glasses. This vixen could have been his own daughter—she certainly had nerve. But he'd always had a weakness for women with character, so he did as she asked. For a moment he lost himself in contemplation of the two portraits then put them back down on the desk without saying a thing. He cleared his throat and tried to avoid Sandrine's gaze, but she wouldn't let go.

"There's a vague resemblance, I suppose. Well, it's above all their heterochromatic eyes that give that impression. But it's a more common feature than you might think, you cannot imagine how often I've run into it in my lifetime. And besides, I know how easy it is to doctor images on a computer, any twelve-year-old child can do it."

Sandrine held back a smile.

"That's true. Here's the negative of the photograph of my husband, have your photography department print it up if you like, I'm sure they still have some traditional equipment."

"But what is the point of all this? You don't honestly think that . . . ?"

A third photograph was now on the table, a fine large color reproduction. Sandrine relished the moment when the old man's jaw literally dropped. Just as he'd done a few minutes earlier with the computer mouse, he seemed to be temporarily paralyzed before he could get his wits about him and close his mouth again. Sandrine had gotten to her feet, and now she was standing right next to him. Gingerly, she took the print from his hands, held it out at a distance so they could both grasp the scene more fully, and nodded her head, with tenderness in her eyes.

It was the type of picture that often features in celebrity magazines: a cocktail party or reception, in the salon of a luxury hotel. In the background, an elegant, carefree crowd, pressing toward the buffet. In the center foreground stood Marcel Lacarrière, in his forties, a champagne glass in his hand, wearing an impeccable suit buttoned over a vintage shirt with a huge pointed collar. His left hand, where you could make out his heavy signet ring, held the forearm of an attractive young woman whom he was devouring with his eyes. She was almost as tall as he was, and looked good enough to eat in her Courrèges outfit: A-line skirt, tight sweater, white patent leather boots. Her thick light brown hair was pinned up in a loose chignon. And that slight come-hither glint to her gaze had something of the singer Dalida about it.

"She hasn't changed much, you know, she's still a real knockout."

* * *

Marcel Lacarrière could not recall ever having felt such contradictory emotions, or at any rate not in a very long time. He wanted both to strangle and take into his arms this pest of a woman who had wormed her way into his office with her twaddle about social contribution exemptions. At the same time, if he had actually used his brain for two minutes instead of thinking with what was inside his briefs, he would never have fallen into this vulgar trap . . . Since when did socialists come to the aid of the press? In one year they had already chipped away at most of the hard-won measures of recent decades, and once again costs were skyrocketing. If it went on like this, he'd have to move his editorial offices to Goa and have the natives do the work. All the more so since speaking proper French did not seem to be the most important skill required in order to blue-pencil a dispatch or upload videos of kittens found on the web.

A wave of melancholy, peculiar to those who refuse to be overcome by their memories—and for good reason—was turning him to jelly. Tickling his bone marrow. Twisting his guts. Marité . . . How could he ever have forgotten her? And yet, how long had it been since he'd thought about her? He met her just after his first divorce. She had a twenty-year-old's perfect skin, magnificent breasts, a mischievous gaze, and lips that melted in his mouth like candy. And above all, an imagination the likes of which he'd never encountered in any other woman. And God knows there had been plenty of them. Masses. A sudden olfactory memory came to him, as powerful as a punch. That Paco Rabanne perfume everyone was talking about in those days, and which he'd given to her, what was it called already? *Calandre*, that's it, *Calandre*. The designer—another nutcase, now that he thought of it—had wanted, so they said, to evoke a couple making love on the hood of a Jaguar during a drive along the sea. Marité? She was all that, and more.

He hunted through his memories for the day they met, at a charity ball *Le Libéral* was sponsoring. Or had he been invited in a private capacity? Some sort of event to do with fashion, that much he remembered perfectly: all the women there were gorgeous, far more elegant than those he saw nowadays at the rare professional celebrations he still attended. Was she one of the models, or a fashion journalist? One of those beauties who hung around that milieu without really doing much of anything? Or maybe she was just a hostess? The detail escaped him after so many years, but it hardly mattered, that night he only had eyes for her, while he himself, in those days, was one of the most prominent bachelors around, constantly in the media spotlight. They had gone off to Trouville right after the gala and hadn't left their suite in Normandy all weekend, having massive platters of seafood brought up by room service.

Their affair had lasted a little over a year, but they'd lived separately all the while. He had the flashy penthouse in Neuilly he'd bought just after his divorce, that he had now passed on to Laurent. Marité, who was fifteen years younger than him, had a studio in Pigalle and that was where he liked to meet her, more than anywhere else. When they strolled down the boulevard de Clichy at night, there were as many clients as pimps, men and women, insistently giving her the eye or blowing him kisses from their fingertips. This added spice to their lovemaking, although it hardly needed it. With Marité he felt as if he was slumming it, but also reliving his youth, recapturing some-thing carefree and energetic after a stifling bourgeois marriage.

He wanted to look more closely at the photograph, to see on her pretty twenty-year-old face all those soft freckles he used to count with a laugh when they made love—he always got it wrong and had to start over again and again, until they fell asleep in a tangle, sated, exhausted. He reached for the pic-ture but Sandrine was quicker. Marcel restrained a grunt and reluctantly got hold of himself.

"An old friend I've lost track of, but it's all ancient history and is of no concern of yours, I think."

"Oh, you're quite mistaken. This old friend of yours is my children's grandmother," retorted Sandrine coldly. "And Laurent looks very much like his older brother, although I pre-fer my Guillaume. So I do think that this does concern me, with good reason, father-in-law."

Marcel almost choked: such familiarity! She would pay for it. He tried to react but the proof before his eyes was con-founding: the two men had the same build, the same high fore-head, the same nose, those heterochromatic eyes that were so special . . . They took after him in every respect even if, he had to agree, Guillaume seemed to have more charm than his younger brother. The fairies had been kinder: Marité's genes had put up a better fight than Mette's. A second son, grand-children . . . And a complete bitch for a daughter-in-law! What an odd sort of gift life was offering him at his age! A one-way ticket for an aneurism, a good paralysis, or even straight to the cemetery? Sadistic punishment for the bad karma he'd been accumulating for several lives? How could he get away from the gang of vultures who would henceforth invade his country houses, plot and scheme to find out the contents of his will, and poison the few remaining Christmases and birthdays he had left to live? And what if, worse luck, which was all too likely, the kids had inherited their mother's temperament? A

cold sweat came over him; he hunted for his Ventolin spray
and took two long inhalations. The horrid woman, at least, had
the decency to remain silent and at a distance: she had sat back
down in the armchair opposite him and was rummaging in her
handbag.

"You don't intend to try and blackmail me, now do you,
with this family business, my dear young lady?" continued
Marcel Lacarrière, his tone half-sententious, half-aggrieved.
"As far as I'm concerned, I have nothing to hide. I am quite
prepared to meet your husband if it turns out that . . . And if
Marité wants to see me again, my door is open wide, I would
be only too glad to see her. You see, she left me without any
explanation. I didn't know she was pregnant."

He was being sincere, but was careful not to mention the
fact that Marité had found out about his escapade with a fit-
ting model from Yves Saint Laurent—in those days, Marcel
was very much into models. Fidelity had never been his strong
point. They'd had a rather acrimonious discussion and she'd
told him to choose. But no woman had ever won at that game.
And yet he cared about Marité, and tried to get back together
with her, but she had moved, and no one in Pigalle could tell
him—or wanted to tell him, perhaps—where she had gone.
These days such a disappearance might seem impossible, with
email and cell phones and all the traces people leave behind
them, but back then it was as simple as that. And she'd never
given any sign of life since.

"Blackmail you because of this family business? No, that
would be unspeakable, father-in-law," said Sandrine, her tone
full of outrage as she went closer to him, her smartphone in her
hand. "You don't know me."

She showed him the screen.

"What's this then, some vacation snaps with the dog and
the motor home? Or the kids' class photo?" said Marcel,
chuckling.

Suddenly full of pep from the turn of events, he put on his reading glasses again. He stared at the screen and frowned, then looked up, disconcerted.

"If that's your place, it seems to be a bit short on light and furniture. It looks like a basement. Not very healthy for the children."

"No, it isn't very cozy at all," Sandrine agreed, "but there's plenty to read. You see, we are very fond of reading newspapers and magazines in our family. Like father, like son. Have a good look, there."

She swiped onto a new photograph. Bales of newspapers and magazines were piled high in what was a garage, perhaps a warehouse. The columns were the height of a man, sometimes higher. Sandrine zoomed in onto one pile, then the cover. *Convictions*. Hundreds of copies.

Marcel Lacarrière stifled an oath with a cough, his voice hollow. This was all he needed . . . But where had this Mata Hari come from? He was thinking as fast as his tired neurons would allow. Raise his head, for a start. He fixed his heterochromatic gaze onto that of his recently acquired daughter-in-law, with the sensation he was playing the toughest poker game of his entire life. For over forty years he had kept the family business prospering, diversifying its activities and making handsome profits. At the head of his professional union, an office he had occupied for four terms, he had acquired a reputation as an uncompromising negotiator. A number of agreements that had proven very favorable for the sector had, moreover, been drawn up during his presidency. The printers and paper manufacturers hugged the wall when they saw him coming: he'd bled them dry for years.

At the magazine, he'd brought the CGT union to heel when the 35-hour work week was imposed, and the present union representative ate out of his hand, in exchange for discreet little favors. His employees feared him, and his management staff did not venture to question his decisions, ever. Even Luc Bricard handled him with kid gloves. He'd gone through three divorces without coming out of it too badly, even preserving good relations with his former spouses. In many ways he was a wealthy man who had a full life, with nothing more to prove or, in many ways, to lose. As a rule, his piercing gaze was enough to destabilize anyone who opposed him, and matters were settled in two minutes flat. As a rule.

Sandrine Cordier had not moved, waiting for her host to speak first. Her attitude betrayed neither awkwardness nor doubt nor impatience, just a slight touch of irony and a great amount of self-confidence. *Poker face.* A real shark, she was! The old man had always been able to tell when an adversary had the upper hand—it was an indispensable skill in the business world—even if it did not happen often. He sighed, regretting just then that she was not the fruit of his love with Marité. He could have left her the keys to the boutique and walked straight to the cemetery with a light heart. And his kid Guillaume had managed to get his hands on a number like this? Either he was very clever, or even more of a half-wit than his younger brother. Marcel decided to stake his all.

"Tell me about my grandchildren," he said, all syrupy, adopting his most innocuous smile.

A gleam of victory flashed in Sandrine's gaze, but she refrained from any audible reaction.

"They're good kids. As it happens, they're trying to find an internship in a company. They're in the ninth grade, so this means just one week of unpaid internship."

"Oh, are they twins?"

"No, not actually," sighed Sandrine. "Juliette is two years ahead and Aurélien is two years behind. He is, how shall I put it, a bit unconventional. Very creative and sensitive, but not really at ease in the school system."

A gifted girl and a half-wit boy . . . well, it was one heck of situation.

"Internship, you said? I should be able to organize something for them. Tell me what sort of things they're interested in."

"Computers and fashion, I think, but they'll tell you themselves, they came with me. They're waiting in your assistant's office."

"Then let's go see them," said Marcel good-naturedly.

One hour ago, he didn't even have any grandchildren, nor did he have the hope or desire, in fact, to have any someday. And now two brats were standing only a few feet away from him, behind that door. He had missed their first words, but also their milk burps on his tie, and all that dreary business with diapers and baby bouncers, and school bazaars and those awful family evenings with everyone going soft in the head over the kiddywinks. To come to know them only today was perhaps a blessing in disguise, all things told. He opened the door with a touch of apprehension, like the first time he'd been alone in a room with a naked girl.

The boy was tall and good-looking, absorbed in reading the magazine on his lap, with a pen in his hand: he must be doing a crossword or a Sudoku. A carefully styled forelock fell over half his face and Marcel did not see at first that he had inherited those heterochromatic eyes. He seemed to have been dressed by one of those morbid designers the chief editor of the *Libéral* fashion pages was always going on about: Von Trusche? Von Musche? The girl was diminutive, neither tall nor pretty, with the face of a little mouse. She was wearing jeans, a pink sweater, and tennis shoes, and had big headphones over her ears, like most girls her age. And yet he couldn't be sure she was altogether normal: her lemur-like fingers were manipulating both a touchscreen *and* a cell phone at the same time, with fascinating speed. Completely absorbed, at first she didn't hear her mother calling. She looked up and hurriedly stored her gadgets in her backpack, mumbling something that Marcel didn't quite understand about the opening of the "*naz-d'ac.*" It had to be slang, clearly.

"Juliette, Aurélien, Monsieur Lacarrière has been kind enough to agree to arrange internships for you in his company. Could you explain to him what you would like to do?"

The mouse mumbled something that sounded like "H'lo." Her brother merely gave a little wave of the hand along with a broad, enticing smile that bore a certain resemblance to Laurent's.

"Hello, Juliette," said the brand-new granddad, somewhat moved to be making the first move. "Your mother said you'd like to come and see how things work in our fashion and beauty department. You'll see, it's instructive for a young lady, and on top of it there are all sorts of pretty little presents from the fashion and perfume brands. You'll have a great time."

"Fashion? No, I'd rather be in the new media department. I've got a web project to wind up, that would be perfect," replied Juliette, in no way impressed. "Princess stuff, that's more up my brother's alley."

"I'll do anything to attend fashion shows and shoots," confirmed Aurélien, stressing the word *anything*.

He'd looked up and closed his magazine: *Madame Figaro*, the special beauty issue. It wasn't a pen he was holding in his hand but a nail file, which he slipped into the inside pocket of his jacket once he had finished his manicure. *Oh dear, this is something else, the kid is one of them*, sighed Marcel to himself. Talk about family! No end of problems, that was for sure.

"Ah, well, why not, you have to move with the times. My assistant will arrange it all with your mother in the days ahead. Goodbye, then, youngsters, be good and work hard at school."

Marcel turned around to take leave of Sandrine.

"We will meet soon, dear lady. We'll be in touch. Until then . . . "

He put on a conspiratorial air, his eyes open wide and one finger on his lips to signal silence.

"That goes without saying, Marcel. And I have another little project I will have to talk to you about soon."

She doesn't pull any punches, the stuck-up harridan. She'd called him Marcel in front of his assistant! And on top of the internships for her snotty-nosed brats, she had some other dirty trick up her sleeve. Was she a nuisance? No, an out-and-out plague—cholera, smallpox, all in one. And she hadn't even left him the photograph of Marité . . . Marcel was still mumbling in his beard when he felt a little hand tugging on his jacket. Juliette had come back in and was handing him a sheet of paper folded in four.

"I almost forgot, this is for my internship. It's super super important. Thanks in advance."

"Oh! You made me a drawing, that's so kind," he said, looking distractedly at the paper before slipping it into his pocket: a sort of collage, maybe a poem. "I'll put it on my desk."

With a clumsy fist he patted the top of the little girl's head, the way he did his Great Danes when they sat up and begged for a snack: she wasn't much taller. Not very gracious, but intelligent and determined, already that. Because of mumps and that other faggot Hedi Von Musche, it was on her frail shoulders that the responsibility of his lineage now rested, he thought with a pang of regret. Juliette shot him an impenetrable look, popped her chewing gum bubble, then turned on her heels to run down the corridor to catch up with her mother and brother.

FINGER FOOD

Tracking down Marcel Lacarrière had been the most exciting chase of her life. When she had encountered Laurent's gaze that day on the rue Myrha, Sandrine felt a sort of dizziness come over her. The driver of the car was her husband's virtual double, a younger version of Guillaume living a parallel life where she did not exist. But how could she locate a man she'd glimpsed only briefly, about whom she knew nothing other than that he bore a disturbing resemblance to her husband? There was no name on the garage door or on their letter box, even though it was emptied on a regular basis. No one in the building seemed to know anything about their discreet fellow tenants. Eventually she tried a search on Google on genetics and heterochromatic eyes. As she searched she came upon pages with rows of portraits of major and minor celebrities who shared the trait. Amid the likes of David Bowie, Elizabeth Taylor, and the Bogdanoff brothers, she spotted Laurent merely by chance; as he regularly frequented upscale restaurants, fashion shows, and gala soirées, he had a fairly significant presence on the web. Once she'd found the son, the father was not far behind. But then things got more complicated: how could she establish the link with Marité?

Sandrine had some half-days off owed to her, so she devoted them to methodically going through her mother-in-law's things. It wasn't easy, because Mamoune was a bit of a homebody, but she eventually managed. Once she uncovered the family booklet containing the birth certificates, she found out for a start that Mamoune's marriage to Raymond took place several months after Guillaume's birth. Guillaume didn't seem to know this, or if he did, he'd never mentioned it. And as she thought about it, Sandrine realized she'd never seen any pictures of the event, nor had her in-laws ever celebrated their anniversary; but she had merely seen this as further proof of her mother-in-law's nonconformist lifestyle. This first discovery sharpened her curiosity. Guillaume was born before his parents got married . . . but did that necessarily mean Raymond was not his father? Maybe they got married to make it official, as they used to say in those days. Big deal . . . Mamoune was seventeen in 1968, and she loved to talk about that period of her life—the lycée deserted for weeks on end, the nights spent partying, the smoky bars, the students she'd met in the street or at political rallies. At the age of twenty she was posing for painters in Montmartre—maybe she'd also done some fashion shoots, or been on the catwalk? Marité never bragged about it, but that could explain all those boxes she'd accumulated her whole life long and which she refused to part with when she moved in on the rue de Clignancourt. So she must have had a few lovers, or more, before she met Raymond.

While delving into her mother-in-law's life, Sandrine couldn't help but wonder why such an attractive woman, who could have gotten any sort of job she wanted in the fashion industry, who could have had any man she wanted, had settled for a dull secretarial and accounting diploma and marriage to a minor civil servant. Raymond was a handsome man, to be sure, but he had neither background nor ambition. Like Marité, he was from a working-class family; their parents and friends lived in the same quartier. He was funny, likeable, clever with his hands, very much in love with his wife, and generous to a fault. Although he was devoted to his family, he had never been able to offer them true financial ease: Guillaume had had to pay for his studies all the way through, and had not prolonged them any further than necessary. When she was widowed, Marité found herself barely making ends meet on Raymond's tiny pension and her meager off-the-books book-keeper's salary. And yet, as Sandrine was forced to admit, her mother-in-law never complained about her situation. Maybe that was true love, wondered Sandrine as she rummaged through the shoeboxes filled with photographs, a tear welling in her eye. But then she came upon the pictures of Marité with Marcel, and all her fine theories about love were demolished in one fell swoop.

A thick A4 manila envelope contained twenty or more color photographs and numerous rolls of negatives. Some of the prints were of a professional quality, taken at society events. In every picture Marité was magnificent. She and Marcel were as awesome as Jane Birkin and Serge Gainsbourg in the late 1960s. Their beauty was pure, raw, elegant; the age difference was serenely absorbed; the whole image was served up to the outside world with all the bold insolence of those who succeed no matter what. Sandrine was able to date the pictures thanks to a stamp on the back of some of them. The resemblance between Guillaume and Marcel was striking, even if Marité's beauty had softened her son's features; it was all the more astonishing in that in the photographs Marcel was roughly the same age Guillaume was now. A tall, elegant man, at ease before the camera lens, very attractive even if he wasn't handsome: his nose too big, his forehead high with a receding hairline, a firm, strong jaw if a bit too square. That gaze, with those eyes that didn't match, was unsettling, of course, but Sandrine was already used to it, after a fashion.

The setting in most of the pictures clearly illustrated a social class very far removed from the Cordiers', or from her own parents': luxury hotels, a yacht, a garden party. But beyond the setting and the tailor-made suits, the man was clearly, naturally, imposing. A *boss*, like the ones she'd met during her internship with the Senior Management Association. Better still: a boss who was at his prime during the glorious postwar expansion years, when selling magazines positioned you in a certain social and economic elite. A pure product of the *Paris Match* glory years. Sandrine smiled when she thought of Guillaume's dodgy business venture, or Juliette's feverish surfing on the web, or Aurélien's piles of fashion magazines: a love of information must be in the Lacarrière family's DNA.

The revelation of Guillaume's father's identity had aroused Sandrine's curiosity regarding her impromptu encounter with Laurent Lacarrière. What could a daddy's boy be getting up to in a sketchy garage in La Goutte d'Or? After working her way through the entire judicial organization chart of affiliates, she had ruled out the possibility—a pretty ridiculous one from the get-go—that they were setting up a business or logistical venture in the quartier. A publisher *sells* magazines, he doesn't keep them in a garage hidden from prying eyes—neither his own nor his competitors' . . . unless? On a second trip to the warehouse, Sandrine's suspicions were confirmed. Nearly all the magazines stockpiled there were issues of *Convictions*. Several thousand in all, and the piles got bigger, on Thursday as a rule, the day the magazine came out. One of the walls was already covered all the way to the ceiling with bundles trussed up like Sunday roasts. Judging by the dates of the oldest issues, this had been going on for over two months. From time to time, the net caught small fry in addition to the main catch, depending on the tides and currents: women's magazines and interior design, dailies, kids' weeklies . . . Sandrine asked Guillaume about *Convictions,* and he was categorical: when it was launched, a few months ago, it made quite a splash. And considerably ruffled the competition. The *Libéral* in particular: the venerable publication was really showing its age. Who stood to gain from the crime? Easier than a game of Clue, concluded Sandrine, as she put together her little file of photographs for Marcel Lacarrière.

YOGURT AND DETOX TEA

Granted, Annabelle Villemin-Dubreuil did look like a reformed porn star. Curvy (very), with an alluring gaze, and a mouth like ripe fruit waiting to be eaten. Granted, her resume, with its mention of some diploma from an obscure Belgian institute of psychology, smelled of pure fabrication a mile off. Granted, her very popular advice column in *Convictions* suggested that she had fully mastered the sixty-four positions of the Kama Sutra and a certain number of regional variations. But appearances can be deceiving. For a start, Annabelle Villemin-Dubreuil was not her real name, either. Her other name was nowhere near as smart, and was much better suited to the pudgy little provincial lump she had been for so long. Véronique Lamoul.[1]

Her parents, though they were full of love and care when it came to their little princess, who had shown up totally unexpectedly and quite late in their lives, had really done her no favors when it came to her name . . . But that was before, a year ago, in her previous life. Rapid rewind: before she became the psychosex ambassador for *Convictions*, Véronique Lamoul had been acquiring experience at the National Institute for Oriental Languages and Civilizations, commonly known as "Langues O," for over twelve years. Initially as a student, the most brilliant in the Southeast Asia

---

[1] La moule = both mussel and cunt (T.N.)

department, then as assistant, then lecturer, and finally adjunct to the head of the department. For she spoke Sanskrit, Hindi, Tamil, and Bengali (and a few very glorified rudiments of Urdu, Sinhalese, and Telugu) and the *Mahabharata* in the original held no secrets for her. So, for her the Kama Sutra was a piece of cake, small beer . . .

Growing up in her sous-prefecture in the Massif central, she had been an endearing only child. On the playground during recess, she added one unforgivable failing to another: tall and plump, awkward, shy, a star pupil, bad at sports and teacher's pet. She had no real friends but she was always ready to help out, to let others copy from her page or to straight-out write their compositions for them. In a region where the smell of brine rarely meant the proximity of ocean spray and the wide open sea, her unfortunate name earned her every mocking phrase imaginable.

"Hey, smell that, Lamoul?"

"No, what?"

"Smells like mussels, that's what! Ha ha ha ha!"

Anyway.

Things calmed down somewhat in the upscale boarding school where she continued her studies from the age of thirteen until she got her baccalaureate degree. Upscale did not mean that her parents, who ran a small but prosperous hardware store, had delusions of grandeur. It was the only place where she could take the various options she'd chosen. Moreover, she had been granted a generous scholarship thanks to her exceptional grades. Les Bleuets was for girls only, a place for the offspring of the well-heeled local bourgeoisie to encounter the haughty daughters of expatriate executives. You had to put yourself in those little foreigners' shoes: they'd been promised France, which for Dad meant the Champs-Elysées, for Mom Avenue Montaigne, for the kids Disneyland Paris, and they had all ended up in Podunc-sur-Bacquouatère . . . As far as quiet went, it was quiet. Dad stayed three years on average, at the head of some subsidiary that didn't even feature in the firm's annual report: two years spent playing golf with the *préfet* and the mayor in order to collect some subsidies, nine months to siphon from the treasury, by way of Luxembourg or Ireland, and three to implement a redundancy scheme before flying off to new adventures. The (exorbitant) tuition at Les Bleuets and Saint-Vincent, the equivalent for boys, was included in the relocation package, as were the maid, the au pair girl, and Mom's hairdressing and manicure budget.

At this school, scorn and sneakiness had replaced outright meanness. The other boarders would snigger and sneer when they saw Véronique's very basic underwear. She'd been landed with the worst spot in her four-bed dorm room: in a draft, near the door. The other girls stopped whispering whenever she came near, and started up again the moment she walked away. Her locker didn't close properly, her toothbrush often fell into the toilet, and that's not all. She didn't make a single friend, not one confidante, and she only managed to ascertain the propensity of girls' boarding schools to foster Sapphic love affairs from a great distance, when she came upon two final-year girls kissing in the locker room in the gym.

Once she got her baccalaureate (with highest honors) she went up to Paris. The fact she'd never been out of her backwater meant that quite early on she'd developed a desire for the exotic, and if she couldn't travel, she would study rare languages. She was still the same Véronique, living in a maid's room: chubby, brilliant, shy, friendless, and desperately virginal. Langues O became a second home to her: she spent her life there. Before long she fell in love with André Agostini, known as Double A, the director of the Finnish and Sami Languages department. An old, married graybeard, twice her age, very full of himself, thoroughgoing woman chaser, misogynist and scornful, he actually had very little going for him, other than a baritone voice in which he recited sagas in the original. She subsequently found out, but too late, that his career was littered with female conquests: assistants, students, administrative staff. Véronique was intelligent and sensitive, but also very naïve, and singularly lacking in experience. She was attracted to men's intelligence more than to their looks, and she'd taken Agostini's arrogance for wit. (And oh well, what the hell, she did think he was handsome.)

He'd deflowered her one evening in his office—she was twenty-five years old, after all—hastily, panting like an asthmatic seal. Their affair had been ongoing, ever since—she had an opulent bosom and was docile and available, which meant, unbeknownst to her, that she was a convenient, attractive stopgap. Their relationship was in no way anything like a love story or even a physical passion, no, or even an extramarital affair which both partners accepted as such. No, it was just quickies in the office, in shabby hotel rooms or, more rarely, in Véronique's little apartment he visited gracelessly. From time to time they met for lunch in self-service places or dreary Chinese delis—they had to be discreet, he said—where they each paid their own share down to the last centime: Double A's miserliness was just one of his many faults. The time between these pathetic trysts was, for Véronique, a great void.

She was in good faith, and believed she had embarked upon a torrid, passionate relationship that would have a fairy-tale ending. She would wait for him, she would be his crutch in old age. She even took classes in Finnish with a view to the trips they would undoubtedly take once Double A retired, a few years down the road. She was lulled by very vague promises of divorce and life together. Promises that had been partly implemented a year earlier when he did indeed get a divorce—only to marry, the moment it was finalized, a young woman who was an assistant professor in economics at the Sorbonne and with whom he'd been having an affair for five years. In the guise of a farewell letter to Véronique, he'd had the boorishness to slip an invitation to the wedding reception in her faculty mailbox, without further ado. Stifling her tears, she'd taken her courage in both hands to ask him for an explanation. Double A had spluttered, to her face, that no one would ever want to marry a frigid fatty like her, and that she'd do better to go back to studying the Kama Sutra. Ha ha ha ha.

She stood for a long while in front of her mirror: at thirty, she did not dwell on the same planet as other girls her age, let alone that of the bombshells in fashion magazines. Her hairstyle was frumpish, she was thirty pounds overweight, did not wear strings or any sort of lingerie that was the least bit sexy, had never waxed her pussy (the one going some way toward explaining the other), and she ordered most of her clothes from mail-order catalogs. Her awakening may have been cruel, but it was salutary. Cooped up at home for three months, eating raw carrots and drinking herbal tea while she sniveled and wept, she had a proper nervous breakdown. Wielding the kitchen scissors in rageful fits she massacred her long blond hair, chopping her locks any old how to just above her shoulders. As she had no girlfriends, only a few acquaintances and colleagues, she was alone during that entire period, with piles of books, and DVDs borrowed from the media library. Most of the time she didn't dare go out and she spent hours perched on an old exercise bicycle she'd found in the building's garbage room.

One morning, after twelve hours of restorative sleep, she saw a stranger in the mirror. A slender young woman whose curves were now principally in her breasts and hips. Slim waist, shapely thighs. Her diet had worked wonders, in a detox sort of way, and she now saw a porcelain complexion and perfect skin. Her short, tousled hairstyle was like that of the model on the cover of a recent issue of *Elle* that she'd bought a few days earlier, between a pack of organic yogurt and a head of broccoli. The ugly duckling's transformation had begun.

She completely reengineered her wardrobe, and after she'd dealt with her pussy she bought a pack of string panties. To be honest, she didn't really like them, they were uncomfortable, but she decided to wear them on principle, as a hard-won right. From now on she would wear strings, stockings, push-up bras, and stilettos, for every Véronique Lamoul on the planet. For all the frigid fatties who'd been humiliated by all the Double As on earth. On the Boulevard Haussmann she discovered there were free coaching sessions available at the makeup counters of luxury department stores. Astonished, amused, she was shuttled from one queen to the next, all of whom went into raptures over her doll-like complexion, her long eyelashes, the perfect line of her eyebrows and her full lips.

"Lips for blow jobs, doll, believe me, I *know*," one of them had whispered to her, swaying his hips, brush in hand. "Even in a bar in the Marais you'd be a hit. Tell me when you're going out, I'll come along to pick up the pieces."

"I never go out, I don't really have any friends," she blurted.

She was careful not to point out that she didn't have much experience in anything else, either. Her relationship with Double A hadn't included any special treats and now she was glad of the fact.

The makeup artist broke off, brush in one hand and a palette of eyeshadow in the other, with his weight on one leg in his tight-fitting black jeans. He wore huge silver rings with a skull design on both thumbs.

"Well then, we're going to fix that, honey. This very evening."

That weekend, Annabelle was born: that was the first name that came into her head when Romain asked her for her phone number, at the end of the makeup session. She was sorry she had lied, because it wasn't like her, she was a simple girl who hated dissimulation. But as that first evening wore on and he introduced her to his friends, in an artists' studio at the end of the rue des Martyrs, she got used to the music of her new name. As many syllables as the previous one, but so much softer . . . Romain became her best friend. Like her, he was a transplant from the provinces, thirsting for love, an unshakable romantic. Like her, he wasn't quite who he seemed to be when you first met him. A gay man who loved to party, obviously, but also very stay-at-home and naively sentimental. She resigned from the Institute and never went back, changed her phone number, and gave no further sign of life to the handful of people she had known. At the age of thirty her life was a blank page. She began legal proceedings to change her last name. Her parents had died a few years earlier and she had almost no family left: she cobbled a name by combining the maiden names of her two grandmothers.

* * *

One evening purely by chance, a friend of Romain's told her about *Convictions*: they were putting their team together and were still looking for a new face for their "sex and psychology" column. She dolled up her resume without altogether faking it, playing her trump card: the Kama Sutra, which she did indeed know inside out and backwards, even if she had never tested any of the positions. As she was conscientious, she signed up for a degree course in psychology, with a view to eventually opening her own practice. What started out as a poorly paid freelance job paid by the line very quickly evolved, given its popularity, into a part-time open-ended contract. Consequently she was earning nearly as much as she had as a teacher. The editors at *Convictions* did not want their rare bird to fly the nest, particularly as they thought she had a wild night-life with a vast network of fellow partygoers among the city's night owls. As no one had yet managed to slip into her bed—she was still resolutely waiting for Prince Charming—some imagined she must be some sort of BDSM dominatrix; others said she was a lesbian. That just goes to show how reputations are forged.

The transformation of the ugly duckling into a beautiful swan was nearly complete. All that remained was the nest. After careful thought, she decided to leave her dark little rental on the rue de la Convention and move to Montmartre. Romain lived in Pigalle and she had succumbed to the charms of the quartier. They strolled through the Marché d'Anvers on Friday evenings, then she slept over at his place; they wandered around all weekend, trying on clothes in designer boutiques, spending hours in sidewalk cafés. They sometimes lost themselves in the crowd on the Place du Tertre, mingling among Japanese tourists and laughing: Annabelle would begin to speak Tamil and Romain would reply in some made-up mumbo jumbo, which elicited astonished murmurs from the people around them. With the money she'd inherited from her parents and a small loan from the bank she hoped to be able to buy a little apartment, fifty square meters or so, somewhere in the quartier.

* * *

She went through the door into the real estate agent's and paused, hesitating. Two young men—black suit a little on the tight side, white shirt a little too open at the neck, Bluetooth earpiece—were looking at her, all smiles, standing by a coffee machine. She did not know which one she had spoken to on the phone.

"Monsieur Benoliel?"

The fleshier of the two walked toward her, hand extended. A gleam in his eye and a damp lower lip testifying to a definite interest. His trousers were close-fitting and twisted at the ankles above black shoes that were too pointy. This was the fifth agency she'd been to that month, and she'd found it odd to discover that all the agents seemed to be cast in the same mold. There must be some sort of specialized vocational training certificate where they were indoctrinated in the utmost secrecy before being let loose on Paris one evening with a GPS. At dawn, the brightest among them would have taken up their positions in premises which, only the night before, had been empty, and that was how, every now and again, new real estate agencies sprouted from the ground one fine morning like mushrooms. They made up a sort of occult brotherhood whose members knew one another from the sheen of their cheap black suits and the tight cut of their trousers. Maybe they even all slept with their clothes on, to produce that little wrinkled effect on the backs of their jackets?

"Good morning, I'm Annabelle Villemin. I'm a bit early; we talked about the little loft in La Goutte d'Or?"

(In private she only used the abridged version of her new name.)

"Yes, of course, I've been expecting you. I'll get the keys and we'll go take a look. You won't be disappointed, it's a superb product."

He wasn't disappointed either: this client was one hell of a nice-looking woman! He was glad he'd answered the phone before Jo did. She was as tall as he was, with one hell of a pair of lips, and as for her boobs . . . A real stunner. He noticed the helmet in Annabelle's hand and he puffed himself up. He'd told her the place was five minutes from there by scooter and she'd thought of everything, the hottie! The apartment really wasn't far, but he'd take the long way round, why not, just to make the pleasure last a while. It was hard to lean into the bends to arouse sensations on a scooter, but he'd try to zigzag, he'd read somewhere that a rolling ride could make a girl horny. With a bit of luck she'd squeeze him even tighter for fear of falling, and her hand might inadvertently brush against his crotch . . . On the way back he could even offer to teach her how to ride a scooter, he'd stick his piston right against her butt and we're all set, pet!

"I see you've brought a helmet, that's great, you can ride with me. But don't worry, I never drive fast with the ladies," he added, injecting warmth and depth in his voice.

"Oh I'm sure you don't drive fast, but in any case, it won't be necessary."

Annabelle raised her pretty finger and pointed across the street. Next to the real estate agent's grimy scooter stood a gleaming Harley-Davidson Sportster 883. A vintage model. Samuel Benoliel almost choked and he cleared his throat with a few coughs to regain his composure. His gaze crossed Jo's: his colleague was trying to hide his hilarity behind his coffee cup, soundlessly mouthing, *Toast.*

At the first red light, Benoliel felt distinctly like a toad lying at the feet of a gazelle. Annabelle, who had caught everyone's eye, took off with a roar, leaving him in a cloud of exhaust. Bitch, he thought, coughing, hoping his erection would disappear, and fast, because the way things stood now, stuck in his tight trousers, he was sure to dislocate something.

HONEY (NOT EVEN ORGANIC)

B itch!" shouted Antoine as he burst into Hervé Schmutz's office, without knocking.

The manager was in the middle of a chess game with Toussaint N'Diaye and the two men did not immediately react. They were used to Antoine mouthing off, and to his theatrical, impromptu entrances. He often came rushing in to make them sign a petition or to try to drag them off to a demonstration. His fellow residents were used to his diatribes against deep-sea trawling, deforestation, and the continent of plastic in the Pacific.

"No, honestly, what a bitch!"

"Might you be referring to your charming adviser over at Pôle Emploi, or am I mistaken?" answered Hervé Schmutz, looking up from the chessboard. "Love story over and done with?"

"Pffff . . . "

Antoine fulminated, pacing like a wild beast in the stuffy little room. He eventually landed on a wobbly stool, the only free seat in the office, a castaway found in the street before the bulky waste collection.

"Did she strike you from the list at last?" asked N'Diaye, holding his bishop in his hand.

The man from Senegal had followed with great interest all the Pôle Emploi sagas of his residence roommates, as they were commonly known. More often than not their adventures ended in failure. Pôle Emploi was even the main reason he was in France: to finish a thesis he'd begun in the early 1990s on the French unemployment benefits system. He couldn't be beat when it came to describing the evolution of the law, the rules governing compensation, and the special regimes of the last twenty years. His father, who in Senegal was secretary of state, provided for him. The reason for his presence at the Darcourt center, when he had the means to stay somewhere more comfortable, remained a mystery. To this day, no one had ever caught him in the act of gainful employment, or even the search for any. On the other hand, he gave an efficient and discreet helping hand to anyone who asked him, his role somewhere between public scribe and social worker. A sort of volunteer offshoot of the prefecture, social security, and Pôle Emploi. He had started off with unemployment issues then branched out, given the bottomless pit of administrative nightmares with which foreigners and the professionally insecure were confronted. He now manned an office several times a week and his reputation had spread well beyond the Porte de Clignancourt district.

"Strike me off the list? Are you joking? No, worse than that," thundered Antoine.

"Another bogus internship, that it?"

Antoine went on shaking his head.

"Don't tell me . . . No. No way. She actually found you *a job*?"

With his white knight in his hand—Toussaint and Hervé had decided to play with matching colors, as they put it, cracking up laughing—Hervé stared at Antoine, a smile on his lips.

"Yes! Yes! Exactly! She found me a job, the bitch!"

Two thunderous peals of laughter greeted Antoine's declaration. Two peals of laughter worthy of their respective owners, who easily stood close to six foot six and weighed well over two hundred and seventy pounds: powerful, enormous thunderclaps, veritable tornadoes.

"Oh, you nasty boy. D'you know how many jobless little kids in France would love to be in your place?" chuckled Schmutz.

"Work is alienation, we agree on that, but we still have the right to choose our alienation, don't we?" answered Antoine. "I refuse to be a puppet in the hands of Pôle Emploi and let them decide what's best for me, on the pretext of my experience or training! This is an infringement of my free will! I refuse to let the system meddle with my life, particularly when someone like Sandrine Cordier is doing the dirty work. I have the right to want to remain a garbageman, even if I have a degree in history. And just because I have a technical school certificate in cooking and now a diploma in organic cooking doesn't mean I have to work in a restaurant no matter what, does it?"

The chuckling grew even more persistent and the chessboard on the desk was no match for their rising hysterics. Toussaint N'Diaye, who was laughing so hard he was in tears, letting out great whoops of laughter, his head in his arms, sent most of the chess pieces flying all around him. Hervé Schmutz was rocking back and forth on his chair, holding his protruding belly as it jiggled up and down. His shirt was stretched so tight that between the buttons you could see his belly button and tufts of blond hair. Between two hiccups he caught his breath and let out a fart, as was his wont. The entire little room resounded, vibrated with their loud voices. Antoine, sulking, glowering, had fallen silent. Hervé Schmutz eventually got to his feet and, still shaking with laughter, went over to give him an affectionate slap on the back.

"Go on, breathe . . . It's a cause for celebration, don't you think? What sort of funeral wake do you want? Shall we invite José Bové and Al Gore?"

* * *

Sandrine Cordier had left him a message the week before, brightly and mysteriously informing him that she had good news. He avoided calling her, sensing some useless ploy or, at the very best, news that would not be all that cheering. In any case, they already had an appointment, her revelation could wait a few days. That morning, he woke up in a foul mood, after a night filled with nightmares: Sandrine Cordier was chasing him down an endless corridor, with a squeegee in her hand. He woke up just as she caught up with him and was trying to ram the handle of the squeegee up his anus, having dipped it in honey that wasn't even organic.

When he walked into the agency he got the premonition that a tsunami was coming. In the waiting room, he tried to focus on breathing exercises. A lost cause. On his right was a man in his fifties calling a friend to tell him in detail all about his hemorrhoid problems—Antoine tried to eavesdrop, but heard no mention of a squeegee. On his left, his neighbor was rummaging noisily through a file, grumbling: he could no longer find the document his last employer had filled out. The yellow paper had landed in the chubby fingers of a fifteen-month-old brat who was crawling around the room while his mother filled out an application form. By the time the man realized where it had gone, most of the yellow paper had been chewed and spat back out into the pot of an artificial house-plant.

* * *

Sandrine welcomed Antoine with a pretty smile and offered him a coffee.

"Since meeting you I only buy organic, free trade coffee, and the same for tea and sugar," she assured him. "Well, tell me, Antoine, how did your internship go? Because I just got the report and everyone was raving about your work there.

Here, for example: *He really has a knack . . . Creative, manages things well . . . Self-starter . . .* I'm really impressed, even if I'm not really surprised, now that I've gotten to know you a little. And what did you think? Was it instructive? Exciting?"

Antoine had already prepared his two-faced little tirade. Not that he hadn't found the internship interesting; on the contrary, it had been fascinating. But ideally, he would rather cut out his tongue than have to thank Sandrine Cordier for anything. What was more, he held access to training to be an inalienable right, without being made to jump through hoops at Pôle Emploi. At the same time, given his situation, he had very little wiggle room in which to go against her. So he felt obliged to blurt out a few banal pleasantries for good measure, his tone half blasé, half pedantic.

"Very interesting. We worked with top quality products, and top level professionals. I hope this enriching experience will prove useful to my future career."

"Oh, but I'm sure it will, Antoine. And sooner than you think, in fact."

The smile on Sandrine Cordier's lips did not bode well.

"Well, for the moment I don't really know. I just finished and I need to think about my future. I was wondering about a little skills assessment, to see where I stand . . . "

"Sure, why not," purred Sandrine, leafing through her file. "But in the short term, now that you've confirmed the theoretical side of your training in *organic and sustainable* cooking, you'll be able to continue with the practical training and get started at your new job."

Aha, so this was the good news! Antoine nearly choked. She'd found him a job! Working in a kitchen, bound hand and foot! A trap, all along! What nerve! Or had he misunderstood? He was seething but he thought he'd better not attack her head-on right away.

"Yes, you're right, that would be a real opportunity, in a

sector that's developing rapidly," he conceded. "But I was wondering if it wouldn't be better to enhance my experience in waste management? I saw several ads for jobs in the inner suburbs and—"

"You didn't hear me, Antoine. You are going to start working in a restaurant two weeks from now, as set out in the work-study contract you signed. You hadn't forgotten, had you?"

God did he feel like strangling her, when she spoke in that scout leader tone of hers! She shoved a document several pages long in front of him, her red witch's fingernail at the bottom of one page.

"Yes, that is my signature," grumbled Antoine, annoyed.

"No, here, higher up."

The paragraph stipulated that Antoine Lacuenta undertook to continue his training, once his internship was completed, for fifteen months at Le Comptoir Bio, located on the rue Myrha in the 18th arrondissement. In exchange, the company agreed to cover the costs of his internship in full. At the bottom of the contract, a stamp and an illegible scribble served as the signature for the company. That was strange . . . Antoine was willing to bet neither was there when he himself had initialed and signed the document. Yet another scam on the part of this scheming shrew!

Sandrine had unearthed a little-used contract in the amended law on finances, intended for highly-trained long-term unemployed individuals who were unable for one reason or another to return to their former professional activity. With his depression and his departure from the Éducation Nationale, Antoine was the perfect candidate. It was a work-study contract: four months of paid internship to bring him up to par, followed by fifteen months of so-called professionalization. The employer was given considerable incentives to create a position once the contract expired, with, in this case, a reimbursement of all the social benefits paid since the start of the contract, and an exemption for the twelve months to come. In the case of a standard business, it would be almost impossible to fulfill the terms: application forms that were abstruse or could not be found, useless but obstructive written proof, deadlines for submission that were almost impossible to meet. At the social security office most of the people Sandrine queried denied that such a contract existed, and kept passing the buck, endlessly, or simply mislaid the files. But it would take much more than that to discourage Sandrine.

How could he have missed it? Antoine swore under his breath. And yet there it was, plain to see, with his signature a few centimeters below. He tried to think on his feet. Le Comptoir Bio had paid for his internship and they didn't even know him; maybe there was someway to wriggle out of it, citing an irregularity? Argue that he had been misinformed, swap places with another intern? Or might it be enough just to give some sort of advance notice to halt the nightmare in its tracks? If he dealt with it right away, he might get off with just one month of work, two at the most. Besides, he knew absolutely nothing about that restaurant; none of it made any sense.

"I don't get it . . . we never spoke about this clause . . . or evidently I blanked on it when I read the contract," he said cautiously. "There must be some provision to terminate the contract, isn't there? All contracts provide for one, no matter the domain . . . It's not like it's a labor camp, this new work-study training scheme?"

"Yes, I think there is something about an early termination, let's see," said Sandrine, picking up the contract.

She put on her glasses and, looking very focused, began leafing through the pages.

"Ah, here it is!" she said after a moment, with a triumphant smile.

Antoine instantly felt lighter. The hussy wouldn't have the final word where he was concerned, not this time, in any case.

"I'll do the math for you."

The math? What math? he wondered, now worried again. Calculator in hand, the bitch began to frown. She typed on it for a few seconds, opened her eyes wide, shook her head, began typing again, and then put it down with a little grimace and a nod. Then she looked up at Antoine and gave him a faint, commiserating smile.

"You're right, it's very simple, all you have to do is reimburse all the expenses incurred. For a start, the internship itself. An internationally-renowned institute . . . you can imagine it doesn't exactly come for free. Moreover, you don't get the VAT back, but you have to pay it for the internship. Then your salary for four months, even if it wasn't very much, which Pôle Emploi took care of. Finally, there is a provision for compensation to the employer, who is now in a tricky situation, since he is obliged to hire someone else on very short notice. If you had given up along the way, it wouldn't be as bad, obviously, but now it's the full amount."

She held up the calculator to show Antoine the figure.

"Forty-six thousand, seven hundred and fifty-eight euros???"

"I can arrange it so that you can pay in several installments. How does that sound?"

Pastéis de Nata

The headquarters of the Lacarrière Groupe were in an uproar. At nine thirty in the morning François Roux, the IT manager, had locked himself in a storeroom and now he refused to come out. Alternating sounds of screeching, invective, and loud sobs could be heard. A quarter of an hour later, his assistant managed to fiddle the lock and found his boss with a wild expression on his face, his eyes bloodshot, a bundle of electric cables in his hand. He had climbed up a mound of old discarded computers that were piled in one corner of the room. The cables, loosely woven together, were connected to various plugs, wrapped around a neon light then slotted through an air vent in the ceiling. François Roux was getting ready to peel back the ends with a penknife before making a slipknot. A few minutes more and he would have been turned into a Christmas tree, twinkling prettily.

The assistant yanked the extension cords from their plugs, gave a hearty kick to the pile of old computers, and took delivery of his boss as he fell from the top of the pile.

"François, you wretch, you want to provide us with the short circuit of the century? Come on, now, let me make you a good coffee. I even have some pastéis de nata my mother made."

The manager let himself go, and sobbed into the arms of his assistant, a sturdy little fellow with tattoos and numerous nose and eyebrow piercings. Thomas Ferreira had started there two years earlier and was also a member of the company workers' committee, and the only union delegate in the place. He dragged Roux to his office at the end of the IT department's open-plan area, and the two men shut themselves in. Curious gazes emerged from behind giant screens as they walked by, but no one said a thing.

"Okay, tell me, what's the matter? Things not going so well with Sylvie? Your teenage kids getting you down? Or money problems? You can confide in me, you know."

François Roux shot Thomas Ferreira a desperate look and burst into tears again.

"If only! It's nothing like that! It's here at work, they want to fire me!"

"You got a letter? That prick from human resources called you in?"

"No, worse than that, they want me to resign, two years before retirement. And they've even found my replacement!"

"No way! What the hell is going on? This is news, the workers' committee hasn't heard a thing about this, and we even went back over all the pending hires and departures just last week! Are you sure?"

"Look at this and you'll see what I mean," sniffled François Roux.

He took a creased sheet of paper from his pocket, unfolded it, and put it on the table between them. Thomas's eyes popped out of their sockets as he looked over the page.

1   Corsair Obsidian 650D Tower Case

1   Cooler Master Silent Pro Gold Power Supply—1200W

1   Gigabyte GeForce GTX TITAN—6 Go (GV-NTITAN-6GD-B) Graphics card

1   Intel Core i7 3970X processor—Extreme Edition

1   Noctua NH-D14 Radiator—Socket 2011

1   G.Skill Kit Extreme3 4 x 4 Go PC17000 Ripjaws Z CAS11 RAM

1 Socket 2011 Asus P9X79 DELUXE motherboard
1 SSD Samsung Series 840 Pro—256 Go Solid State Drive
1 Western Digital WD Black 3,5—SATA III 6 Gb/s—1 To Internal Hard Disk, 3.5 inches
1 Blu-Ray Pioneer BDR-208DBK—OEM optical burner
1 Akasa EPS12V adapter
1 PC Silverstone internal adapter cable USB 3.0—CP09—accessory for case
2 PC LCD Iiyama ProLite XB2776QS-B1 27-inch screens
1 Roccat Le Méga Pack combined mouse—keyboard
1 pair Logitech PC 5.1 Z906 loudspeakers

"Fuck, what the hell sort of sicko hookup is this?" choked Ferreira.

"For the new guy, dammit. He's moving into that empty office by the elevator, between us and new media. No need to draw you a picture, is there: they've hired one boss to head the two departments. Some young guy, who has his sights fixed high and who'll be paid two to three times as much as me, you can bet your bottom dollar."

"But all this stuff?"

"The old man's secretary handed me the list a few days ago, but she'd already ordered everything on the sly. She asked me to get the computer ready this morning, because the guy is coming this afternoon. When I started unpacking everything just now, it gave me a real shock. It left me numb, borderline paraplegic. Do you realize how far a boss will go these days to humiliate an employee and give him the boot, after he's spent over thirty years working his ass off for the place? Obliging him to hook up all this stuff for the guy who's going to take his place? It's sort of as if, I don't know, some guy made you buy your wife sexy underwear and change the sheets on your bed then went on to fuck her right there in front of you . . . So you see, when I started putting everything together I just lost it . . . "

"Fucking hell, they won't get away with this. You say the guy's coming this afternoon? You go home, get a medical certificate from your doctor. In the meantime, I'll get the word out not to touch any of this equipment and I'll find out what's going on."

GULAB JAMUN

As he had done every day since the beginning of the week, Toussaint N'Diaye took a seat at the Khédive, in the spot he'd chosen years ago: a corner booth slightly off to one side but which had a broad view over the entrance and the street. He nodded a greeting to the owner, and put his imposing self down on the red leatherette. He was wearing a three-piece suit in fine quality wool with a white shirt and cuff links: he looked every bit the lawyer. He had spent ten minutes buffing his shoes with a soft cloth, after polishing them the night before along with a dozen other pairs.

"The usual?" asked the owner from behind the counter, where he went on wiping glasses.

"Yes, a cappuccino and a croissant. Thanks, Momo."

N'Diaye took out his laptop from a crocodile-skin document case and checked the bar's Wi-Fi connection. He always thought of everything, so had brought a 3G key just in case. Next to the laptop he placed a portable printer and a pile of blank paper. 7:45 A.M.: he was ready. He just had time for a first sip of coffee when Vairam came in, followed by a dark little woman with a shy smile, her gaze one of amused curiosity.

She spoke broken French, with a heavy accent that made Vairam's seem almost imperceptible in comparison. Vairam quickly explained her situation, then, at Toussaint's request, questioned the woman in their language to obtain a few additional clarifications. Several minutes later she left the café with two folded sheets of paper in her shopping bag and a broad smile on her face. Before leaving she bade the two men a solemn farewell.

"Thank you, Vairam," said Toussaint, "I would have had difficulty managing without you, I didn't understand much. Coffee, tea?"

"No, thanks, I can't stay, I'm working the morning brigade now and I might be late at the brasserie. Yesterday already I almost got caught. I'm really sorry but I'm not going to be able to help you much more than this, these days. It's bad timing because I know you're working twice as hard, but I don't really have the choice."

"Bah, I'm making out fine already with the Arabs and Africans. I'm sure I'll manage with your compatriots as well, if any more come by today. I'll let you know this evening. And Antoine?"

"As planned. He'll stop by from time to time during the day. For now he's acting the tout."

The young cook left when another client, an African this time, came to sit down across from Toussaint. A new interview began. The man put a thick file on the table, and Toussaint leafed through it for a good ten minutes, pausing occasionally to question him. He then did a search on the Internet, printed out a document, and handed it to the man once he'd explained what it was about.

* * *

The director had summoned his most experienced advisers half an hour before the agency was due to open. They all looked sleepy and grumpy, and the bitter coffee from the dispenser, exceptionally on offer from the management that morning, did little to dispel their mood.

"Right, I didn't want to create a panic by bringing everyone in and revealing the agenda too far in advance, but the situation is very serious," declared Michel Zadkowski. "Let's see: have any of you noticed what has been going on this week?"

A long, stupid silence greeted his question.

"No? Not the slightest idea? No one picked up on anything in the latest statistics? Let me help you: have any of you had an incomplete file over the last ten days? A poorly filled-out application? A complaint with information missing? When was the last time anyone was struck off the lists?"

Again an embarrassed silence. Sandrine raised her hand, looking uncomfortable.

"I had one, on Monday."

"Okay, well, yours don't really count, you'd manage to strike off a person who is not even signed up with us. Having said that, you usually have two a day, so things are getting slack. Okay, the rest of you, as a rule, how many suspicious cases a day? Césaire?"

"I don't count them . . . I don't know, maybe one out of three?"

"Céline?"

"There are usually elements missing in about a third of all cases, I think."

"Okay . . . And you, Sandrine?"

"As a rule, half the files are incomplete, and as for the others, if I look carefully, I manage to eliminate another third, or a bit less, on the grounds of various irregularities."

"And this week?"

"Dead calm. But now that you mention it, I did notice two or three weird things. A new freelance journalist who had all his documents in order. And a few independent entrepreneurs with several things on the go at the same time, who actually managed to explain their situation perfectly clearly to me, something I've never seen. So that got me thinking, and I've kept their files handy so I can go through them, but I would never have suspected such a widespread plot . . . "

"You're wrong! You should have rung the alarm bell right away. You know very well you're our sniffer dog. Right, Philippe, Elsa, I suppose you've had more or less the same results?"

"In fact, I found the clients very relaxed these days, *Hello, Thank you, How are your kids*, that sort of thing. Not a single insult, no weeping, people chatting quietly in the waiting room . . . But not for one moment did I imagine it would come to this," sighed Elsa.

"Well, I can see it's putting your brains to sleep to work in a zen sort of atmosphere. I'll turn the heating down and replace the elevator music with recordings of car horns and sirens. In one week, while you were all being led up the garden path, and I'm being polite, now, the number of unemployed receiving benefits through our agency went up by twelve percent. Two or three more months at this rate and the shop will go under. And the shop, in this case, is all of France, in case you need reminding. You can bid farewell to our first place in the annual regional challenge and the little bonus that goes with it. Come on, now, we open in five minutes, you know what you have to do! From now on the program is blood and tears!"

The team left the meeting room and headed for their offices. As they crossed the hall, they could not believe what they saw. Instead of the usual glum crowd fussing and shoving one another to get in, there was a well-mannered, relaxed, smiling line outside the door. People were chatting amiably and one mother was handing out *chouquette* pastries to those around her. While Césaire opened the metal shutter, Sandrine stood for a few moments in the hall, frowning. Two men on the opposite sidewalk had caught her attention. They were having an animated discussion and seemed to know each other well. One was Pakistani or Sri Lankan and he reminded her vaguely of someone, but she couldn't say who. Was he an unemployed jobseeker who had been through her office at one point, perhaps? But the second one, with his satchel slung over his shoulder, and in spite of the hoodie that concealed his long hair, she had instantly recognized. It was none other than Antoine Lacuenta.

* * *

Toussaint tried to articulate more slowly, but to no avail: the two women did not seem to understand him any better, and once again they launched into their frenzied chatter. They interrupted each other, laughed, then looked at him with a hopeful gaze after their long tirade. Just his luck, the day that Vairam had left him in the lurch, the entire Indian subcontinent decided to flock to the Khédive. Just before, he'd managed all right with a Pakistani newly arrived from London by switching to English. But now, with these two ladies—a woman and her daughter, or her niece, he wasn't quite sure—English didn't work. After they'd said *Bonjoul-Melci* several times over, the only words of French they seemed to know, they set a thick file down in front of him. Both anxious and smiling, they expected him to help solve their problem. Problems, rather: as he leafed through the documents, Toussaint saw that the issue was one of access to free health care as well as residence permits for a very large family. Many of the documents were written in a foreign alphabet, with pretty, exotic stamps he could not decipher. For over ten minutes he had been trying to explain to them in his best pidgin French that he could not proceed without Vairam. He asked them to come back later. Stubborn and smiling, they nodded vehemently, appealed to him in their impossible dialect, but did not budge from their seats.

Finally Toussaint got fed up and decided to send an SMS to Vairam. He typed away on his smartphone—the size of his fingers did not facilitate the task, and slowed him down—but the ladies' chattering only got louder and more insistent. What a strange language, all the same; to him it sounded as if he were listening to a tape recording both backwards and speeded up. Then he raised his eyes and almost dropped his phone in astonishment: a magnificent blond woman had come over and was speaking to the two women in their own language, while they looked at her, both intrigued and very eager. She asked them a question, which she had to repeat until the older woman finally answered. The younger one observed them, her mouth agape. Continuing the conversation all the while, the blond pulled over a chair and sat down at the table. At last she turned to Toussaint and gave him a pretty smile.

"Do you mind if I take a look?"

Not waiting for his reply, she started leafing through the documents and lingered over several pages. She then took a blank sheet and wrote down a few words, then handed it to the older woman. After a short exchange, she took the paper and added her telephone number. Toussaint wanted to memorize it, but could not make it out upside down. The two women said goodbye with broad smiles, nodding to Toussaint with a burst of giggles and a final, somewhat mocking *Bonjoul-Melci*.

"Don't worry, that's for the hidden camera, stay calm," said the blonde.

Toussaint lost his composure and began to stutter.

"No, don't worry, I was joking," she said. "You should see your face . . . Forgive me for interrupting, I didn't want to be indiscreet, but I could sense you might not sort things out on your own. Your friends were of the opinion that you were slow to understand. They said the men around here are not very bright."

"You speak . . . that stuff?" he said at last, after a long silence.

The young woman smiled at him, amused.

"That stuff, as you call it, is Tamil, a language spoken by roughly eighty million people around the world. To be honest, my accent is not perfect, but I don't have many opportunities to use it. Having said that, since I moved into this quartier things have been looking up."

"Thank you, in any case, you got me out of a tight spot."

"Oh, don't mention it. I told the ladies I could go with them to the prefecture and the social security for their documents, it will be simpler. There are interpreters at the prefecture but they're not always available. At the social security, on the other hand, they would have come up against a brick wall, for sure. It's not easy to adapt, so far away from home, when you've lost all your points of reference."

"Thank you very much, for their sake. By the way, allow me to introduce myself: Toussaint N'Diaye. I'm very glad to meet you, Mademoiselle."

He held out his enormous mitt. She placed her own slender fingers in it, with pretty almond-shaped nails, and he kissed it ceremoniously.

"Annabelle Villemin."

* * *

While she dealt zealously with the day's files—already four applicants struck from the list—Sandrine thought about the bystander she'd spotted on the sidewalk across the street the day before, and then again this morning on the corner. What was that damned Lacuenta doing around here, all smiles, chatting away while he cast meaningful glances at the clients heading into Pôle Emploi? Was he trying to recruit activists for one of his dodgy collectives? Or, worse still, was he going to come and harangue the crowd right there in the waiting room, at peak hours, then threaten to turn himself into a human torch? Just let him dare complain even a smidgen about the fact that

he'd found a job, goodness, he'd be lynched on the spot . . .
When he'd left her office last week, anxious, crestfallen, he did
not seem at all in a hurry to come back. He'd asked her for
some time to think it over before giving her a definite answer
regarding Le Comptoir Bio, under the pretext that he had a
medical appointment. Above all, without having to spell it out,
he had threatened to file a complaint for improper contract.

She knew that neither of these strategies had any real
chance of succeeding. There had been several long spells of
sick leave, so the doctor at social security was hardly about to
reimburse still more sick leave: budget restrictions were the
order of the day. As for filing a complaint . . . It would be a real
uphill battle. Lacuenta, with his many years of graduate-level
studies, would find it hard to prove that he'd been forced to
sign a contract and hadn't read the fine print. And besides,
how many long-term jobseekers could afford the luxury of
turning down a definite contract for fifteen months of work?
Still, she had to give him time to think it over, and she was getting worried, because the deadline was approaching. Next
week she would be taking leave to start up her business, initially part-time, then full-time. And in three months at the latest, Le Comptoir Bio would be opening its doors.

The biggest jobs were under way, but now she had to deal
with the finishing touches—cleaning, decorating, finding furniture, signing for deliveries of dinnerware. Where the actual
food was concerned, it meant tracking down the best suppliers, designing a menu, and testing recipes. She had to come up
with some marketing strategies to draw custom and create a
loyal customer base. She could not accept the fact that one
grain of sand might now try to jam such a perfectly oiled
machine, her dream taking shape after so many years of careful thought. Perhaps she'd gone too far, enlisting Lacuenta
without his approval, obliging him to work for her. Perhaps
she should have tried gentle persuasion, instead of trapping

him, forcing his hand? But she was sure he would have refused—out of pride, regardless of whether the project was interesting or not. He had already exploded when he saw the work-study contract; what would happen when he found out that Sandrine had engineered the whole thing from the start? And what if he caused a scandal and handed in his apron, right in the middle of his service? Or reported her little scheme to Pôle Emploi? There was nothing really illegal about it, but she would rather they kept it to themselves . . . Well, the time had come for an explanation: it was up to her, now, to find forceful, persuasive arguments.

Since the latest budget restrictions there had been no more security guard at the Darcourt residence. Instead, the boarders took turns putting in a few hours in exchange for a modest reduction in rent. It was Saturnin Doucouré who informed Sandrine of this when she showed up at the end of the day. Although she did not reveal the purpose of her visit—she wanted to remain incognito—Doucouré could tell she must be some sort of efficient bureaucrat. Maybe even a cop, with a bit of luck? Ever since the final of the cooking contest, he had nurtured a hatred toward Vairam and his friends that was as secretive as it was deep, and now he saw an opportunity to play a mean trick on Lacuenta. He suspected him not only of abusing the system instead of doing an honest day's work, but also of being involved in some fishy business. He was a terrorist, no less, hiding his dangerous activity behind his fine speeches about protecting the blue whale. Or the white one. It hardly mattered. Thus, ever so obsequious, Doucouré gave Sandrine the address for the Khédive, and even offered to go with her. Which she declined: she could manage on her own. She knew the café well: it was only two blocks from her office.

* * *

They saw her before she saw them, and by the time she spotted Antoine, six faces were already turned toward her. Definitely a funny bunch of lazy idlers. She recognized the dark-skinned little man she'd seen in the street the day before. He couldn't have been older than twenty-seven or twenty-eight, and his eyes sparkled with mischief. Honestly, his face looked so familiar, but for the life of her she could not recall why. The others were strangers, in any case not one of them had ever been through her office. Two over-the-hill rugby prop forwards stood on either side of Antoine like bodyguards. One was black as ebony, wearing a handsome three-piece pin-striped suit, his thumbs tucked in the pockets of his vest. The other man was not nearly as elegant, and looked more like a butcher boy: pink skin, shaved head, wearing an ugly synthetic shirt that was too tight and clearly showed the sweat marks in his armpits. A third man was wriggling next to the African man: platinum blond, plucked eyebrows, rings on every finger. Then a blonde in her thirties. Tall and sexy, a pleasant, frank expression that Sandrine thought she'd already seen somewhere . . . Not on television, couldn't be. Sandrine was wary of women who were too attractive, but she had to admit that this one looked rather likeable. She seemed a bit out of place among the five rogues but perfectly at ease in spite of it all. Was she Antoine's girlfriend? Not a very romantic sort of meeting-place . . . And anyway, there were no signs of intimacy between them. With a faint smile on his lips, her favorite job-seeker watched as she walked over to them with a sure stride.

"Well, hello, Sandrine. You're right on time."

He held out his palm toward the pink rugby player who deposited a yellow coin in it with a nod. Visibly she'd been the object of a bet for ten or twenty centimes . . . Charming! Without waiting for anyone to offer, she pulled up an empty chair and sat down just behind the blonde and the dark little man.

"So this is the monthly meeting of your association for the tax exemption of dry toilets, I suppose?"

The two giants exchanged a look with a stifled laugh—which in their case was anything but discreet. Antoine gave them a dark look and the two men composed themselves, avoiding each other's gaze. The tall black man slid his glasses from the top of his head onto his nose and concentrated on consulting his cell phone. The other man, coughing, started rummaging in a briefcase, and put a cardboard file down in front of him.

"So you see, Madame Cordier is my very nice adviser from Pôle Emploi," said Antoine. "May I introduce a few dear friends," he continued, holding his arm out to sweep around the table, naming each one of them quickly.

"Antoine has been telling us about you for a long time, you know," the blond man who had lost the bet observed, with a big smile; he had an Alsatian last name. "You really went to bat to get him back into the workforce. If all your colleagues were that diligent, unemployment in France would be no more than a bad memory . . . "

The tall black man nodded, solemnly.

"It's true, to go so far as to hire a long-term unemployed worker *yourself*, I cannot find the words to commend such generosity," he said, with a little smile. "I take my hat off to you."

The Alsatian opened the cardboard file in front of him, took a sheet of paper between his thumb and index finger, and gently shoved it in Sandrine's direction. The company registration certificate for Le Comptoir Bio, with her name in capital letters right in the middle. She hadn't foreseen this but, oh well, at least now everyone knew where they stood. They'd be able to proceed with the discussion.

"Everyone has to help in any way they can, don't you think? Moreover, I've noticed that your fine team are also working for the common good, and on a volunteer basis, no less . . . You dream of a paradise for overworked, stressed out civil servants, where, from now on, all the applications will be properly filled out and complete? And never mind if now and again it incites people to work the system rather than find a job?"

"In my country, there is a saying: *Whoever waits a long time at the well will eventually find a bucket*," answered the tall black man sententiously, putting on a thick African accent.

"Such a poet!" laughed Sandrine. "Are you getting ready for some literary competition, to boot? The Goncourt Prize for the Unemployed, perhaps?"

N'Diaye observed the little brunette with growing interest. What a temperament! A petite, almost skinny little thing, a gazelle amidst a pride of famished lions, and she remained as proud and arrogant as could be. She certainly was pretty when she got angry, her black eyes practically firing missiles. Between the tall gentle blonde joking with Vairam in Tamil and this one here, who stood up to them in spite of a situation that wasn't really to her advantage, his heart swung back and forth. What a pair! And speaking of pairs, both of them were equally well-stacked . . . He sighed, casting a concupiscent glance over his eyeglasses. What a pity there's no touching allowed, not even a little . . .

"Having said that, although we may not have been after the same thing at the outset, our interests might end up converging," continued Schmutz, putting the certificate away. "We also have a project that means a lot to us. And your talent might just help us bring it about."

"I see . . . And in exchange?"

"You need professionals for your future restaurant: we can offer you two chefs for the price of one. Regarding the first one, it's really up to you, there are no guarantees. But anyway, as you're the one who chose him, you will know where to go to complain. As for the second one, however, you really will end up better off: he's a pearl, a real chef."

Everyone had turned to look at the little man on her right. He must be Sri Lankan: the community had settled just nearby, in the quartier of La Chapelle . . . Indian vegetarian cuisine was renowned, of course, but did this young fellow know anything about it? Did he even know how to cook? What was his name, already? Vishnu? No, Vairam. What a funny name, anyway! Looking for something to help her place him, Sandrine studied his friendly face, the way he screwed up his eyes. Then the memory surfaced, all of a sudden, like a cork from a pool of water. Of course, that was it! He was the former lodger of the maid's room on the eighth floor, the one she'd encouraged to leave, with her veiled threats . . . More than veiled, now that she thought of it . . . The situation was getting interesting. Had he recognized her? And how in heaven's name had he ended up in partnership with Antoine Lacuenta? The Sri Lankan, with a mischievous smile, nudged a small box full of tiny sweets over to her. Some were shaped like apples and pears, with little green leaves on a stem. There were lozenges and cubes in three colors, white balls dusted with grated coconut, and other ones, brown and spongy, that seemed to be glazed with sugar or honey.

Sandrine had never seen anything so delectable. Cakes for a dollhouse, exotic candies, little bites for a fairy-tale princess: she knew she couldn't resist. So what if they were poisoned, or off—maybe this would be the little gang's ultimate revenge, some friendly little germ that would keep her in bed for several days or give her a good case of diarrhea. She bit into a little pear, a delicate almond paste covered with a fine silver leaf. Nothing bitter, no suspicious smell . . . Just yummy. Then when the chef gave her an encouraging look, she picked up a white ball. Unctuous, a mixture of condensed milk and sugar scented with rosewater. A hint of something else she could not place. But the boy was just a dishwasher, a potato peeler, a simple *commis*, no more than that, wasn't he? And he could make such divine *mignardises*? Unless he'd bought them in some specialty patisserie? There must be one somewhere between the Gare du Nord and the Passage Brady; maybe it even belonged to some cousins of his. Eyes half-closed the better to enjoy it, to finish she chose a brown ball that melted in her mouth. It was like nothing she had ever tasted; she could not identify a single ingredient, but it was delicious. She could not help but give a little sigh of satisfaction, and she kept her eyes closed to prolong the pleasure; she was in no hurry to meet Lacuenta's ironic gaze. Annabelle's gentle hand came to press lightly on her own.

"It will be the death of you, poor thing. I've been eating nothing else for days, and I have not yet recovered."

A feeling of immense well-being came over Sandrine. She could sense her blood throbbing gently in her fingertips, on her lips. She would have liked to lie down, to relax every muscle. Sounds came to her as if through a filter. She opened her eyes slightly and looked around: these people looked rather nice, after all. She recalled she had come to have it out with Lacuenta, but it all seemed so pointless, of no interest. She smiled back at the pretty blonde woman and put her head on her shoulder, sighing with contentment.

GRANOLA BARS

J uliette trotted along behind Marcel Lacarrière's secretary, a backpack on her shoulders. The woman jabbered away, wriggling her rump, stopping from time to time to point something out to the girl. Before taking her into the office where she would spend her week as an intern, she took her on a quick tour of the company. They went through the editorial offices, nearly deserted at this time of day, then distribution, and they walked by the advertising department. They took the elevator to the fifth floor, where the new media department was located.

"Here, young lady, you can put your things here. Your internship coordinator will come and see you a bit later. I see your computer hasn't been hooked up yet," she said, giving a little pout of annoyance. "In the meantime I brought you our latest issues. There's a drinks and candy machine at the end of the corridor, and here's a card so you can choose whatever you want. If you need anything call me at 62 25. My name's Isabelle. See you later."

Juliette put down her bag and looked all around her. A funny little room, glassed-in on every side, with an oeil-de-boeuf overlooking a courtyard. The glass walls were frosted up to roughly one meter sixty, so she had to stand on her tiptoes to look out: an open-plan office on either side. To the right, all the floor space and desktops were cluttered with computer junk: giant screens, towers, external hard drives, CD burners, loudspeakers, power cables, extension cords, and servers. Two tall portable PC towers were piled like books on a table. A mountain of scrap equipment filled one corner. An old calendar was hanging from a wall: a girl in tight shorts and a scanty top, her mouth open with a funny lubricious expression, was lying in the hay surrounded by piglets and hens.

To the left, two huge plasma screen televisions hung from high up and broadcast the latest news nonstop, on mute. Posters featuring the front pages of magazines, a few gadgets scattered here and there: the decoration was more sober but basic. In comparison, the little office where Juliette was had been lushly decorated, with a thick carpet and imposing furniture, including a bookshelf filled with DVDs and books. A little round table stood under the window. But it was hard to move around, the room was cluttered with cardboard boxes set down at random all over the place. Some were half open but most were still closed. She started wandering around, looking at them, nibbling on a granola bar. Then she took a little pouch from her backpack, removed a cutter and various sizes of screwdrivers. After she'd licked the last crumbs from her fingers and adjusted the barrettes in her hair, she attacked the first box with a broad smile of satisfaction.

* * *

"Carry on like this and I'll get the labor inspection people on you," shouted Thomas Ferreira, pounding his fist on the desk in the huge office Luc Bricard shared with Laurent Lacarrière. "We've been asking you for ages to do something about the degradation of working conditions and the risks to workers' health, and you haven't done a thing."

"Tsk, tsk, Monsieur Ferreira, you have a short memory. On the contrary we give your working conditions the utmost care. We provided you with a nice little car so you wouldn't have to take the métro at rush hour, if you recall. With a nice little gas allowance on top of it. Did Madame Ferreira like the color, by the way? But . . . oops . . . maybe your comrades don't know about it?"

The union delegate slipped lower in his seat, staring daggers at Bricard. Laurent Lacarrière, who had been struggling for over an hour with a Sudoku puzzle (level: easy), looked up and was following the conversation with interest.

"Is this blackmail?"

"Blackmail for what, my poor Ferreira? Remind me how many card-carrying members you have in the company? And I don't seem to recall that you exactly raised armies of supporters at the general assembly, even when it came to complaining about a lack of restaurant coupons or the size of the Christmas tree. There were fourteen of you last time, including the mole I sent so there wouldn't be thirteen, because I didn't want you to have bad luck."

"Look, enough cynicism, and stop obstructing procedure. Five minutes more and you would have had a suicide on your conscience: François Roux."

"What, he tried his hanging trick again? Or was it the Christmas tree lights?"

"Uh, both at once . . . But how—???"

"It was a specialty of his, before you started here. An old bondage fantasy, maybe. Everyone knows about it."

Luc Bricard leaned across the desk and lowered his voice.

"He's a chronic depressive, management knows it, has always put up with it, and will do so until he retires, two years from now. That's why you've been hired as an assistant, to take over from him when the time comes. So why did he blow a fuse this time?"

"He said you'd hired someone to head IT and new media at the same time, and that you're forcing him to resign."

Luc Bricard let out a little hyena's laugh.

"A single boss for IT and new media? And why not let the

head of fashion take over the maintenance department, on the pretext that her team also uses couriers? You want to set the place on fire? Come on, be serious. You have my word that there is no plan to hire someone or to replace François Roux. He will retire according to schedule and if all goes well, the job will be yours. If however, he begins stirring up shit . . . "

"But then who is that office for? The old man . . . er . . . Monsieur Lacarrière's secretary asked for a workstation to be set up by this afternoon. An incredible amount of equipment, I might add. Whoever is going to be using it must be a high-flyer. A deluxe geek. There's no smoke without fire."

"Ferreira, I am not consulted every time a worker goes to the john: human resources is there to take care of hiring, and the maintenance department for all office and workstation matters. And besides, computers are your department, aren't they? I don't know what is going on, but there is surely a very simple explanation. I'll look into it, if that will make you feel better. Let me get to the bottom of it with human resources and I'll keep you posted."

"Okay, thanks. We have to clear it up. Otherwise I'll mobilize the workers."

"If you say so."

Luc Bricard had great difficulty suppressing a nasty smile, and he walked Ferreira to the door.

Once the union delegate was out of earshot, Laurent Lacarrière said, "Really, Luc, you sent a mole to the last personnel general assembly? Who was it? Can I go next time?"

"Laurent, how to explain it . . . " sighed the deputy CEO. "You could be spotted, don't you think?"

Very proud of what he'd said, Bricard couldn't restrain himself and burst out laughing.

"Of course not, what are you thinking, there was no mole. I just said that to freak him out. Not only do his union activities have virtually no effect on the workers, but he'll go thinking that one of the few civvies who actually follows him is a scab, without knowing who. It'll poison the atmosphere within the workers' committee."

"Oh? But then how do you know there were fourteen of them?"

"Oh dear, I do have to explain everything to you . . . The glassed-in landing on the second floor, on the restroom side, overlooks the hall. I stood there and counted them, bingo, none the wiser."

"Sneaky spying, I get it! Like a ninja, sort of. That's great! I'll have to use that sort of tactic to keep an eye on the new fashion assistant. I don't think she's wearing a bra."

"Yes, I mean, no," said Bricard, getting annoyed, his tone pontifical as he shook his head. "What you have to remember is that this is yet another victory of mind over force. Take a page out of my book: if the bogeyman doesn't get you, it could prove useful down the line."

"If the bogeyman is a bogeywoman, I don't mind . . . "

"Forget it."

TORTILLA

Well, sweetie, are you happy with your internship?"
Juliette grinned at her father. Her front teeth—
wide, short, and jagged—looked like those of a
baby beaver. Touching, but not very graceful. The family were
sitting around the dinner table, eating a tasty omelet: potatoes
sautéd golden in olive oil, then mixed into a bowl of beaten
eggs before finding their way back into a sizzling frying pan.

"Yes, I'm off to a good start."

"I hope the people are nice and they look after you, at least.
Because where I work, sometimes when they have young
interns they don't lift a finger," he added, turning to Sandrine.
"They stick them in a corner for a week with something to
read, and that's it."

"No, I'm sure they're more professional at the Lacarrière
Groupe, they made a very good impression when I met them,"
said Sandrine. "Didn't they, Juliette? And what about you,
Aurélien, will you be starting soon?"

"Yes, in ten days, for the fashion shows. I'm also going to
take part in a photo shoot for the next beauty feature. At last
I'll see a professional makeup artist and a fashion photogra-
pher at work, close up . . . "

"Is it really necessary for the kid to go to fashion shows and
hang out with queers?" grumbled Guillaume, turning again to
Sandrine. "Is this how he is going to make it into the lycée and
get his baccalaureate degree someday? Or is it not on the agenda
anymore?"

"It's not just fashion, Dad, it's haute couture," sighed Aurélien, rolling his eyes. "It's not at all the same thing. These are unique pieces, made to measure and outrageously expensive, for ultrarich clients who come from all over the world in their private jets. The editor in chief promised me I could go with her backstage at Hedi Von Musche's show. It's supertrendy, I know, I could have had to pay for an internship like this one."

"And that's another thing, young people these days are prepared to pay to go to work . . . What next?! But what about you, Juliette, what are you doing, then? Will they let you use a computer, at least? Because sometimes they don't want minors touching their equipment."

"No problem, Papa, I have everything I need."

* * *

The kid had taken four hours, stopping only once to use the restroom, to hook up the computer and its accessories. Betting was brisk when the entire team came back from lunch and found her in the middle of all the boxes with her screwdriver in her hand. Several of the company nerds had wanted to intervene but Thomas Ferreira had spread the word not to get involved, secretly hoping it would be a catastrophe. The IT workers had placed their bets, and only two of them had bet on Juliette. Those two were now sharing over three hundred euros in winnings. All afternoon, more and more people trooped by the office, but nobody went in. The spectacle was both heartening and depressing: a little imp in a pink sweatshirt, with barrettes in her hair, valiantly tackling equipment that was worth, at the very least, two months' salary, net. At around three o'clock, by the coffee machine, the assistant from general management told her colleague from the IT department that the kid was a recent recruit to the new media department, hired directly by the old man. By four o'clock, the rumor had spread the Juliette was a prodigy, with a degree from MIT. One hour later, people were whispering that she had come straight from Google—or Yahoo!, or Facebook, opinions differed—and that she looked much younger than she really was.

The union delegate champed at the bit until nine thirty that evening before he went to ferret around. It was the day the magazine was put to bed, so he had to wait for the corridors to empty before he could sneak into the bubble without being disturbed, carrying a handful of cables in case someone spotted him. On first sight, the computer seemed to have been put together perfectly, and all the connections and peripherals were where they should be: power, network, printer, loudspeakers. He turned on the PC; it was password-protected. With twenty seconds to enter it. Shoot, it really made you feel old . . . And what if the kid actually had been hired to replace Roux? She was too young, but still . . . Or could she be a hacker on a mission to audit their computer system? Apparently that was common practice in big American companies, brainy high school students showing up for a week or two, turning everything upside down, cracking all the procedures, getting through all the firewalls, and reconfiguring all the security systems in the twinkling of an eye.

With three or four geeks like this brat in her pink sweatshirt, he could have the IT department running like a Swiss clock. Except he risked, above all, landing at Pôle Emploi in no time if she was too good at what she'd been sent to do! He would really have to keep an eye on her . . . While trying to crack the password, he triggered the next level of security. Things were heating up, now: the machine's camera switched on, projecting a close-up of his face onto the two twenty-seven-inch screens. The angle distorted his face, like a caricature. His nose shone like some huge toadstool between two beady little eyes.

His balding brow and protruding chin didn't help matters. A faint tinkling noise sounded, and the face of an imp appeared at the top of the screen. Wearing pink flannelette pajamas, holding a security blanket, the girl examined him calmly, chewing on her gum. She had installed a distance surveillance system that she could run from her smartphone.

"Ah, um . . . well, good evening, how are you?" said Ferreira, clearing his throat. "I just wanted to make sure everything was up and running. So that you can, uh, use it tomorrow. I'm the assistant director of the IT department, you see. The equipment is my responsibility."

To put on a bold front he brandished the cables he had left on the desk. *What an idiot*, he thought, too late, seeing his gesture on-screen. He bore a striking resemblance to a mountain troll, some sort of ogre shaking a bunch of bananas, and he looked anything but clever.

"That's very kind of you, but the gear has already been turned on and tested," answered the little voice.

"Okay, then, well, see you tomorrow . . . "

The little devil popped a huge bubble with her gum and the screens went blank all of a sudden, to the sound of a sardonic little laugh that echoed for a long time in Ferreira's ears.

FARMED MUSSELS

Have you thought about dry toilets?" asked Toussaint N'Diaye with a solemn expression as he walked over to the restrooms, which smelled of fresh paint.

Sandrine observed him attentively, without answering. The tall black man had arrived a quarter of an hour earlier with Schmutz to visit the restaurant. The renovation work was nearly finished. He had set a big bag down in one corner and was docilely following Sandrine as she commented on her plans for outfitting and decorating the place. He squinted attentively at her buttocks, but could not determine whether she was wearing a string or not. He also kept an eye on her nipples, which were protruding (not freely enough to his taste) beneath her tight sweater.

"I merely ask, Sandrine, because it seems logical, in a place like this, to act as an evangelist for such an important issue. Not to mention the subsidies."

Hard to tell where you are with him, thought Sandrine. She glanced around her. Antoine, who had helped her unload equipment all day long, was still digging around in the kitchen. He came over with a broad, tender smile. Schmutz, in one corner of the room, seemed very busy lacing up his shoes. In fact, he was doubled over with laughter, not making a sound. His body shook, his eyes shone with tears, and he tried as best he could to hide his mirth. When she caught his eye, he raised one finger to his lips and winked. She repressed a smile in turn: they made an amusing pair.

"Personally I've never seen any," continued the clever man from Senegal in muted tones, addressing Sandrine and ignoring Lacuenta, who stood behind them. "To be honest I don't even know how they work, but Antoine has talked about them so often at the residence . . . For an African like me, you see, saving water resources is of primordial importance. But now it concerns everyone, even in the West."

Schmutz, still bent down, had started on the second shoe and was emitting stifled little spurts of laughter. Sandrine felt his mirth start to overcome her and she got ahold of herself, trying to concentrate on a subject that was less amusing: the bills for the most recent work.

"As far as I'm concerned, I have decided to be a responsible citizen," said N'Diaye. "Whenever I can I will use dry toilets and encourage others to follow my example. Which reminds me . . ."

He reached for the big bag he had put down and took out a big rectangular plastic container and a bag of biodegradable cat litter.

"Antoine, could you give us a little demonstration? I'm not quite sure how to go about it, but if you could show me to start with . . ."

Lacuenta's smile froze before it faded into a sullen pout. He crossed his arms and glared at Toussaint, outraged.

"You can be such a jerk sometimes, a real asshole."

A sudden shriek came from the other side of the room, a veritable war whoop. Hervé Schmutz had collapsed on the floor. He was shaking violently, his spasms punctuated by particularly loud farts—which was always his way of showing he was in a good mood. With an impressive sound like the whooshing of bellows, which modulated the popping of wind in the manner of a piece of experimental music, Schmutz seemed to be bouncing on his large behind. He was pointing a shaking finger at Antoine, guffawing and slapping his thigh, unable to get to his feet.

"José Bové!"

He repeated this performance several times, dying of laughter, red in the face, out of breath. He pointed at Antoine and chanted the name of the global justice leader once he actually managed to catch his breath. Unable to restrain herself any longer, Sandrine collapsed in fits of laughter, careful not to meet Lacuenta's stormy gaze.

"No, I mean just a little wee, Antoine, not number two . . . and Sandrine won't watch, will you, Sandrine?" continued N'Diaye, holding out the bag of kitty litter. Absolutely deadpan calm. "I made sure it was organic, and it has a pine scent, you're not allergic I hope?"

"You want to preserve water resources? Hey, I'll give you some to preserve, dammit," grumbled Antoine.

He grabbed a bucket from the kitchen and tossed it at Toussaint. With a swiftness and dexterity surprising for his size, Toussaint ducked and hurriedly hid behind Sandrine, letting out little cries in a falsetto voice. A spray of soapy water splashed the wall behind them and dripped down to the floor.

"Help, Sandrine! Sandriiiiine!"

Toussaint had to crouch low down in order to hide behind her, and he held her by the waist as if he were brandishing a shield. He pivoted her this way and that to protect himself from Antoine, who was trying to grab him. This was his chance to feel the goods. Her waist was slim and supple—he could almost put his big hands all the way around it—and her hips spread tenderly beneath his palms. Instead of wriggling, she pinched him ruthlessly, twice, and with a shout he withdrew his big hands, to his everlasting regret. He stood up straight and backed away from Antoine, who was now armed with a mop.

"N'Diaye, hands off," growled Sandrine, outraged. "Does he think he's still in Africa, the minister's son?"

"I am sorry, o princess of my heart . . . it is love that has led me astray, my flower of the islands . . . my tropical sun . . . "

"Flower of the islands? N'Diaye, have you had a good look at me? I was born in Charente-Maritime. Flattery will get you nowhere!"

Sandrine went on scolding him, frowning, trying to focus on the bills to keep from exploding with laughter. Antoine stood watching them, amused, satisfied at the turn of events. Toussaint's pranks were aimed at the vixen now, so much the better, it would teach her a lesson. Besides, his friend was not out of danger of feeling the backlash: this woman knew how to defend herself. And ever since he'd been seeing her every day, he had to admit she had other things besides faults.

"Charente-Maritime with its little mussels? And you want to make me believe there are no islands there? Of course there are: Oléron!"

Toussaint began to hum, carefully detaching each syllable, *O-lé-ron, O-lé-ron, O-lé-ron.* He accompanied his little song with swaying hips, to a merengue beat and suggestive movements with his big hands. He held them chest-high and rounded, as if they were about to grasp a coconut or a cantaloupe. Sandrine reached for the bucket Antoine had set down on the floor. This time, the man from Senegal was not quick enough: the dregs of the dirty water got him right in the face. Hervé Schmutz, who had just managed to get to his feet, toppled heavily to the floor and onto his bottom, for a new score of experimental music.

The imp was already at her desk when Ferreira came out of the elevator. The two twenty-seven-inch screens were lit and the kid was busily typing away. Jesus Christ, what could she be working on so furiously and so early in the morning? She was wearing pink again. With her velvet trousers and barrettes, she looked harmless, a simple schoolgirl. His own daughter was about the same age; he wasn't about to let himself be smoked out by some little minx, on the pretext that she knew how to put together a computer worth five thousand euros as if it were some vulgar Lego set.

"Hello young lady! How's it going? Do you need anything?" he said, putting his head around the door.

"Hey. Fine. No."

"Looks like you've already got plenty to do," he said, trying to relax the atmosphere. "You're sure you don't need anything? Don't hesitate to ask, alright? My office is at the end of the open-plan sector, come and see me and I'll fill you in on everything we do here. I'm an engineer, you know."

"Wow, I'm impressed," went Juliette, yawning ostensibly.

"I'll show you the servers and a few other things, since you seem to be interested," he continued, not giving up.

"It's fine, I have everything I need here, it's okay. Actually, last night at my place I tested your firewalls, they're regular Swiss cheese. Does the old man know he's paying you to sit around on your asses?"

Did they diagnose them before birth, munchkins like this?

Because by the looks of it that might be a good reason for therapeutic abortion, thought Ferreira. Or maybe attenuating circumstances, in the event of the ill treatment of minors.

The defense now has the floor.

"Your Honor, my client caught the plaintiff red-handed, several times, encoding Linux."

"Ah!"

A shocked murmur arises from the courtroom, full to overflowing.

"She was preparing to install free collaborative tools that might have enabled salaried employees in the company to save time."

"Oh!"

The murmur grows, between stupor and incredulity.

"Moreover, we have at your disposition a report from the Central Department of Internal Information which has formally identified the munchkin here present as a leading spokesperson for Anonymous in Western Europe."

The hubbub among the crowd swells, cries and insults come from every side: "Terrorist!" "No more family benefits to parents!"

"Order! Order in the court! Or I will have everyone dismissed and the trial will be held in camera!" thunders the chief magistrate, striking raging blows with his little gavel on the sound block on his desk. "Please continue."

"Thank you. The latest messages posted by Anonymous have been analyzed using biometric software, in collaboration with MI6 and the Americans. Taking into consideration the framing of the videos, the size of the face, the positioning of the camera, and the average height of a desktop, the conclusions of the General Directorate for Internal Security are categorical: the hacker stands between four foot eight and four foot nine. I would like to question the plaintiff on this significant point."

"Can you enlighten us?"

"Uh, well, my client is . . . let me check my file . . . four foot eight and a half inches."

A murmur of excitement spreads through the courtroom.

"Do you realize," said the judge, "the impact of your declaration at this stage in the trial? This is now a matter for national security! And to create a diversion you have been suing Thomas Ferreira for torture and barbarous acts, on the simple grounds that he supposedly, I quote 'hung your client upside-down above a toilet bowl full of excrement, wrists and ankles bound with scotch tape, wrapped in high-tension electric cables corroded by acid?' Facts for which there is no proof other than a photograph of the toilet bowl, taken from above with the plaintiff's smartphone. This is very flimsy evidence. The prosecution will not follow you!"

The judge turns to the prosecuting attorney, who nods knowingly while picking his nose.

"Well, we might accept an amendment of the charges . . . Assault and battery?" ventures the lawyer.

"Hazing at the very most, and even then, I've seen far worse in the military," yawns the prosecuting attorney.

"May I remind the court that the victim is a minor under the age of sixteen and that she owes her life only to her sangfroid and uncommon intelligence. She managed to switch off all the power supply on the floor thanks to an ingenious little program she developed on her smartphone and which she then ran using voice recognition since, need I remind you, her hands were bound," said the plaintiff's lawyer this time, sweating more and more profusely.

"MacGyver in the kingdom of free software! Ah! Ah! The judicial system of the Republic will not get involved in such mystification," roared the judge. "The defendant will be discharged and the plaintiff is ordered to pay costs for obstruction to the proper execution of the law. And do not think you have gotten off lightly, we will see each other again very soon regarding the investigation of the Anonymous case. Next!"

There's no harm in dreaming.

"And you're cute and funny on top of it. Okay, I have to go, I have a lot of work, you know," he said, putting on his most serious voice. "Go on having fun, but don't blow the server with any of your nonsense, okay?"

"Just so you know, I also have the access codes to your three mailboxes and the logins and passwords for your Facebook and Match.com accounts. By the way, you don't really look like your photos on Match, I think it amounts to false advertising. Anyway, I'll hang on to them just to be on the safe side, but if you go snooping around in here again I'll give your real contact information to the lump you've been bamboozling for two weeks telling him you're the boss's son. And I'll also post your secret videos on the company intranet."

Juliette stressed the word "secret," her voice dripping with irony, along with the conventional little gesture to signify quotation marks, holding up the index and middle fingers of each hand.

"It was child's play to decode, by the way. And you're being closely watched everywhere on the network and in the cloud, you're about as discreet as an elephant in a mud puddle. Have a nice day anyway. You can close the door on your way out."

She readjusted her barrettes and disappeared behind her giant screens.

"In the end, the court has decided to proceed with a re-enactment of the crime scene in the courthouse toilets, which, unfortunately, are blocked," announces the chief magistrate, rubbing his hands, a faint smile of satisfaction on his lips. "Will someone fetch me the acid and the electric cables?"

I'm dreaming, this is just a nightmare, it will pass, said Thomas Ferreira to himself over and over until his computer was up and running. His desktop wallpaper had been changed, and he gave a start: a threadbare security blanket, some sort of hideous weasel, was looking at him slyly and making a horrible little snigger.

He logged in as administrator but couldn't identify Juliette's computer. Impossible to get his hands on it. And yet she had to be connected to the network? The junior piss-artist had managed, therefore, to set up her own firewall, she was undetectable, a regular submarine. He scrolled through every directory, to no avail. How could he find out what she was up to? At one point he thought of informing Luc Bricard, but she must also be able to read his mind: via instant messenger she sent him one of his *secret* videos. A file he would have done better to destroy, to be honest . . . That would teach him to be sentimental!

The previous year, Thomas Ferreira had hidden a miniature camera in the largest of the women's restrooms, the one that was wheelchair accessible, on the fashion editorial floor. It was hidden behind the spotlight above the mirror and the sink, opposite the toilet bowl. On casting days the catch was particularly tasty. Long-legged girls waited ages for their turn in the corridor, drinking organic green tea from tall Thermos bottles: guaranteed admission to the Ladies'. Some of them were also sent there to get changed by the fashion editors, who wanted to check their figures ahead of the photo shoots. Quite often those teases didn't even wear a bra, and they all seemed to prefer the tiny strings that were imperceptible beneath their tight trousers.

Ferreira had nicely supplemented his income by streaming his videos to a Japanese website devoted to sexual fetishes. But he had to dismantle the camera in a hurry when the website, which had ties to yakuzas, was closed down; it was a cover for a juicy traffic in escort girls and drugs. Ferreira couldn't help keeping a few of the videos. They were coded in a format he thought was extremely rare—but not all that rare, in the end, he'd have to have a word with the Pakistani guy who'd given him the information on a forum. All of it was protected by a randomly generated password, and he'd stored them in the cloud for evenings when he was hard up.

As a precaution, he had been erasing his personal browsing from all his computers: in theory, the file should have been impossible to find. It had better be, particularly as the video that excited him the most, and by far, was the one where a tall redhead, standing firmly on her vertiginous heels, her mane of hair tossed behind her, her miniskirt pulled up above her perfect buttocks, was having a wee, resonant like the rush of a waterfall. When she turned around to adjust her clothes and cast a greedy eye at the mirror, the handsome rod she held in her hand had given Ferreira, the first time he watched the video, the most violent and delicious erection of his life. And in spite of multiple screenings, the video continued to be quite effective.

* * *

Ferreira spent the day trying to unearth Juliette on the network, which turned out to be mission impossible. She didn't budge from her two screens. She had brought a sandwich for lunch and only left her office to run quickly to the restroom. At this rate he'd never manage. At the beginning of the afternoon Ferreira decided therefore to try a new strategy, and he headed casually over to the office of Léonard Trân Lê, the head of new media, to try and find out a bit more.

"Hey! I saw you managed to debug the Android tablet app," he said, by way of an introduction, with a big, honeyed smile. "Good job."

"Oh, yeah, you saw? You may laugh, but it's that kid who did it. You know, our little intern, next to your office."

"Oh, was it? Actually I was wondering what the kid was up to, what sort of internship she's doing."

"I think she's got some project for school, she wants to start an e-commerce site."

"Really? And she's in ninth grade? She thinks she's the cat's meow, the brat. Tell me," he added, lowering his voice, "isn't she some great-niece of the old man's or a friend of the family, because it seems to me she's really making herself at home . . . I don't know if you've seen the gear they gave her, but—"

"No idea," interrupted Trân Lê curtly. "But hey, my team of developers are swamped and the kid really did me a favor sorting out the bug in that app, so whether she's at home or on vacation, I really don't care one way or the other . . . I'm not that picky, especially at such a price. And between you and me, if you had even a few guys half as good as her, instead of your lamebrains on the hotline . . . "

Ferreira shot a dark look at Léonard Trân Lê. The enmity between the two men had been part of the Homeric war waged between the two departments since time immemorial. Even their predecessors couldn't stand each other. For the developers, the computer technicians in the IT department were, select one: a) civil servants, b) big lazy bums, c) has-beens, or d) (most frequently) all three at once. Jokes went flying as soon as the IT herd trooped out, on the stroke of half past twelve, to occupy the local bistro or the cafeteria. The new media team never set foot in the cafeteria. They had trays of sushi or bento boxes brought in from whichever noodle bar was trendy at the moment. In response to the jibes and rebuffs they were subjected to, the IT department narrowed the bandwidth on the sly, particularly on days when there was a scoop, or new digital products were being launched. They also kept supreme control over the servers where the group's websites were hosted, and the slightest crash required a torrent of procedures and complex validations to be fixed, and that could take several days.

"Ah! Trân Lê, Ferreira, we were looking for you," interrupted Luc Bricard from the door to the office. "Monsieur Lacarrière would like to stop in and say hello to your intern, to see if everything is going well. Will you come with us?"

Four men walked across the open-plan office in single file to the bubble where Juliette was installed. She had left her screens and was doing something at the round table at the back of the room. The blinds to the single window had been lowered and big white screens overlooked the table, the kind that studio photographers use. A powerful halogen lamp lit up the scene, and the girl was shooting rapid-fire from every angle with a big digital camera. From the threshold of the room no one could see what she was taking pictures of. The four men trooped in one behind the other, Bricard in the lead, followed by his boss, and Ferreira bringing up the rear behind Trân Lê.

The deputy CEO stopped short, stunned, when he saw up close what was going on. Behind him, the old man hadn't seen anything yet, absorbed as he was by the two twenty-seven-inch screens, where psychedelic kaleidoscopes revolved nonstop as screen savers. It was too late now to retreat from the show.

"Good morning, young lady," said Marcel Lacarrière good-naturedly, hunting in his pocket for his eyeglasses. (He was very nearsighted but refused to wear them all the time, out of a concern for his looks.) "So, how are you getting on with your website project for school? So what nice things are you taking pictures of? Little ducks?"

Juliette turned around, and an enormous bubble of pink gum expanded in front of her little face.

"Butt plugs is more like it," she said, ever so blasé, after popping the bubble.

On the table were half a dozen sex toys of various shapes

and colors. The box at her feet was filled with any number of accessories: fur handcuffs, whips, feather dusters, black satin eye masks, geisha balls.

"But, um, is this really appropriate for your age, young lady?" asked the old man, gingerly picking up a little duck with a boa around its neck.

He looked at it from every angle. In his day, dildos looked like big fat cocks, there was no mistaking the merchandise. But here, a duck . . . ? And how the devil did you use it? (He would have found out if he had taken a look at the latest special issue of *Intimate Convictions*.)

In the meantime, Léonard Trân Lê was discreetly retreating on tiptoes. She might be his intern, but he wasn't the one who'd hired her. He didn't want anything to do with this nauseating business. He had always suspected that old Lacarrière was a bit nuts, and his harebrained ideas were not improving with age. This was on the verge of pedophilia, all they needed now was for the unions and the labor inspection people to get involved. What a pity, the kid was really very talented. He bumped into Ferreira, who was trying to get closer, not to miss any of the show. Stuck at the entrance to the room, shorter than Trân Lê, he had not yet managed to get a glimpse of the items on the table, and he had a hunch, judging from the faces the fussbudget in front of him was making, that it was something he would really like.

"Oh, no, of course it's not appropriate for my age," snapped the brat, rolling her eyes. "It's my grandma's special range, models just for senior citizens. We think there's a potential market."

Little Pear, Little Plum

Did you ever think of selling films?" she said, straight off the bat, when they met for the second time.

"My dear, we haven't had any success with DVDs for a long time, either as a bonus with the magazine or sold separately, even at a bargain price," sighed Marcel Lacarrière, a hint of regret and annoyance in his voice. "For at least two years. Nowadays people download stuff onto their computer or store it in their box, if I've understood correctly. And most often for free, on top of it. We tried classic Westerns, and musical comedies, Jacques Tati, New Wave, Charlie Chaplin, Alfred Hitchcock, the usual," he explained, ticking the names off on his fingers. "But no one's interested anymore, unfortunately. All our stock ended up as Christmas presents for the personnel. Three DVDs per person for two years, and two extra for each child in the family."

"And this?"

Sandrine held up a dusty VHS cassette she had taken from her bag.

"What planet are you on? Nobody even has a player for those things anymore. Even old fogeys like me know that much!"

"I'm not interested in the format, but the film."

She slid the VHS over the waxed surface of the big desk, like a hockey puck over ice. A pirated cassette, and on the cover was an old-fashioned black-and-white photograph of a convertible parked outside an English manor, with a stylized X made from a red rose with a long stem thick with thorns placed against a black satin garter strap. Marcel felt an unpleasant twinge all up his spine; he closed his eyes for a moment, opened them, then glanced at the title, holding his breath. *His Lordship Likes His Part Down the Middle.* Papa's porn movies! This was all he needed! The nightmare had begun, once again. In the blink of an eye she had managed to dig up an affair that Marcel had gone to a great deal of trouble to bury when he'd taken control of the group, over forty years ago now. In those days, his rivals had worked themselves into a frenzy. But now most of the people who'd been involved had passed away or, as regards those who had the misfortune of still being alive, were lost in the mists of dementia. And now here she was, like a flower, with her videocassette in her hand! God, she was a pest!

"Where the devil did you find that thing? It's at least . . . "

He bit his tongue just in time, afraid he'd already said too much.

"I mean, by the looks of it, it must be very old."

"Fifty years old exactly, this year. It calls for a celebration."

"And what does it have to do with me?" asked Marcel innocently.

He turned the box every which way, dreading he might find some incriminating label. At first glance, there was nothing, apart from the logo: no name, no address.

"I hope this isn't a present, because it's not at all the type of movie I enjoy," he said, somewhat reassured. "I'm even a little bit shocked to find you're interested in something like this, to be honest . . . "

"Now, now, Marcel! Let's have none of that between us! AML Productions . . . Do I really have to refresh your memory? A for André, M for Marcel, and L for . . . ? Do you give up?"

The CEO of the Lacarrière group tried to think on his feet.

What sort of fib could he come up with? He was tired of all this pretense, tired of constantly having to put on an act for the business world. A world of sharks, that was for sure! After all, that was all ancient history, he'd digested it long ago. A strategic error, which did not, for all that, make the Lacarrières captains of the sex industry. Not to mention the fact that there would have been a lot to say if he dug around in the pasts of a certain number of his rivals, who were colleagues all the same.

"An unfortunate little diversification from Papa's days," he said, with a weary smile, after holding Sandrine's gaze for what seemed an endless minute. "He was a fan of . . . soft-core porn, you see, and after he divorced Maman he fell for a young actress. He wanted to support her career, along with that of two or three other gutsy young actresses. But it only lasted a few years, and then everyone forgot about it, thank God. These films were never sold as videos, we stopped production in the late sixties, long before video recorders came on the scene. They were only ever shown in the cinema, well, sort of clandestinely, a little network of private screenings, to be exact. I personally opposed this strategic trend, and it did turn out to be a financial fiasco. We even had to sell the manor house— this one," he said, tapping the cassette, "and the stable of Thoroughbreds. Having said that, Papa was a bit of a trailblazer, in his own way . . . This was long before the porn king Marc Dorcel, you know. But where did you get this? I thought I'd found all the reels and destroyed them, I'm surprised there are any videos."

His daughter-in-law certainly had more than one trick up her sleeve. A formidable adversary. A regular killer.

"On eBay. There is a market—proof being that pirated copies were going around in the eighties and you can still find a few on the Internet."

"Have you watched it?" asked the old man with a worried gaze.

"Of course. This one and two or three others. Well, I skimmed them, a lot of fast forward."

"Ahhh. And?"

"Really bad. Not the least bit erotic. Hackneyed as hell. But very funny, at the same time. So dated and old-fashioned they are actually quirky."

"If you say so . . . Which means?"

"Which means? That quirky is *the* moneymaker in today's entertainment business, Marcel. You're holding a gold nugget in your hand. A future cult series. I'm not saying you're going to transform your business model, but it might be a way to get your head above water and get rid of *Convictions* for good, instead of pillaging their copies from every kiosk in Paris. It might be worth a try, don't you think?"

Marcel Lacarrière frowned when she mentioned his rival. He had to acknowledge that the strategy Luc Bricard had put in place at his request had not really paid off thus far, other than to stir up ill will among publishers, parcel services, unions, and sales networks. Everyone was passing the buck regarding the lack of organization in the chain of distribution over the last few weeks, and the financial cost was affecting them all, in the end. *Convictions* had even managed to make the most of the situation, ranting like an offended matron about the publishers' lobby; their sales had gone up.

"Well . . . I don't really know. They are X-rated films . . . Readers might be shocked. And we risk losing our press accreditation."

"Honestly, Marcel, they wouldn't dare dismiss one of the last family publications in the Paris region! Besides, you know those films. Even back in the days they couldn't have offended that many people. It's soft-core, the sort of thing you can leave on in the background when you have friends over, to create a relaxed atmosphere during the aperitif. David Hamilton, with a few slightly risqué scenes, nothing more. Those clips of rappers that play nonstop on YouTube these days are a lot more hard-core, I assure you."

"Why dig them up, then?"

"Precisely because there is a certain old-fashioned freshness about them. The actresses are charming, they really fit that category of silly women and debutantes. And there are refined costumes, and lovely settings, the manor house, racehorses, vintage automobiles . . . It's a real lifestyle, a cliché, of the picture-postcard sort!"

"Papa did have taste when it came to decorum, I have to admit," said Marcel with a smile, easing pleasurably into his memories. "He died in the same four-poster bed that was used in the film, wearing red pajamas and black velvet slippers embroidered with his monogram, and surrounded by rose petals. At the end of his life, after sipping a little plum or pear brandy on the sly, he would fall asleep in this stage set, hoping the grim reaper would come for him while he slept. And that is just what happened. I imagine he left this world a happy man, in a way. He was the one who wrote the screenplays for the films."

"I'm not surprised," said Sandrine. "The stories are full of fantasy and humor. Real collectors' items. Marité and I really enjoyed watching them."

"You watched them with Marité?" said Marcel, alarmed.

"Yes, why not? But rest assured, I didn't let the cat out of the bag. I wanted her opinion. After all, she is a dead-center target for your ideal audience: a senior citizen, very active, perfectly in sync with her time."

"Well, if anyone's in sync with their time, she is," grumbled Marcel.

The project for senior sex toys often woke him up in the middle of the night. In a recurrent dream that took him back to the days of his affair with Marité, he found himself in a bed, waiting for her. She came toward him, naked, magnificent, and lifted up the sheet to slip in next to him, only to burst out laughing: his penis had disappeared and in its place was a little plastic yellow ducky. She squeezed it carelessly, eliciting a raucous quacking. The first time, he woke up in a sweat and slid his hand down into his pajama bottoms, not without a certain anxiety, to make sure his equipment was still there—and that it wouldn't start quacking.

"She agrees with me. You can cause a sensation and catch *Convictions* in their own trap. They sell sex tarted up in a pseudo-psychological sauce. But you could offer sex that's tongue-in-cheek, and it wouldn't just be sex. Because these films also evoke an era. All the esthetics and culture and carefree lifestyle of the sixties, you know what I mean? You won't be selling porn, but analysis, the unraveling of a decade smack in the middle of the glorious postwar years, seen through a lens of X-rated films. You need to set it all up, of course: produce shorter versions and work with a film historian to add a little cultural veneer. I know half a dozen or more guys like that who clock in at Pôle Emploi, and they're pretty smart as well. It won't cost you much."

How did she come up with all this? She made his head spin! And yet her energy was a joy to behold. And the way she didn't question anything, either, but charged straight ahead. When was the last time his management committee had proposed a project that was even slightly original or enthusiastic? Every meeting started off with moaning and groaning about the crisis and ended with long self-pitying declarations. It was the fault of the unions, of the cut in subsidies, and of the competition, not to mention those bastard readers who got their news online for free! And it wasn't Laurent who would ever have the ghost of an idea, even a harebrained one. Maybe he'd have to consider hiring this pest of a daughter-in-law of his, before she started working for the competition . . .

"Yes, all right, maybe. But let me reiterate that I destroyed all the copies that were in circulation at the time, precisely in order to keep this business from harming the expansion of the group. Not long after, I became head of our professional union, and I didn't want any scandals dogging me. You won't be able to make a DVD with the three or four cassettes you'll find on eBay. Forget the whole thing."

"Oh, but you're wrong! I found a guy who used to work for AML Production, and he kept a copy of every film, including the rushes. Years of work stockpiled in his garage, if you could see it, there are reels from floor to ceiling. We're going through them to keep the best ones. Two a month at the most, with a little booklet co-written by the cinema columnist and the historian I'll find for you. You sell it at the magazine stand with the magazine, and a soft version of the DVD; in addition, on the website, you make the X-rated scenes available for download. That will give you one season to get your head above water, maybe two if you're lucky. At the same time you can shake up your teams: a new formula for the magazine, accelerate development of the digital version, and all the usual stuff."

"And how can I get hold of the tapes? I'm not about to bring a lawsuit against some former employee over an issue like this!"

Sandrine's face lit up with a broad smile.

"Not to worry, I already took care of it."

"Oh dear, you do worry me, young lady. And in exchange?"

"The old man confessed that to preserve your father's work, he'd kept everything, because he was very attached to him. He's thrilled with the project, of course. He'll be very happy to help out with postproduction for the DVDs. He's over eighty-five years old and he lives alone: this would be, sort of . . . fulfilling his last wish."

"I meant, what would be required in exchange . . . for your idea."

There was a flash of mischief in Sandrine's eyes. She took a file from her bag. *Le Comptoir Bio, Media Plan and Press Kit*, read Marcel when she showed it to him.

"Did I tell you I've left Pôle Emploi to start a restaurant?"

SEA BASS WITH FENNEL AND GINGER

The couple went up to the window where the large slate with the menu was clearly visible. The man put on his glasses, the better to read, and questioned his companion warily.

"What are we entitled to, exactly?"

The woman took a leaflet from her bag and unfolded it.

"It says . . . chef's menu with house aperitif, a half bottle of wine per person, coffee or tea, all included."

"Oh, right, not bad," said the man after thinking for a while and nodding his head. "They're not ripping us off. It's a pretty good deal. We'll save about ninety euros."

"What a stroke of luck! On the very day we've come to Paris. But tell me, what sort of cuisine is it? I think I can see a black man inside. Do you suppose it's African or West Indian? I wouldn't have thought so, given the name. What if it's not fresh?" she said, making a grimace. "Because this quartier . . ."

She accompanied her last words with a vague wave of the hand to encompass the nearby buildings. The man peered through the window; a tall, portly African was waiting on the tables. He was dressed to the nines: an impeccable dark suit and a long sommelier's apron, shoes highly polished. The room was tastefully decorated, and the chairs looked comfortable. He glanced again at the menu.

"No, I think there's no danger where that's concerned, the restaurant looks clean and brand-new," he reassured her. "And there's a lot of choice, even some vegetarian meals. It says everything's organic, to boot. I don't think it's necessarily better, but it's the in thing and it allows them to raise their prices. As for the type of food, they call it 'world cuisine.' In my opinion that's bogus marketing so you can mix Chinese noodles with stew from the Auvergne. But hey, the main thing is that it's free."

That was indeed the main thing: this God-given meal would enable him to recoup the standard twenty-euro deduction for business meals without having forked out a centime. And if he ate voraciously, which he intended to do, he could skip supper and save an additional twenty euros. Trafficking expense claims was his specialty. He could inflate the number of kilometers he traveled by devising outlandish itineraries, and he would not hesitate to drive through the night to save on a hotel that he got reimbursed for all the same. But as his relatively sedentary position gave him only scant opportunity to claim costly professional expenses, he soon learned to diversify his activity. He sold all sorts of invoices on eBay (which he'd snatched here and there, and doctored if need be) to guys trying to con their insurance company pursuant to a burglary or some other incident. He was in the process of calculating the profit from his little escapade to Paris when his companion's voice brought him back down to earth.

"Just so long as it's not too spicy . . . I have rather sensitive intestines, you see," she sighed. "But anyway, it will be a change from the cafeteria and I'm sure I'll find something suitable. And besides, it's on the house, as you say, we mustn't turn it down. Let's go!"

She opened the door and the man followed her in. The gigantic black man came to greet them with a professional smile.

"Do you have a reservation?"

"Well, yes, in a way," gushed the woman, unfolding her

leaflet again. "In fact, you invited us. I'm Madame Chauvin, I confirmed last week. It is an invitation for two, correct?"

A worried shadow passed over her gaze and she felt for her handbag unconsciously, as if to make sure her wallet and credit card were where they should be, even though she had no intention of using them.

"Absolutely, Madame Chauvin. The restaurant opened just recently and the management decided to send out invitations randomly selected from a mailing list of professionals and opinion makers. Welcome to Le Comptoir Bio."

Toussaint N'Diaye led the couple to a round table, which he pulled to one side to allow the woman to slide in onto the bench. Then he set a tiny bouquet on the table. Nadine Chauvin, already flattered by his allusion to opinion makers, puffed herself up at so much consideration. She was a tall, chestnut-haired woman in her fifties, rotund and slightly nearsighted. Her stringy, shoulder-length hair was thick with spray in an effort to obtain some sort of volume, and the effect had been more or less ruined that morning by over three hours on the train. She was wearing a cheap woolen pencil skirt that was far too tight, and her synthetic blouse was stretched over an impressive bosom. A costume necklace disappeared into her deep décolleté; N'Diaye could not help but peer at it. She was wearing thick ankle boots that she intended to change for a pair of heels in the evening. In her travel bag she had also slipped a lace nightgown that she'd bought by mail order two years earlier, and in which she placed a great deal of hope— Chauvin was unmarried.

"I'll bring you your aperitif right away."

"Not too strong, I hope," she said with a laugh to her companion. "I don't drink all that often, and we have to have our wits about us this afternoon, don't we, Bernard?"

"It's nearly all settled, Madame Chauvin," he said reassuringly. "The last file was sent off yesterday by e-mail. And there won't be any other serious offers, according to Mazard anyway. Two or three little glasses won't do our concentration any harm. On the contrary, you always need a little bit of fuel for a good performance!"

"Between you and me, I'm glad the hearing was postponed an hour," purred the woman, lowering her voice. "It leaves us a bit more time to enjoy this nice free meal. Otherwise we would have probably had to turn down the invitation . . . That would have been a pity. And besides, the good news is that we'll be spending an evening together in Paris," she murmured with a knowing look. "A little relaxation won't hurt, after all the overtime we've devoted to these complicated cases."

The man gave a faint, sly smile, careful not to part his lips. Even though he was a good ten years younger than her, he hardly looked it. He was prematurely gray, and the way he dressed didn't help: a tight black suit that had seen better days, shoulders sprinkled with dandruff; a light blue shirt with frayed cuffs; sturdy, clumpy ankle boots with crepe soles that looked as if they were left over from his military service. (Toussaint, who only ever bought his shoes from English bootmakers, made a face when he caught a glimpse of Gomez's clodhoppers.) His slightly greasy hair was carefully combed over to hide an incipient bald spot. Ugly blotches spread across his nose and cheeks, marbling his skin, with its dilated pores, with a particularly dense network of tiny blood vessels.

"We're going to have to share the same hotel room, the prices in Paris are exorbitant, and it's still only a two star place," he said, wryly cautious. "I reserved a room with twin beds, I hope you don't mind."

"We'll just have to make do, Bernard," she sighed.

The man wondered whether it was his mention of the shared room or the separate beds that had triggered her sigh, and he decided it was wiser not to speak of it until later. He was counting on combining business with pleasure, and he was already rubbing his hands at the thought that thanks to this trick of a double room he'd be able to get reimbursed for a lump sum per diem that would cover more than his actual expenses.

"Indeed."

Toussaint had come over and was clearing his throat, menus in his hand.

"Today the chef's special is sea bass with fennel and ginger, baked in the oven, with stewed vegetables. As a starter may I suggest the sweet potato samosas with coriander and Espelette pepper. And of course we have all the usual dishes on the menu," he said, handing an open menu first to her, then to him.

"Well . . . we'll take a closer look, what do you think, Madame Chauvin?"

"Take your time," said Toussaint. "I'll come back for your order as soon as you're ready. In the meanwhile, here are your drinks: sparkling kir with a hibiscus cream."

"Bernard, don't be silly, call me Nadine," she scolded, giving him a sharp little tap on the hand once she had swallowed her entire drink in one shot.

Her pudgy fingers, nails painted bright red, were covered in cheap rings. She gave a sigh of delight, her little pink tongue showing obscenely between her fleshy lips, and she shot him a concupiscent look. The man did not take offense: for many years now, no woman had ever looked at him with anything but a hint of repulsion, and things were not improving with age. To be sure, this woman had neither youth nor beauty to recommend her, but he knew full well that he wasn't exactly born yesterday. He was sure that they would spend a memorable evening together. The aperitif was delicious, already a real tonic. And what luck! Two more full glasses had just appeared on the table as if by magic. Like a pair of raptors they swooped down on their drinks without saying a word, sharing a knowing little smile.

"We've been working together for such a long time, perhaps we ought to get to know each other better, don't you think?"

"But that's just the problem, the fact that you're my supervisor. So I'm afraid I won't be up your level, that you'll get bored," said Gomez flatteringly.

"What nonsense, Bernard! I hope at least it's not the fact that I'm two or three years older than you?" she simpered, putting on a sulky look.

She turned away with a flutter of her eyelashes, unaware that as she did so she exposed to the overhead light her gray roots and the traces of foundation that had leaked onto her ear and neck. She'd put it on hurriedly in the bleak morning light, and now her makeup formed a thick mask that immobilized her chubby face.

"Not at all, Nadine, where did you get that idea? Two or three years older than me? You must be joking. I had never realized. And besides, I like women with a bit of experience. As they say, old pipes give the sweetest—"

"Oh, come on," laughed Nadine, tapping him on the arm again.

He gave her a hideous smile, this time unveiling his irregular, nicotine-stained teeth. Before he'd even taken his first sip of the aperitif his breath already stank of the red wine he'd drunk on the train, on the pretext that coffee early in the morning gave him acid indigestion. He promptly closed his mouth again when he saw that Nadine Chauvin was putting on her glasses to have a better look at the room around her.

"Excuse me," coughed N'Diaye, who had come back to their table almost immediately. "I'll take your coats and put them in the cloakroom. You'll be more comfortable."

"Oh, yes, thanks."

The woman handed Toussaint her fake fur and a little travel bag she had placed on the bench next to her, keeping only her handbag. Bernard gave him a horrible worn leatherette bomber jacket and a big briefcase where he had stuffed a change of underwear and a toilet bag, next to their work documents. At the bottom of the toilet bag he had hidden—just in case—a box of condoms. In the drugstore at the shopping mall farthest from his house—a comical precaution, given that he was single—he had wandered up and down the aisle, slowing down when he came alongside the shelf in question, only to continue immediately in the opposite direction, first toward the toothbrushes, then toward the shampoo. An impassive store detective kept a watchful eye on his circus; Gomez eventually reached for a toothbrush then suddenly, in a rush, grabbed from the shelf the first box of condoms he saw. When he reached the checkout he was dismayed to discover that they were scented, but as he didn't have the courage to go back and exchange them, he had nevertheless placed the box on the conveyor belt.

The bar code didn't work. The checker, a young goth with a white complexion, chewing gum as if she were excruciatingly bored, turned the box over, then with a sigh shook it several times in front of the optical scanner, to no avail. She shot Gomez a look heavy with innuendo, as if it were his fault. Reaching for the microphone next to her she eventually summoned a colleague to the rescue. Her message was broadcast throughout the entire store (*Sandra, can you check the price on the strawberry condoms please? The gentleman seems to be in a hurry. No, not lemon, straw-beh-ree*) while the line got longer and longer behind him. Only women, he noticed, housewives of all ages, staring at him with stern, disapproving gazes. He left without further ado, after paying cash, careful not to meet the checker's gaze. At the sudden thought—even though it was unlikely—that his bag might inadvertently spill and scatter the precious contents of his toilet bag and other documents right there in the middle of the restaurant, he changed his mind and reached out to stop Toussaint.

"I think I'll keep my briefcase after all, I would rather have my laptop here with me. I have two or three things to check before our meeting this afternoon. It's a very important business meeting," he told the waiter, as if in confidence. "We're here in Paris on business, you see."

"But of course, Monsieur. In that case, let me give you the password for our Wi-Fi, you'll need it. Don't hesitate to connect, it's free."

With a knowing air he leaned closer and lowered his voice, trying to ignore as best he could the man's fetid breath.

"I'll give you the code for the high-speed connection, which we reserve for our best customers."

Gomez puffed himself up, jangled the change in his pocket, and slipped a fifty-centime coin into the waiter's large palm. Toussaint had to refrain from shrieking with laughter, and after making an obsequious bow he went off to the cloakroom. He hung up their things and placed the bag on the floor. Inside the virtually empty little room an imp in a pink sweatshirt was sitting cross-legged on the floor with a laptop open on her knees, a printer next to her.

"Plan B," he whispered, giving her a wink. "We have one hour."

BOUILLABAISSE

"I hope we're not going to spend ages going over this file, Mazard, I promised my wife I'd take her shopping," huffed Leonetti between two spoonfuls of soup.

Now he was slurping the last of the bouillabaisse directly from his bowl, making a horrible sucking noise. Little pieces of fish clung to his thick black mustache, which was also damp from the broth. Mazard could not tear his eyes away, watching him with a slightly nauseated fascination, ignoring his own steak-frites.

"We have only two offers and one of them is out of the running."

"Remind me who that is, again?"

"It's one of the salaried employees who wants to take over the business; he's in charge of the site. A hothead who has had any number of disputes and differences of opinion with his bosses. He's probably a good worker, but he has no scope . . . And besides, he has no backers. He claims he can make it with a standard loan from the bank, he wants to remain independent."

"Much good may it do him. And the other offer?"

"Immo-Ardennes, a property management firm in the provinces, specialized in student residences. The head office is in Charleville-Mézières. They're not very influential in the sector, but they've been diversifying with social residences. They've already got two or three in the Paris region. As a rule they buy the property at the same time. In fact, it would seem that Immo-Ardennes has had its eye on this residence for a long time, precisely because it's small and doesn't interest the big players in the sector. They've got a solid financial base and some good people on the board. Friends of ours, very understanding," added Mazard.

"Ah, you should have said so from the start," laughed Leonetti with a sniff; he was a bankruptcy judge. "Who's coming to the hearing?"

"The general director and the head accountant. They've been on the case from the start."

"Am I supposed to have met them?"

"No. I don't even know them personally, we've only been in touch by email and telephone. But Behr dealt with them in Nanterre last year. Very competent, but an odd couple, by the sound of it: the accountant is a real lush and the general director, well, how to explain, is straight out of one of those soaps set in the provinces. Well, that's *la France profonde* for you."

Leonetti shot Mazard a dark look; Mazard remembered, too late, that the man was from Piana, in Corsica, and could be quite sensitive. He hurried to change the subject.

"Anyway, the accountant drinks like a fish, but he's also a regular shark, after a fashion. Immo-Ardennes renovated all the sites they took over. They're listed on the Stock Exchange and they've had very satisfactory results. Given how serious the group is, as is the plan they submitted, the hearing should be just a simple formality. I can't imagine your opinion won't be respected. It's not like any former employees have to be given jobs, other than the guy who's in charge at the moment and who is presenting his own plan, which leaves us more room to maneuver. They don't have many creditors, either, it's mostly just tax and social security debt."

"Excellent, excellent," said Leonetti approvingly, wiping the last of the broth from his bowl with big chunks of bread. "And our little arrangement?"

He rubbed his hands, a broad smile on his still-damp lips. Mazard tore a scrap from the paper tablecloth; the two men were having lunch in the cafeteria at the commercial court. He scribbled a number on it and set it down, still holding it, in front of Leonetti. Leonetti frowned, didn't say anything, nodded, then, making a more abrupt gesture with his head, indicated to Mazard that he could put the paper away. The recipient was about to slip it into his pocket but the other man again motioned with his chin, more firmly. Mazard sighed, crumpled the paper, and placed it discreetly on his tongue, then went on to chew on it slowly, with bad grace. He was used to the Corsican's paranoid behavior, and he was grateful for the poor quality of the tablecloth, as thin as cigarette paper. But the taste was no less abominable for all that.

"A little coffee to wash it all down?" suggested the bankruptcy judge, busy cleaning his teeth with a huge fish bone. "My treat."

* * *

"Tell me, Vairam, are you sure your magic potion will work? Because that woman has gone stark raving mad: she just asked me if blacks were really as well endowed as they say. I had to clear out of there before she tried to find out for herself. The last time, with Sandrine, things went more smoothly. Good thing there aren't any other customers because they would have ended up attracting attention, those two bozos."

"Some people are more receptive than others to ayurvedic principles," said Vairam reassuringly, with a faint smile. "It was different with Sandrine, she only had to feel a bit more relaxed. Today this is more serious, a regular truth serum. You'll see, it's like using a plunger when you've got a blocked toilet: all the shit will rise to the surface in no time. The main thing is that it has to have the same effect on both of them."

"Well, don't worry about that. They're both crazy. And besides, they drink like fish. Antoine is putting a nice photo album together for us, as well," he said, nodding toward Lacuenta, who stood by the door to the kitchen taking pictures with his smartphone.

"Hey, Uncle Sam!" scolded Nadine Chauvin. "Are you neglecting your favorite customer? My glass is empty and I'm really thirsty!"

She was fanning herself with the dessert menu, tossing imaginary ringlets. Her foundation had been slowly decomposing in the heat, which made her look haggard, as if she'd spent the night with an upset stomach. Dark shadows were spreading under her armpits. And yet she seemed perfectly at ease. Bernard Gomez, eyes half-closed, was watching her attentively. Yes, she was chubby, even more than that, but perfectly edible . . . the memory of his box of condoms came back to him and his gaze darkened with annoyance. What if either of them turned out to be allergic to strawberries? He didn't eat them very often, they were too expensive. The thought of an edema made him curse himself for not going back to swap the box, and he swore he'd buy another one on the sly, later in the day. But for the time being he had to concentrate on their business matters, particularly as the matter that had brought them to Paris ought to fetch him a nice little bonus. Once he'd connected to the restaurant's Wi-Fi he downloaded his latest emails and tried to recapitulate all the key points for that afternoon: present his bid to take over the residence in a favorable light, cleverly sidestep any awkward questions from the court. And in the end, as always, hand out the little envelopes, behind two padded doors: bankruptcy judge, receiver, lawyer from the Francilienne Sociale. He was used to the procedure. But this time the arrangement was ruffling his feathers. The amount that would vanish into thin air, the consequence of some obscure negotiation by the board at Immo-Ardennes, was far more substantial than his bonus. That was nothing new, but today for some reason the pill was hard to swallow. The thought that he would spend his entire life in the shadows as a simple underling rankled. No, Bernard Gomez would not be doomed to spend the rest of his time on earth fiddling his expense claims to have a decent income.

"I think our bribe is a little high for a den of unemployed immigrants: in this rotten quartier it's a waste of money," he told his companion in a conspiratorial tone. "It's not as if someone is going to make a better offer . . . Just wait and see, the court will have no choice, anyway. Our shareholders had a poor grasp of the situation."

She gave him a puzzled look. As a rule their conversations were limited to technical details, exchanges of no interest. They cautiously avoided discussing the financial wheeling and dealing which had been determining the fate of their company for years, in particular outside the office. But after two aperitifs and two bottles of wine, the situation was different. Her vision, too, had changed: over the last few minutes her thoughts had been in line with his. They had to see things on a larger scale.

"Well, to be honest, I was thinking the same thing, Bernard. We do all the work, but who goes home with all the winnings? Need I ask?"

She had always found her head accountant completely unremarkable, but now she was seeing him in a new light, full of an authority and virility that caused her to quiver with pleasure. Elegant restaurant, lace nightgown, good bottles of wine, and secrets . . . This ordinary business trip was gradually turning into a veritable adventure. She liked the way Gomez was making the first move, and it gave her hope there'd be other surprises later on that evening. James Bond had just better watch out.

"Yes . . . I wonder whether Mazard didn't overstate his case by taking us for some country bumpkins. The rue de Meulières is not far from here and I can see that the quartier is not as fancy as he would have had us believe. He said it was gentrifying. Gentrifying, my ass, if you'll pardon the expression."

Chauvin shivered at the mere thought of Gomez's big, white, hairy ass.

"And it's full of black people around here," she added, lowering her voice and pointing toward the kitchen. "The waiter, for a start, but even there in the kitchen, look at that little guy. They may even live in the residence."

They both looked toward the kitchen where Vairam was wielding a huge wok above a bright flame. Their eyes met and they began laughing uproariously.

"No, you're right, who do they think they are," said Chauvin. "We do all the work: why should we make do with the stem of the cherry? Give me your briefcase. This will be our little secret."

Gomez hesitated, but Chauvin's determined air overcame his reticence. Besides, he was beginning to like the idea, and he wanted his piece of the pie. He handed her the briefcase. She opened it with a chuckle of satisfaction, while her fellow diner looked on, his expression salacious but full of admiration.

KULFI

T
he arrangement: what size bills will it be?"

The two men had just left the cafeteria to head into the labyrinth of the commercial court, on their way to Leonetti's office.

"As usual, five hundreds."

"Next time, tell them to use twenties and fifties, it's more convenient for everyday shopping," fussed the Corsican judge. "And delivery?"

"Right after the hearing, even if the final decision has not yet been made," said Mazard, not displeased with his little negotiation. "That's the advantage of working with people you trust, you've got all the procedures down pat."

"Marvelous! Just in time for my wife's birthday. And what do they plan to do with the residence? Not that I'm really interested, they can do what they like with it as far as I'm concerned, but that pest of a Josyane Nakache is bound to be a drag about the whole thing . . . she's presiding today. As far as I know. Isn't it a center for foreign workers at the moment?"

"Foreigners, yes, for the most part. Workers . . . It's above all a den for the unemployed and welfare scroungers of every stripe, as far as I could tell. The level of outstanding payments has gotten worse and worse over recent months."

"Spare me the details, Mazard, I can't stand it, especially numbers," said Leonetti. "We all have our cross to bear, right? Take me, for example, I have a social conflict on my hands because of some insignificant little restructuring, one hundred jobs axed. So, I won't make a song and dance about it: I handled it fair and square with some buddies from Piana who came and talked to my lily-livered union people. As regards this business of ours, I just want to know if there are any specific plans for the place, just so I don't show up looking totally ignorant. I have a certain ambition, here, and a reputation to preserve. Not only do we have to put up with Nakache, but Sylvie Wang, too, the prosecutor. Two harpies, they've given me a headache already."

Leonetti was at the head of a major logistics company that owned several sites in the Paris region. For six years he had managed to carry out his duties as bankruptcy judge with a minimum of involvement, a great deal of bad faith, and a healthy dose of dishonesty. A good number of lawyers, even the ones who were not very particular, did not like dealing with him: his decisions were often arbitrary, and disastrous for companies that were struggling; he would change his mind several times over during the procedure. In conciliation procedures he took sides, and heaped insults on the adversary. He was the bailiffs' pet peeve: incompetent, vulgar, misogynistic, muddled, and always late. The inane rubbish he uttered in the middle of a hearing went on to do the rounds of every corridor in the court, but those who were prepared to confront him head-on were few and far between. Moreover, his incompetence and bad faith had not hurt his career, and he had his sights set on a position as president of the chamber. It was rumored that he owed his nomination to an unofficial quota for regional minorities—along with one Basque, one Breton, and one Catalan; they were called, behind their backs, "the 2B2C"—and apparently he was impossible to budge.

"To sum up, they want to convert the place into women's housing, for young foreign students from good families, with money. A sort of home where they'll be looked after, with a governess or some such, to reassure the parents. It's a load of rubbish, of course, but the two American pension funds putting up the capital liked the idea. They want to use the image of Montmartre—painters, Sacré-Coeur, and so on, even if the residence is nearer to the Porte de Clignancourt. But the view from New York or Romorantin—it's all the same. A few cosmetic touch-ups to hide the slummier aspects and they'll open in time for the next academic year, it's all planned."

"Aren't they clever, those people from eastern France, I like them. They're silent, they look stupid and may be a bit nearsighted, but they get things done."

"With the leaseholder they've planned an unofficial moratorium on the rent freeze, and have arranged to buy the building on a depreciated basis. In exchange, the Francilienne Sociale increased the rent due by the current management. That was what triggered the failure to pay, I will admit. But this is all off the record. Don't breathe a word about it in the presence of the presiding judge, it mustn't get out, it would ruin everything."

"Ha ha! What did I tell you? I'm all in favor of speeding up the procedure. They should give training sessions, those two. It's Darwinian, Mazard: survival of the fittest."

The bankruptcy judge glanced at his watch.

"We should get a move on, that menopausal old bitch of a bailiff will send for us if we dawdle."

* * *

Toussaint set two dessert bowls on the trolley, as well as a new bottle of wine—the fourth since the beginning of the meal.

"Here are your desserts. This is homemade kulfi—it's Indian ice cream made from condensed milk and spices," he said, not without a hint of pride. "And who will be having the bottle of wine?"

"Pleazhe," said the woman, her voice furry, as she held out her empty glass.

As he leaned over to serve her, Toussaint spied a wad of bills tucked between her enormous breasts. Everything was imprisoned in a bra that seemed to be made from Kevlar. The most imposing bosom he'd ever seen in his entire life, as impressive as a Russian tank. As for Gomez, he had removed his shirt and for the last few minutes had been flaunting a dubious wifebeater. Under the combined effect of the cocktail and the wine his nose had tripled in volume. Fortunately, the shutters of the restaurant had been lowered some time before, hiding the spectacle from view. At regular intervals, between two glasses of wine, the pair chuckled, then laughed hysterically.

"Fuck, man, they really are dumb," said N'Diaye, going back to the entrance to the kitchen where his followers were standing, to watch.

He didn't even need to lower his voice: the two customers were in a fourth dimension.

"I've gone on a few benders in my time, some far-out trips with every drug under the sun, and I've been to voodoo rituals and a bunch of other weird stuff, but this . . . really, hats off, Vairam! It's *Alice in Wonderland*! Complete delirium. Tell me, how much longer will it last?"

"Oh, all afternoon, don't you worry. This is just the beginning, the grand finale is for later. I'm preparing a special coffee to enhance the effect."

According to the chef, the special coffee would act as a booster, erasing any last remaining unconscious barriers, opening the floodgates that imposed social relations and rules of propriety. The two bozos would go into a tailspin, revealing all their failings, petty faults, and shameful little secrets. Then they would collapse into a near-coma. When they woke up, all that remained would be a good hangover and a few vague memories.

"Okay, we're going to have to time the moment they leave the restaurant. The kid is already cleaning their computer: in principle there won't be any trace of their visit here. She's a real prize, that kid, the worthy daughter of her mother."

When he thought he was connecting to the Wi-Fi, Gomez was actually on a network with Juliette's computer. She had gotten into his laptop and gone over it with a fine-tooth comb. She had siphoned off a certain number of documents, and uncovered precious information about the relationship between the buyers and the bankruptcy judge. As she dug a bit further, other dubious matters came to light. Gomez refused to save his sensitive files on the Immo-Ardennes network, and stored them solely on his hard drive. It took Juliette one minute to crack his passwords. In her net she caught at least half a dozen affairs involving indiscreet lawyers, politicians who were greedy but hardly scrupulous, company bosses as corrupt as they came, and an entire swarm of go-betweens, each more crooked than the next. Enough to keep the taxman and the financial brigade busy for several weeks.

Nadine Chauvin had just spotted the kulfi. She reached for her bowl and tasted it, while rattling on to Gomez about the board of Immo-Ardennes. They both agreed they were a bunch of limp-wristed candy-asses. Then she got going on her favorite topic: the hidden microphones at headquarters, planted in order to spy on the employees. Clever, nodded Gomez; sensing he had won her trust, he began to describe in detail how he trafficked his expense claims. As she listened, she dipped her pudgy fingers in the ice cream, then went on to lick them, casting sidelong glances at him that left no doubt as to her intention.

"But what I like best is getting rid of the union people," she said greedily, after an exposé on the best way to get one's hands on freeway vouchers. "First the carrot, a little bonus or some vague promise of promotion, something that doesn't cost much, to put them to sleep. Then the stick: have them transferred to a faraway location, change their schedules, send warning letters, use personal attacks or explosive missions: there's no shortage of ideas. See, there is only one union sector left nowadays, as opposed to five, fifteen years ago."

Gomez listened admiringly while he finished his ice cream. He nodded approvingly at Chauvin's endless supply of ruses for cleverly circumventing the labor laws. The entire company, beyond her own department, feared and despised her, and now he knew why. Together, they would be invincible. The Bonnie and Clyde of social housing.

"It's coffee time, and then we close," said Toussaint. "You mustn't miss your appointment."

He put two small coffees down before them, which his customers slurped noisily. The woman didn't stop laughing, telling terrible stories about the various ways she had harassed her coworkers. Her makeup was completely ruined, and her disheveled, sweaty hair, sticking in clumps on her scalp, made her look like a scarecrow. Gomez was enchanted. He scratched his inner thigh with conviction and gave a grunt of pleasure. The bitter black brew was working wonders. He was already thinking of the underhanded way he would trim his team's bonuses and deprive them of the days off they were entitled to, just as soon as he got back.

The taxi pulled up ten minutes later at the corner where the rue Myrha met the rue Stephenson. Toussaint bundled them inside—pressing them together to make sure they didn't fall over—before heading back to the restaurant, where he was overseeing the operation. "Another pair of clowns," the taxi driver had sighed when he pulled over to the fare waiting on the sidewalk. The woman looked as if she'd been parked for several hours under a dripping gutter. Her eye makeup had run halfway down her cheeks, and the driver thought she must be wearing a wig, the way her hair was stuck to her scalp this way and that, in clumps. The man was tearful, his cruel little eyes staring into space, a grimace on his lips. A visible rivulet of snot was dangling from his unusually large wino's nose. In one hand he held a Post-it with an address and in the other a fifty-euro bill. Could they be transvestites? In any case, he'd stake his right hand that the wino was wearing a woman's fake fur coat. In the cloak room, Nadine Chauvin had pinched Gomez's leatherette bomber jacket (even though she couldn't close it), simperingly pleading with him to agree to the exchange.

They had fallen into the car, amid a strong odor of sweat and booze. "Fucking job," sighed the driver, "I really ought to have studied harder at school."

Madame Chauvin and Monsieur Gomez, representing the Immo-Ardennes company," announced the bailiff in a shrill, tight voice, after she had closed the double doors.

The couple came in arm-in-arm, as if they were marching down the aisle of a church for their wedding, and took the seats the bailiff indicated to them. A murmur of surprise arose from the small audience as they came closer, followed by an awkward silence. In spite of his white hair, the man had to be in his early forties. The woman was older. They were a perfect match: slovenly, vulgar, dirty, anything but the idea a person might have of the managers of a small to medium-sized company listed on the stock exchange and summoned to attend an official hearing at the commercial court. A heady perfume, mixed with a heavy smell of alcohol (and could that be sex, wondered some, not really daring to formulate their suspicion), wafted into the room in their wake. They both seemed to have just gotten out of bed and not slept in at least twenty-four hours.

"Well then," said the presiding judge, clearing her throat, somewhat irritated by the pair's inappropriate and offhand attitude. "The court has examined attentively the bid made by Immo-Ardennes to take over the Darcourt residence, located at 13 rue des Meulières, in the 18th arrondissement in Paris. The court and the parties here present before me would like to question you regarding several additional issues. I believe you are already familiar with this procedure, since your company has taken over several other locations, including one last year at the commercial court in Nanterre."

"Myeah," answered the man, yawning with his mouth open wide, letting out a resounding burp along the way.

The size of his nose, which was a true oddity, suggested he had been the target of a swarm of wasps.

A blast of fetid air broke over the little room, obliging the bailiff, who was closest to the pair, to fan herself with a manila folder. Sylvie Wang, who was two and a half months pregnant, suddenly felt nauseous. The others turned to one side, making faces they could scarcely hide.

"Whoops, sorry," said the head accountant with a nasty smile that revealed his bad teeth. "We've been making the most of our stay in Paris to fill our bellies on the cheap, and we're going to do it again this evening before we get down to the serious stuff."

His last words were accompanied by a thrust of his hips from front to back and a balancing motion of his arms: this left little doubt as to the nature of their projected nocturnal activity.

"But you don't have to write that down, okay, Thérèse," he added with a wink in the direction of the bailiff.

He licked his ring finger and began smoothing his eyebrows. His odd coat, a vintage model that evoked a mangy old rabbit, smell included, seemed to have come straight from the flea market. He was wearing it over a dingy wifebeater. After his little tirade he put his briefcase down next to him then stood up again, spreading his coat theatrically, spaghetti western style. He took the time to scratch his privates at length, grunting with pleasure, then adjusted them with a determined gesture before sitting back down. The bulge at his fly (he clearly wore on the left) was most impressive, and the bailiff gave a little cry.

"Your project is banking on a change of activity," continued the presiding judge, her tone severe, after a stunned silence. "Could you explain this strategic choice to us? It's not as if space for social housing is exactly abundant in the Paris region, particularly for single men, so why do you want to leave this sector to create a residence for young women?"

"Social housing, we don't give a fig," replied the man with a knowing smile. "It's fine for our promotional brochures, for our nitwit shareholders, for financial communication . . . But it's no great shakes where the dough's concerned."

Leonetti looked around for Mazard and they exchanged a questioning, slightly worried gaze. The bankruptcy judge, ill at ease, gave an awkward little grimace.

"So, no more single workers, then?"

"That residence is full of blacks and Arabs. Just between you and me, no one is crazy about them, 'specially not our shareholders. No, there's nothing better than the petit bourgeoisie with plenty of cash—foreign students, little girls from the sticks who live off Mommy and Daddy. They're more solvent and what's more, you can raise the rates. Our business plan is for twelve percent growth already the first year, without increasing the number of rooms. Pretty clever, huh?"

"So you intend to ensure the durability of the Darcourt residence through a radical change of economic model," said Josyane Nakache, somewhat irritated. "I must say that while the management of Immo-Ardennes undeniably speaks in your favor, the arguments you have presented here do surprise me, all the same. I thought your board had approved of a strategic direction that would be more . . . socially responsible, so to speak."

The general director of Immo-Ardennes got to her feet with difficulty, hiccuped, burped, then let out a little laugh in apology. She was no longer in the full bloom of youth. But while most women her age played the card of discreet elegance, she aggravated her case with a very vulgar style. Tall and sturdy, she was teetering on ankle boots, in a tight short skirt of red wool. Her leatherette bomber jacket was too small, and opened onto a plunging neckline in a blouse stained with sweat marks. Her dyed hair, hastily teased, looked like some cheap wig rescued from a garbage dump. Her makeup was that of an over-the-hill hooker in a bad film: dark smudgy eyes, smeared lipstick, and bright red fingernails. There even seemed to be a few two-hundred-euro bills sticking out of her décolleté. So this was *la France profonde?* thought Leonetti with a smirk. He wasn't hard to please. But this was beyond him.

"Monsieur Gomez"—she turned to her associate with a complicit smile and gave him an obvious wink—"has a financial approach, you mustn't hold it against him, he's our head accountant. Whatever the case may be, our project is very innovative. We want to promote a radically new approach toward social integration and to do that we'd like to create a pilot residence: for both students and prostitutes, in the same location. It's the perfect quartier for it."

"And why not a fix room, while you're at it," Leonetti mumbled to himself.

"Did you have something to add, Monsieur Leonetti?" inquired the judge. "To be honest, what we have just been told is not all that obvious in the case you presented to us."

"No, no, we're fine. Madame Chauvin can explain it better than I could," he said, giving the pair a dark look.

"You see, I know the milieu quite well," said Chauvin, her tone ambiguous. "I profess to have a certain number of connections there, and—"

"You would like to do what you can to help with the rehabilitation of young prostitutes, if I've understood correctly, by inciting them to take an example from the students they would meet at the residence," interrupted Sylvie Wang. (Overcome again by nausea, she was trying to bring the discussion to a rapid conclusion.) "Is that it?"

"Yes, and vice versa. To have two strings to one's bow, to be versatile—that's very important in the workplace in this day and age—"

"Come on, Nadine, stop beating around the bush," interrupted the head accountant, giving her a sharp slap on the butt before turning to the judges. "Whores are good for the working capital requirement, it's as simple as that: they pay top dollar, in advance, in cash, and they never complain."

"Can you say that again?" said the prosecutor, aghast.

"Absolutely, Madame. We work really hard to get the mix right: the student is for the image, and the whore is for the working capital requirement. Not to mention that we don't declare the cash, and we pay part of our employees' salary with it under the table. Well, the ones we pay, that is. Because, as a lot of the time we hire undocumented workers, they're just happy to be fed and watered. And that's how we screw the tax man across the board: VAT, social contributions, company tax. If they don't see you, they can't catch you."

He delivered a suggestive gesture to accompany his tirade, ramming his right index finger in and out of the little circle formed by his left hand.

* * *

Romain was having a hell of a time. He hadn't had this much fun in ages. What a terrific idea Annabelle had had, asking him to help out his new friends! He immediately understood that she had fallen in love with that Antoine guy, even if Antoine, head in the clouds, still hadn't realized. Something had to be done, and quickly—these straight guys could sometimes be beyond redemption. Yes indeed, he really enjoyed being part of the operation, and had played his role to perfection. He'd intercepted the couple when they emerged from the taxi outside the courthouse, pretending to be an usher there to greet them. He'd dragged them down a corridor off to one side under the pretext of examining their various documents one by one, and he'd muddled them up brilliantly, checking their IDs and all the documents at great length, obliging Gomez to open his briefcase several times. While he was fiddling with the files, he'd inundated them with fantastical judicial precedents. In the whirlwind, the envelope that had been in the briefcase disappeared. Then he had accompanied them to the courtroom, slipping away discreetly before the bailiff spotted him. As he was saying goodbye, Romain deposited a little spy microphone in the pocket of Gomez's coat. Now, sitting in a corner bent over a magazine, with headphones over his ears, he was catching every word of the discussion in the courtroom.

This flagrant display of bullshit and bad faith, this immersion into the world of business to which he'd never belonged, was a real delight. He would have liked to watch the show, and even take over the artistic direction, as if it were a fashion show. But hearing the conversation live was still a hell of a consolation. And something he'd be able to share with his mates, later: it had all been recorded. The hubbub in the courtroom was growing louder: the dénouement was drawing near.

* * *

"Incidentally, I would have you know that as a representative of the creditors, I find it deplorable that no plan has been made to take responsibility for at least part of the liabilities," protested a discreet little man who had not spoken until now.

"Creditors? You want to know what we say to the creditors?" Gomez reiterated his obscene gesture with a broad smile. "Up yours, huh, while we're at it!"

For once Leonetti was speechless. He'd attended all sorts of hearings over the years, but this was beyond belief, beyond even his own capacity for bad faith and vulgarity, by a long shot. As for that head accountant, what a treasure . . . Maybe he should try and hire him away. He was a weirdo, with his fur coat, but he definitely had balls, too. He liked him!

"Okay, we're not going to spend all afternoon on this either, we'd like to have a naughty little nap before we go back to work. So, now, shall we get going with the little handouts as planned, Monsieur Mazard? I haven't had time to prepare the little presents for everyone, but it won't take me more than two minutes."

To illustrate his words, the head accountant opened his briefcase and took out a huge envelope; a stream of Monopoly money fell out. Initially he seemed surprised, then put his hand deep in the envelope and rummaged around, desperately searching for his vanished booty. Nadine Chauvin stared at him, not understanding at first, then she tried to grab the envelope from him to check for herself. The envelope got torn and its contents scattered around them like confetti at a carnival.

It was like the starting shot at the World Championship 100 meters. The judges and all the other participants leapt to their feet in a caterwauling frenzy, swooping onto the fake bills. Insults flew in every direction. The creditors' representative was spluttering at Mazard, whom he'd grabbed by the tie and shoved up against the wall. Leonetti was tussling with the prosecutor (who was throttling him with her raging little hands) and the presiding judge (who was kneeing him below the belt). All of this as the second judge looked on, not daring to try and part them, for fear of getting walloped in turn. The bailiff did not know where to turn and was trying, unsuccessfully, to call for calm in her bleating voice as she circled helplessly among the warring parties. Sylvie Wang felt another wave of nausea, let go of Leonetti, and rushed to throw up in a wastebasket behind the bench. But she stumbled on her long gown and landed in the arms of the second judge, whom she splattered copiously with bitter bile and fish remains (she, too, had had bouillabaisse at the cafeteria). Leonetti seized the opportunity to get away from Josyane Nakache, knocking her to the ground with a nasty thrust of his shoulder into her throat, and he rushed over to Mazard, who was already in the clutches of the creditors' representative. He gave Mazard a slap and the other guy a punch: he had just realized that their little arrangement was off, and he was squealing like a piglet for his vanished lucre. The bailiff then took the initiative to expel the representatives of Immo-Ardennes, shoving them unceremoniously out the door.

"This is a disgrace! An insult to the law of the Republic! Go back and wallow in your mire, you bunch of inverts! Go back to Germany!" she shrieked.

Gomez swiftly swung her around and immobilized her against the nearest wall with her back to him. Panting, he made vigorous thrusts against the elderly woman's skinny behind. She struggled (feebly, nevertheless pushing her hips backwards) while crying for help. Before trying to get away he tossed at her the reason for the huge swelling behind his fly: a thick wad of banknotes, all that remained of the original envelope. But he instantly regretted his gesture when he realized his mistake. He swept down on the bailiff, who was about to pick up the money, and pinned her to the floor, screaming like a rugby player scoring a decisive try in a relegation match. Next to them, Leonetti was trying to rip out the banknotes he'd discovered in Chauvin's bra, but the she-devil was fighting him off tooth and nail. At the same time, hearing their shouts, an usher came down the corridor at a trot, with two policemen in tow. The three men set about disposing of the Immo-Ardennes agents in a muscular fashion, shoving them forward with the help of their truncheons.

218 · PASCALE PUJOL

"Leonetti, Mazard, we have a few things to take care of at the end of this hearing," barked Josyane Nakache as they were closing the door; she glowered, massaging her ribs. (She had just gotten to her feet and was adjusting her gown.) "In the meanwhile, are there any other bids, so we can get this nightmare over with?"

* * *

Eight pairs of eyes focused simultaneously on the two clowns, who had been expulsed from the courtroom by force.

Romain was still hiding behind his magazine, rocking with laughter.

Marité, reading glasses on her nose, was trying desperately to begin a second row of garter stitch, in the hopes of knitting a scarf for the first time in her life.

Sandrine and Annabelle, sitting a little further along on a bench, were discussing the best positions of the Kama Sutra. They hardly looked up when Gomez and Chauvin went by but, continuing to chatter, they did exchange a wink of complicity.

Vairam, Toussaint, and Antoine were pacing up and down at the other end of the corridor, still breathless from the race against the clock they had run since closing the restaurant. Toussaint had insisted they wear disguises so that Gomez and Chauvin would not recognize them. All three of them were wearing ample white boubous of bazin riche fabric, little embroidered skullcaps, and enormous dark glasses. For ten minutes, Toussaint had been counting his prayer beads and quietly chanting, beneath the disapproving, worried gaze of all those who walked by. Antoine finally nudged him sharply in the side (which gave him tendonitis for several weeks) to shut him up.

Juliette was sitting on the floor with her laptop, moderating a live discussion on crisiswhatcrisis.com about the increase in VAT. She looked at Gomez and Chauvin and winced with disgust, burst one of her ever-present bubbles of chewing gum, and turned back to her screen.

Only Hervé Schmutz did not dare look up at the door. Sitting all alone on a plastic chair that felt as if it were about to collapse under him, ill at ease in a suit Toussaint had lent him and shoes that were too tight, he was sweating and exuding his stubborn scent of cabbage. He was gripping a folder containing all the elements of his case; suddenly, his professional future and the continuity of the center seemed not to carry much weight at all.

Marité stood up, put down her knitting needles, and walked over, catlike, to adjust Hervé's tie and give him a mischievous wink.

"They've warmed up the room for you. Your turn, now."

T ake that out of your pocket at once and go give it back, you little brat," hissed Toussaint, not even looking at Juliette.

The girl had just pocketed the two-euro coin an African mama had left surreptitiously on the table at the end of a consultation with Toussaint about daily allowances.

"Your business policies are hopeless," snapped the girl smugly. "How do you expect people to respect you if it doesn't cost them anything?"

"Those are my rules, and everyone who comes to see me knows them. I don't make myself useful for money. Go on, go give her back her coin. Hurry up."

Juliette groaned and rushed out of the restaurant in a huff, catching up with the woman on the sidewalk. She came back a few seconds later and triumphantly slapped a five-euro note onto the table.

"Now what's that?"

"Your new rate. She agreed with me, she thought it was kind of fishy it was for free. Nothing is free in France, she said, or if it is, it's crap."

N'Diaye glanced out at the sidewalk: the woman had vanished and he didn't feel like running after her in the noonday heat. In spite of his tropical linen suit, his shirt in cotton voile, and his soft loafers in braided leather, he was sweating profusely. He reached for the five-euro bill and with a sigh tucked it away in the fob pocket of his vest.

"And my commission? I get half, now, and you still come out ahead," fussed the elf. "We'll make a fine team, you'll see."

N'Diaye looked around: the restaurant was empty. When he was sure that Sandrine was nowhere in sight, he showed the kid his middle finger.

"Let this be today's lesson, little viper: there will always be a bigger crocodile in the pond," he hissed quietly. "You've been warned, so don't try again."

The kid suddenly burst noisily into tears, and this brought her mother from the depths of the kitchen.

"What's going on?"

"Toussaint stole my five-euro bill, the one Mamoune gave me to buy candy, she drew a little heart on it," sniffed the kid. "He won't give it back."

N'Diaye discreetly unfolded the bill without removing it from his pocket: a little red heart leered at him. What a disaster this kid was! For weeks now she'd been sticking her nose into his consultations, and didn't hesitate to give her opinion on everything. The changing of the guard, where Sandrine was concerned, was guaranteed. The end of summer vacation couldn't come soon enough, let the kid go back to school so he'd be rid of her!

"I just picked it up off the floor, I didn't realize," he apologized, handing the bill to Juliette with an insincere smile. "Here, pest . . . uh, pet."

Juliette waited for her mother to walk away then she gave Toussaint the finger in turn, flashing her big baby beaver smile.

* * *

Toussaint had moved his quarters to Le Comptoir Bio in the spring, when the Khédive changed owners. He came early in the morning or late in the afternoon, outside the hours when the restaurant was serving. Sandrine had pestered him for weeks to upgrade his unofficial activity into a nonprofit association, and listed all the advantages it would bring. He had surrendered, wearily, and along the way got himself a little subsidy from the town hall, which covered his expenses: supplies, telephone, and so on. As a result his consulting hours were more professionally organized. Once a week, now, they were reserved for Indian, Sri Lankan, and Pakistani nationals, and Annabelle came to help out. Also within the framework of the association, she had started literacy classes for adult migrants. Juliette had created a website for each of them, and a Facebook page.

As for Vairam, he was giving regular cooking classes. *Master classes with a real chef*, specified Sandrine on the brochures that Juliette had designed and printed; she had asked the children to distribute them in the buildings around the quartier. But Juliette had persuaded her brother to go on his own—she hated going out—and he had done the job on his rollerblades throughout Montmartre, vaunting the aphrodisiac virtues of Vairam's recipes. When the first workshop was held, the kitchen was full of a cross-section of effeminate young men, most of whom were wearing Hedi Von Musche and could not tell the difference between a vegetable peeler and a bread knife. They let out little cries, exchanging knowing glances every time Vairam picked up his mincer or switched on the electric eggbeater. Romain officiated by his side like a flight attendant demonstrating safety procedures. He wandered among the apprentice cooks, describing each ingredient he held out in front of him (carrot . . . zucchini . . .) in a neutral voice, encouraging the most intrepid among them to verify that yes, the sea bream was indeed dead. Now Le Comptoir Bio had become one of the requisite new addresses for Montmartre's gay community. Given all these activities, the restaurant was always as full as a beehive, even when it was closed. The Green councilors were delighted.

Annabelle came in the door, bringing with her a breath of fresh air. She was radiant, her cheeks pink, in full bloom in a long, light dress. She was holding a big envelope. Sandrine rushed up to greet her and the two women kissed each other on the cheek.

"Well? Antoine wouldn't tell me anything, he said you'd tell me yourself."

"Guess."

"Go on . . . "

"It's a girl!"

Sandrine put her hand on her friend's belly, which had become quite round. She was not nostalgic for her own pregnancies, but Annabelle's reminded her of the days when she was expecting Aurélien and she wandered all over Montmartre without a care in the world, other than to find sweet things to nibble on, and to sleep like a dormouse. With Juliette, things had been different: Aurélien had just started kindergarten and her days were busy. The two women sat on a bench to look at the pictures from the ultrasound. Juliette crept soundlessly up to Annabelle, peering now at her belly, now at the pictures.

"It looks like a tadpole," she said sulkily after staring at the pictures for a long time. "Three minutes of intercourse for that . . . Yuck . . . It's nothing to be proud of."

"Would you like to feel the baby moving? Put your hand there," suggested Annabelle kindly; she no longer took offense at Juliette's caustic remarks.

"Nah, I really don't feel like it," sniffed the elf, disgusted. "I just wanted to ask: you're not really going to keep it, are you?"

"Honestly, Juliette!" said her mother. "Don't say things like that. You're old enough to know better than to behave so childishly!"

"So what? It's just that Antoine is always going on about negative growth. As a rule, supporters of negative growth act in a coherent way and don't fill the planet with more mouths to feed. So I figured that maybe it was an accident and now you'd like to get rid of it?"

She slid a folded sheet of paper over to Annabelle.

"Because I found this clinic in Switzerland that deals with this sort of thing even when you're in the fifth month and—"

"Juliette, you're going too far! Leave us alone, go pester Toussaint for a change!"

"Okay, okay," grumbled Juliette, taking the paper with her. "Can I babysit, then, when the tadpole is born? I don't like babies but I have to get more pocket money. There are things I need and nobody cares. The entire planet is exploiting me but Mom won't let me get paid for all the stuff I do—Mamoune's website, blogs, brochures, Facebook pages, all the secretarial work for the association . . . So as soon as I go back to school, I warn you," she said, raising her voice, "it's either babysitting, or walking the streets."

"God help us!" said Toussaint, alarmed, from the far end of the restaurant, making the sign of the cross several times in a row. "Just when the 18th arrondissement is beginning to be trendy, you want to scare away the tourists and bohemians and even the immigrants!"

"Hello, everyone! What's this business about streets? Are you having a problem with the road maintenance people?" Marcel Lacarrière had just arrived, together with Marité.

"Nah, it's nothing, Gramps, it's just Toussaint, he only just discovered streets, he thinks he's still in the bush."

She went to sit back down with him and acted as if she were busy reading the copy of *Le Figaro* that had been left on the table. She unfolded the paper until she could hide behind it, and then she leaned over to Toussaint, who was working on his laptop.

"The old man is sleeping with my grandma," she whispered. "It's gross. Can't you put some spell on him? The pharmacist won't sell me any bromide. I brought you something that belongs to him so you can do the business. I hope you're as good at it as your ancestors were."

Quicker than smallpox infecting the lower clergy of Brittany, she reached in her backpack and took out an object which she tossed onto Toussaint's keyboard, then ran off to the kitchen for a glass of milk. Just as Marité came over to kiss him hello, Toussaint found himself holding an enormous pair of white Y-fronts with dubious yellow streaks in one hand, and a clump of grayish hairs in the other.

* * *

In the spring, Marcel had made his entry in the Cordier family official. There had been a rather hasty and incredible reunion the evening of the official inauguration of Le Comptoir Bio, when he had showed up unannounced, on his own, on impulse—something that was not at all like him. No sooner had he come through the door than he ran into Guillaume, who was helping to greet the guests. The two men stood there for a few minutes not saying a thing. The younger one furious and increasingly upset as his mind formulated the only sensible response to the mute question he did not dare utter; the older man stood stiffly in his tailor-made suit, as if he were confronting his accusers on Judgment Day. They had blocked the entrance, the two tallest men there that night other than Toussaint and Schmutz, who were busy in the kitchen, until Marité came and slipped between them, taking each of them by the arm and guiding them gently toward the back of the restaurant. They sat down at a little table off to one side and she spoke to them for a long time. Sandrine watched the scene from a distance, worriedly; that night, Guillaume couldn't fall asleep and she went to join him on the sofa in the living room. He had buried his face against her chest for a long time, not saying a word, then they made love, passionately—the restaurant coupon racket had ended long before, and the fly-swatter had disappeared. Juliette shrieked when she found them the next morning, half naked, limbs tangled beneath the old throw that was full of the dog's long gray hairs.

Now Juliette took fiendish delight in calling Marcel "Gramps," particularly in public, something he had expressly asked her not to do, while he tried to tame her with a certain number of exorbitantly priced digital gadgets. Aurélien had opted for "*Granddad*", in English. Brother and sister spent part of their vacation wandering around the corridors of *Le Libéral*; they felt at home. She beat her uncle (whom she called in private "the big doofus") hands down at Sudoku. Aurélien was the darling of the fashion and beauty department. He followed the editor in chief everywhere as her zealous assistant, and his initiatives were greatly appreciated. Juliette was too young for a paid internship, but she had nevertheless commandeered the bubble office. From there she expertly administered crisiswhatcrisis.com and her grandmother's erotic website for senior citizens. When the site was launched, Marité had appeared on the cover of several magazines (including *Lui*, with the title, "The Sexiest Grandmother on the Web"). Just before summer, Sandrine had advised Marcel to buy shares in Plug SA, Marité's venture, which had gotten off to a great start. The soft-core DVD campaign was going well (newsstand sales had nearly doubled) and *Convictions*, which Annabelle had left, was in serious difficulty: now was the time for *Le Libéral* to catch the wave and not wipe out, to ride it as long as it was at its crest. Marcel had decided to progressively hand over the reins to his sons, and Guillaume was now on the board of the group, where at last he was able to display his intuition and talent for everything press-related. But the old man still kept Sandrine on as special adviser: he adored his daughter-in-law, but he would rather bite off his own tongue than admit it.

Champagne

Samuel Benoliel rubbed his hands as he walked down the rue des Martyrs. At last he had managed to pick up one of those little American dolls who wandered around Montmartre in minishorts and sneakers, her suntanned legs prepared to climb the hill at the crack of dawn. He had come upon her the day before at the exit to the Pigalle métro: she was trying to find her way, staring at the map she held in her hands, an enormous backpack on her shoulders. He had helped her in the right direction and had offered to meet her today to show her around the quartier. He'd had to negotiate a day off with Jo, not easy on a Saturday, but business was quiet in August. Not long before ten he'd met the girl, Lana, at her hotel near the Saint-Georges métro, where she was sharing a room with her best friend. He had missed this detail during their conversation the day before, due to his bad English. And worse luck, the best friend was stuck in bed with a sore throat, which reduced to nil his hopes of any leisurely morning shenanigans. Lana was eager to explore Montmartre, and was ready and waiting, out on the sidewalk; she didn't even invite him into the lobby.

While he had been hoping to get his way with his American before lunchtime (and at the same time save himself fifty euros on lunch, and have a drink on her hotel account), he found himself wandering endlessly around the quartier instead, in the ever more blazing sun. North to south, east to west. She wanted to see every *ruelle*, every *impasse*, every unusual spot, to climb up the slightest little stairway, to weave her way through all the typical buildings. They had gone up and down Abbesses with its boutiques and designers, from Bateau Lavoir up to the house where the singer Dalida used to live, before turning off to the Place du Tertre, where they got lost in the crowd and indulged—begrudgingly on the part of the real estate agent, who financed the operation—in the tradition of having their caricatures sketched. Tireless, her guidebook in hand, she had continued on to Sacré-Coeur, then to the Marché Saint-Pierre, where she spent a long time rummaging through the displays of bolts of fabric. She stayed as fresh as a rose and looked like a golf or tennis player in her little skirt and tank top, her ponytail emerging from her cap. Samuel Benoliel, on the other hand, was melting a bit more with each step, his shirt sticking sweatily to his back. His black suit was made of a synthetic material whose thermal properties far exceeded those of most solar panels on the market.

The plus side was that she seemed neither hungry nor thirsty: she had two big water bottles and cereal bars in her little shoulder bag—no two ways about it, these girls were organized. Maybe he'd manage to take her at last to the apartment on the boulevard Barbès, a big three-room place from the Haussmann era; it was empty and he had the keys. He wanted to show it to her, on the pretext that she'd be able to admire typical Parisian architecture from the inside. He'd had the foresight to stop by the night before to deposit a big blanket in the living room for their frolics, even supposing they had time to make it as far as the living room. He felt rather like holding her up against the wall of the corridor but hey, he was prepared to make a minor concession to sentimentality. But now, just as they were approaching the fateful address, lo and behold she wanted to go off and visit Barbès and La Goutte d'Or!

He had drunk two coffees and two beers before going to meet Lana, and now he had just finished a bottle of water: he felt that his gauge had just gone into the red. This was usually a girl problem. But not for this American: she seemed as impervious to the need for a little wee as she was to the heat or the steep gradient of the streets of Montmartre. Shoot, she'd be tireless in bed, wouldn't she! Oooh, he couldn't wait to get her up against the wall and show her what he could do! He wouldn't even need to undress her, with that ridiculously short skirt of hers.

The streets they were going along now were dirty and narrow, and in his opinion were not all that interesting, but they elicited cries of enthusiasm from the young woman nevertheless. At the Marché Dejean she observed everything very attentively, wrinkling her adorable little nose at the fish counters, and trying out her hesitant French with a fruit vendor—bananas, obviously. With her smartphone she fired away at the tiniest graffiti, the slightest peeling wall, every passing African woman wearing a boubou. Card players and hawkers of fake Chanel perfume, kebab stalls, music, fresh laundry hanging from the windows in the narrow streets: everything sent her into raptures. They went deeper and deeper into the quartier. Lana, delighted, indulged in the enormous *banane tigrée* she'd bought at the market. Samuel Benoliel watched in a haze of concupiscence as her fleshy lips closed on the fruit, but he was beginning to feel the time dragging. And his bladder was sending its kindest regards. Things were getting urgent, in fact, and now there wasn't a single bistro in sight. Was he going to have to urinate in the street—behind a door into a courtyard, or between two parked cars—so he wouldn't wet his pants? If he didn't find a solution, and quick, his entire plan would go up in smoke.

That was when he saw the sign for Le Comptoir Bio at the end of the street. Well, well, that was the restaurant he'd rented out a few months ago! A ridiculous commission for some bogus program from the town hall, but it looked fairly

230 - PASCALE PUJOL

welcoming now, nothing like the dive it had been in the old days. It had never occurred to him to go back there, and yet it was right next to his aunt's garage. Which reminded him, the most recent tenant had vanished without notice, dropping off the keys at the agency one day. He went up to the restaurant and looked at the menu. Lana opened her eyes wide, intrigued. *Wow, what a nice place! Is this a surprise for lunch?* Benoliel nodded, relieved, going through the door. Okay, there went his fifty euros (and maybe even more if Lana was the hungry type), but never mind, he had no choice, now.

There were a dozen or so people in the restaurant. Between two champagne buckets at either end of a long table was a platter of little fried triangles and a big plate of grilled vegetables.

"We'd like a table for lunch."

"I'm really sorry, but we're not open, this is a little family gathering, we're celebrating a happy event," answered the woman he supposed was the owner. "But this evening we're open, if you'd like . . . ? I'll give you our card so you can reserve for next time."

Samuel Benoliel thought he would pass out. He could see the door to the toilet all the way at the back of the room, leering at him. He was only a few steps from paradise, but the way in was still blocked.

"Do you mind if I use your toilet, at least?"

He looked around him. A family gathering? What a bunch of cretins . . . he'd recognized the woman, a pretty brunette with a good figure, not very tall, but the ballbreaker type: she had driven him up the wall in the course of several visits, with her endless demands for details and explanations. Right behind her was a tall, sinister-looking guy who looked like a rugby player. The pregnant blonde in the armchair reminded him of someone . . . of course, she was the bitch with the Harley! She was still sexy in spite of her bump, as well! Sheesh, she hadn't even bought the apartment he'd shown her, nor had she ever come back to the agency. Next to her was a thin little guy with long hair, gazing lovingly at her, surely the baby's father. Good luck, mate. A bit further along, two guys were playing chess: a huge tall black man dressed like a fat cat, and another guy who was just as impressive, with pink skin, close-shaven hair, a beige short-sleeved shirt . . . was he a soldier, a mercenary? Probably a bodyguard for the black guy, who looked like a minister in his three-piece suit of grayish-beige linen. Next to them another man was sucking on his pen, absorbed in a Sudoku puzzle.

A little Sri Lankan man came out of the kitchen with a huge steaming platter. A peroxide blond in tight trousers followed in his wake, swaying his ass. He was holding a spoon up in the air and keeping time with the pop song playing in the background, and he gave Samuel an emphatic wink that made him feel ill at ease. It was impossible to see what was in the platter but the delicious aroma reminded Benoliel that he hadn't eaten anything all day—though he'd drunk plenty. An adolescent with impeccably blow-dried hair brought up the rear with a pile of plates and began to set the table. On the bench, a couple in their seventies were billing and cooing, lost in each other's gaze, champagne glasses in hand. Shoot, even old people managed to have it off! And here he hadn't laid a finger on a girl in over six months! But now it was his big day, and at last he had a nice little prize in hand, a real hottie, her skirt level with her goodies, and his bladder was blown up like a basketball, ready to explode like a suicide bomber there in front of a bunch of dingbats. What sort of luck was that . . . Besides, he was sure the urine he couldn't evacuate was beginning to poison his blood. For the last few moments he'd been having visions, the sure signs of an intoxication: the men's eyes were blinking, like in a zombie film. Or rather, they were changing color, like an intermittent light, now brown, now blue. First the owner's husband, who was looking at him suspiciously.

Then the old man, too, from behind his champagne glass: blue, brown, blue, brown. Now the kid who was setting the table, now the Sudoku player, who had finally raised his head and was staring at him with an inane smile . . . Samuel Benoliel was beginning to feel weak at the knees.

"Please?" he said again, pointing toward the door, feeling distinctly unsteady.

"I'm afraid that won't be possible," said a little voice behind him.

He turned around and saw a girl of twelve or thirteen with a mousy face, her hair pulled back by a multitude of barrettes, flat as a flounder in her pink dress. She was so tiny that he hadn't seen her sitting there at the screen of a laptop computer. She was glaring at him perfidiously.

"Those are dry toilets," she said emphatically, as seriously as possible, emphasizing the penultimate word. "They're only for the initiated, you have to have a membership card from the Green Party."

Samuel Benoliel heard a stifled laugh, without being able to determine where it came from: the walls, the chairs, the tables? After his eyes, now his ears were playing tricks on him! Then the laughter filled the entire room, everyone smiling and chuckling louder and louder, every gaze focused on him. The four pairs of blinking eyes made his head spin, he felt unbearably dizzy: he was sure his kidneys had stopped filtering anything and were about to break down. He beat a retreat as hasty as his basketball bladder—still about to explode—would allow. Never mind, he'd make it to the agency. Just as he opened the door he heard, quite distinctly, a high-pitched fart, followed by another that was more of a bass note; then came the finale, a resonant spluttering noise, echoing the fit of hysterics of the entire company.

ABOUT THE AUTHOR

Pascale Pujol grew up in Perpignan and now lives in Paris. *Little Culinary Triumphs* is her first novel.